NON SANS DROICT.

William Shakespeare

AS YOU LIKE IT

Edited by Albert Gilman

The Signet Classic Shakespeare
GENERAL EDITOR: SYLVAN BARNET

PUBLISHED BY THE NEW AMERICAN LIBRARY,
NEW YORK AND TORONTO
THE NEW ENGLISH LIBRARY LIMITED, LONDON

Fourth Printing

SIGNET TRADEMARK REG. U.S. PAT. OFF. AND FOREIGN COUNTRIES
REGISTERED TRADEMARK—MARCA REGISTRADA
HECHO EN CHICAGO, U.S.A.

SIGNET CLASSICS are published *in the United States* by
The New American Library, Inc., 1301 Avenue of the Ameri-
cas, New York, New York 10019, *in Canada* by The New
American Library of Canada Limited, 295 King Street East,
Toronto 2, Ontario, *in the United Kingdom* by The New
English Library Limited, Barnard's Inn, Holborn, London,
E.C. 1, England.

Contents

Shakespeare: Prefatory Remarks

Between the record of his baptism in Stratford on 26 April 1564 and the record of his burial in Stratford on 25 April 1616, some forty documents name Shakespeare, and many others name his parents, his children, and his grandchildren. More facts are known about William Shakespeare than about any other playwright of the period except Ben Jonson. The facts should, however, be distinguished from the legends. The latter, inevitably more engaging and better known, tell us that the Stratford boy killed a calf in high style, poached deer and rabbits, and was forced to flee to London, where he held horses outside a playhouse. These traditions are only traditions; they may be true, but no evidence supports them, and it is well to stick to the facts.

Mary Arden, the dramatist's mother, was the daughter of a substantial landowner; about 1557 she married John Shakespeare, who was a glove-maker and trader in various farm commodities. In 1557 John Shakespeare was a member of the Council (the governing body of Stratford), in 1558 a constable of the borough, in 1561 one of the two town chamberlains, in 1565 an alderman (entitling him to the appellation "Mr."), in 1568 high bailiff—the town's highest political office, equivalent to mayor. After 1577, for an unknown reason he drops out of local politics. The birthday of William Shakespeare, the eldest son of this locally prominent man, is unrecorded; but the Stratford parish register records that the infant was baptized on 26 April 1564. (It is quite possible that he was born on 23 April, but this date has probably been assigned by tradition because it is the date on which, fifty-two years later, he died.) The attendance records of the Stratford grammar school of the period are not extant, but it is reasonable to assume that the son of a local official attended the school and received substantial training in Latin. The masters of the school from Shakespeare's seventh to fifteenth years held Oxford degrees; the Elizabethan curriculum excluded mathematics and the natural sciences but taught a good deal of Latin rhetoric, logic, and literature. On 27 November 1582 a marriage license was issued to Shakespeare and Anne Hathaway, eight years his senior. The couple had a child in May, 1583. Perhaps the marriage was necessary, but perhaps the couple had earlier engaged in a formal "troth plight" which would render their children legitimate even if no further ceremony were performed. In 1585 Anne Hathaway bore Shakespeare twins.

That Shakespeare was born is excellent; that he married and had children is pleasant; but that we know nothing about his departure from Stratford to London, or about the beginning of his theatrical career, is lamentable and must be admitted. We would gladly sacrifice details about his children's baptism for details about his earliest days on the stage. Perhaps the poaching episode is true (but it is first reported almost a century after Shakespeare's death), or perhaps he first left Stratford to be a schoolteacher, as another tradition holds; perhaps he was moved by

> Such wind as scatters young men through the world,
> To seek their fortunes further than at home
> Where small experience grows.

In 1592, thanks to the cantankerousness of Robert Greene, a rival playwright and a pamphleteer, we have our first reference, a snarling one, to Shakespeare as an actor and playwright. Greene warns those of his own educated friends who wrote for the theater against an actor who has presumed to turn playwright:

> There is an upstart crow, beautified with our feathers, that with his *tiger's heart wrapped in a player's hide* supposes he is as well able to bombast out a blank verse as the best of

you, and being an absolute Johannes-factotum is in his own
conceit the only Shake-scene in a country.

The reference to the player, as well as the allusion to
Aesop's crow (who strutted in borrowed plumage, as an
actor struts in fine words not his own), makes it clear that
by this date Shakespeare had both acted and written. That
Shakespeare is meant is indicated not only by "Shake-scene"
but by the parody of a line from one of Shakespeare's plays,
3 Henry VI: "O, tiger's heart wrapped in a woman's hide."
If Shakespeare in 1592 was prominent enough to be attacked
by an envious dramatist, he probably had served an appren-
ticeship in the theater for at least a few years.

In any case, by 1592 Shakespeare had acted and written,
and there are a number of subsequent references to him as
an actor: documents indicate that in 1598 he is a "principal
comedian," in 1603 a "principal tragedian," in 1608 he is
one of the "men players." The profession of actor was not
for a gentleman, and it occasionally drew the scorn of
university men who resented writing speeches for persons
less educated than themselves, but it was respectable enough:
players, if prosperous, were in effect members of the bour-
geoisie, and there is nothing to suggest that Stratford con-
sidered William Shakespeare less than a solid citizen. When,
in 1596, the Shakespeares were granted a coat of arms, the
grant was made to Shakespeare's father, but probably
William Shakespeare (who the next year bought the second-
largest house in town) had arranged the matter on his own
behalf. In subsequent transactions he is occasionally styled
a gentleman.

Although in 1593 and 1594 Shakespeare published two
narrative poems dedicated to the Earl of Southampton,
Venus and Adonis and *The Rape of Lucrece*, and may well
have written most or all of his sonnets in the middle nineties,
Shakespeare's literary activity seems to have been almost
entirely devoted to the theater. (It may be significant that
the two narrative poems were written in years when the
plague closed the theaters for several months.) In 1594 he
was a charter member of a theatrical company called the
Chamberlain's Men (which in 1603 changed its name to the
King's Men); until he retired to Stratford (about 1611,

apparently), he was with this remarkably stable company. From 1599 the company acted primarily at the Globe Theatre, in which Shakespeare held a one-tenth interest. Other Elizabethan dramatists are known to have acted, but no other is known also to have been entitled to a share in the profits of the playhouse.

Shakespeare's first eight published plays did not have his name on them, but this is not remarkable; the most popular play of the sixteenth century, Thomas Kyd's *The Spanish Tragedy*, went through many editions without naming Kyd, and Kyd's authorship is known only because a book on the profession of acting happens to quote (and attribute to Kyd) some lines on the interest of Roman emperors in the drama. What is remarkable is that after 1598 Shakespeare's name commonly appears on printed plays—some of which are not his. Another indication of his popularity comes from Francis Meres, author of *Palladis Tamia: Wit's Treasury* (1598): in this anthology of snippets accompanied by an essay on literature, many playwrights are mentioned, but Shakespeare's name occurs more often than any other, and Shakespeare is the only playwright whose plays are listed.

From his acting, playwriting, and share in a theater, Shakespeare seems to have made considerable money. He put it to work, making substantial investments in Stratford real estate. When he made his will (less than a month before he died), he sought to leave his property intact to his descendants. Of small bequests to relatives and to friends (including three actors, Richard Burbage, John Heminges, and Henry Condell), that to his wife of the second-best bed has provoked the most comment; perhaps it was the bed the couple had slept in, the best being reserved for visitors. In any case, had Shakespeare not excepted it, the bed would have gone (with the rest of his household possessions) to his daughter and her husband. On 25 April 1616 he was buried within the chancel of the church at Stratford. An unattractive monument to his memory, placed on a wall near the grave, says he died on 23 April. Over the grave itself are the lines, perhaps by Shakespeare, that (more than his literary fame) have kept his bones undisturbed in the crowded burial ground where old bones were often dislodged to make way for new:

> Good friend, for Jesus' sake forbear
> To dig the dust enclosed here.
> Blessed be the man that spares these stones
> And cursed be he that moves my bones.

Thirty-seven plays, as well as some nondramatic poems, are held to constitute the Shakespeare canon. The dates of composition of most of the works are highly uncertain, but there is often evidence of a *terminus a quo* (starting point) and/or a *terminus ad quem* (terminal point) that provides a framework for intelligent guessing. For example, *Richard II* cannot be earlier than 1595, the publication date of some material to which it is indebted; *The Merchant of Venice* cannot be later than 1598, the year Francis Meres mentioned it. Sometimes arguments for a date hang on an alleged topical allusion, such as the lines about the unseasonable weather in *A Midsummer Night's Dream,* II.i.81–117, but such an allusion (if indeed it is an allusion) can be variously interpreted, and in any case there is always the possibility that a tropical allusion was inserted during a revision, years after the composition of a play. Dates are often attributed on the basis of style, and although conjectures about style usually rest on other conjectures, sooner or later one must rely on one's literary sense. There is no real proof, for example, that *Othello* is not as early as *Romeo and Juliet,* but one feels *Othello* is later, and because the first record of its performance is 1604, one is glad enough to set its composition at that date and not push it back into Shakespeare's early years. The following chronology, then, is as much indebted to informed guesswork and sensitivity as it is to fact. The dates, necessarily imprecise, indicate something like a scholarly consensus.

PLAYS

1588–93	*The Comedy of Errors*
1588–94	*Love's Labor's Lost*
1590–91	*2 Henry VI*
1590–91	*3 Henry VI*

POEMS

Shakespeare's Theater

In Shakespeare's infancy, Elizabethan actors performed wherever they could—in great halls, at court, in the courtyards of inns. The innyards must have made rather unsatisfactory theaters: on some days they were unavailable because carters bringing goods to London used them as depots; when available, they had to be rented from the innkeeper; perhaps most important, London inns were subject to the Common Council of London, which was not well disposed toward theatricals. In 1574 the Common Council required that plays and playing places in London be licensed. It asserted that

> sundry great disorders and inconveniences have been found to ensue to this city by the inordinate haunting of great multitudes of people, specially youth, to plays, interludes, and shows, namely occasion of frays and quarrels, evil practices of incontinency in great inns having chambers and secret places adjoining to their open stages and galleries,

and ordered that innkeepers who wished licenses to hold performances put up a bond and make contributions to the poor.

The requirement that plays and innyard theaters be licensed, along with the other drawbacks of playing at inns, probably drove James Burbage (a carpenter-turned-actor) to rent in 1576 a plot of land northeast of the city walls and to build here—on property outside the jurisdiction of the city—England's first permanent construction designed for plays. He called it simply the Theatre. About all that is known of its construction is that it was wood. It soon had imitators, the most famous being the Globe (1599), built across the Thames (again outside the city's jurisdiction), out of timbers of the Theatre, which had been dismantled when Burbage's lease ran out.

There are three important sources of information about the structure of Elizabethan playhouses—drawings, a contract, and stage directions in plays. Of drawings, only the so-called De Witt drawing (c. 1596) of the Swan—really a friend's copy of De Witt's drawing—is of much significance. It shows a building of three tiers, with a stage jutting from a wall into the yard or center of the building. The tiers are roofed, and part of the stage is covered by a roof that projects from the rear and is supported at its front on two posts, but the groundlings, who paid a penny to stand in front of the stage, were exposed to the sky. (Performances in such a playhouse were held only in the daytime; artificial illumination was not used.) At the rear of the stage are two doors; above the stage is a gallery. The second major source of information, the contract for the Fortune, specifies that although the Globe is to be the model, the Fortune is to be square, eighty feet outside and fifty-five inside. The stage is to be forty-three feet broad, and is to extend into the middle of the yard (i.e., it is twenty-seven and a half feet deep). For patrons willing to pay more than the general admission charged of the groundlings, there were to be three galleries provided with seats. From the third chief source, stage directions, one learns that entrance to the stage was by doors, presumably spaced widely apart at the rear ("Enter one citizen at one door, and another at the other"), and that in addition to the platform stage there was occasionally some sort of curtained booth or alcove allowing for "discovery" scenes, and some sort of playing space "aloft" or "above" to represent (for example) the top of a city's walls or a room above the street. Doubtless each theater had its own peculiarities, but perhaps we can talk about a "typical" Elizabethan theater if we realize that no theater need exactly have fit the description, just as no father is the typical father with 3.7 children. This hypothetical theater is wooden, round or polygonal (in *Henry V* Shakespeare calls it a "wooden O"), capable of holding some eight hundred spectators standing in the yard around the projecting elevated stage and some fifteen hundred additional spectators seated in the three roofed galleries. The stage, protected by a "shadow" or "heavens" or roof, is entered by two doors; behind the doors is the "tiring house" (attiring house, i.e., dressing room), and above the doors is some sort of gallery that may sometimes hold spectators but that can be used (for example) as the bedroom from which Romeo—according to a stage direction in one text—"goeth down." Some evidence suggests that a throne can be lowered onto the platform stage, perhaps from the "shadow"; certainly characters can descend from the stage through a trap or traps into the cellar or "hell." Sometimes this space beneath the platform accommodates a sound-effects man or musician (in *Antony and Cleopatra* "music of the hautboys is under the stage") or an actor (in *Hamlet* the "Ghost cries under the stage"). Most characters simply walk on and off, but because there is no curtain in front of the platform, corpses will have to be carried off (Hamlet must lug Polonius' guts into the neighbor room), or will have to fall at the rear, where the curtain on the alcove or booth can be drawn to conceal them.

Such may have been the so-called "public theater." Another kind of theater, called the "private theater" because its much greater admission charge limited its audience to the wealthy or the prodigal, must be briefly mentioned. The private theater was basically a large room, entirely roofed and therefore artificially illuminated, with a stage at one end. In 1576 one such theater was established in Blackfriars, a Dominican priory in London that had been suppressed in 1538 and confiscated by the Crown and thus was not under the city's jurisdiction. All the actors in the Blackfriars theater were boys about eight to thirteen years old (in the public theaters similar boys played female parts; a boy Lady Macbeth played to a man Macbeth). This private theater had a precarious existence, and ceased operations in 1584. In 1596 James Burbage, who had already made theatrical history by building the Theatre, began to construct a second Blackfriars theater. He died in 1597, and for several years this second Blackfriars theater was used by a troupe of boys, but in 1608 two of Burbage's sons and five other actors (including Shakespeare) became joint operators of the theater, using it in the winter when the open-air Globe was unsuitable. Perhaps such a smaller theater, roofed, artificially illuminated, and with a tradition of a courtly audience, exerted an influence on Shakespeare's late plays.

Performances in the private theaters may well have had intermissions during which music was played, but in the public theaters the action was probably uninterrupted, flowing from scene to scene almost without a break. Actors would enter, speak, exit, and others would immediately enter and establish (if necessary) the new locale by a few properties and by words and gestures. Here are some samples of Shakespeare's scene painting:

> This is Illyria, lady.
>
> Well, this is the Forest of Arden.
>
> This castle hath a pleasant seat; the air
> Nimbly and sweetly recommends itself
> Unto our gentle senses.

On the other hand, it is a mistake to conceive of the Elizabethan stage as bare. Although Shakespeare's Chorus in *Henry V* calls the stage an "unworthy scaffold" and urges the spectators to "eke out our performance with your mind," there was considerable spectacle. The last act of *Macbeth*, for example, has five stage directions calling for "drum and colors," and another sort of appeal to the eye is indicated by the stage direction "Enter Macduff, with Macbeth's head." Some scenery and properties may have been substantial; doubtless a throne was used, and in one play of the period we encounter this direction: "Hector takes up a great piece of rock and casts at Ajax, who tears up a young tree by the roots and assails Hector." The matter is of some importance, and will be glanced at again in the next section.

The Texts of Shakespeare

Though eighteen of his plays were published during his lifetime, Shakespeare seems never to have supervised their publication. There is nothing unusual here; when a playwright sold a play to a theatrical company he surrendered his ownership of it. Normally a company would not publish the play, because to publish it meant to allow competitors to acquire the piece. Some plays, however, did get published: apparently treacherous actors sometimes pieced together a play for a publisher, sometimes a company in need of money sold a play, and sometimes a company allowed a play to be published that no longer drew audiences. That Shakespeare did not concern himself with publication, then, is scarcely remarkable; of his contemporaries only Ben Jonson carefully supervised the publication of his own plays. In 1623, seven years after Shakespeare's death, John Heminges and Henry Condell (two senior members of Shakespeare's company, who had performed with him for about twenty years) collected his plays—published and unpublished—into a large volume, commonly called the First Folio. (A folio is a volume consisting of sheets that have been folded once, each sheet thus making two leaves, or four pages. The eighteen plays published during Shakespeare's lifetime had been issued one play per volume in small books called quartos. Each sheet in a quarto has been folded twice, making four leaves, or eight pages.) The First Folio contains thirty-six plays; a thirty-seventh, *Pericles*, though not in the Folio is regarded as canonical. Heminges and Condell suggest in an address "To the great variety of readers" that the republished plays are presented in better form than in the quartos: "Before you were abused with diverse stolen and surreptitious copies, maimed and deformed by the frauds and stealths of injurious impostors that exposed them; even those, are now offered to your view cured and perfect of their limbs, and all the rest absolute in their numbers, as he [i.e., Shakespeare] conceived them."

Whoever was assigned to prepare the texts for publication in the First Folio seems to have taken his job seriously and yet not to have performed it with uniform care. The sources of the texts seem to have been, in general, good unpublished copies or the best published copies. The first play in the collection, *The Tempest*, is divided into acts and scenes, has unusually full stage directions and descriptions of spectacle, and concludes with a list of the characters, but the editor was not able (or willing) to present all of the succeeding texts so fully dressed. Later texts occasionally show signs of carelessness: in one scene of *Much Ado About Nothing* the names of actors, instead of characters, appear as speech prefixes, as they had in the quarto, which the Folio reprints; proofreading throughout the Folio is spotty and apparently was done without reference to the printer's copy; the pagination of *Hamlet* jumps from 156 to 257.

A modern editor of Shakespeare must first select his copy; no problem if the play exists only in the Folio, but a considerable problem if the relationship between a quarto and the Folio—or an early quarto and a later one—is unclear. When an editor has chosen what seems to him to be the most authoritative text or texts for his copy, he has not done with making decisions. First of all, he must reckon with Elizabethan spelling. If he is not producing a facsimile, he probably modernizes it, but ought he to preserve the old form of words that apparently were pronounced quite unlike their modern forms—"lanthorn" "alablaster"? If he preserves these forms, is he really preserving Shakespeare's forms or perhaps those of a compositor in the printing house? What is one to do when one finds "lanthorn" and "lantern" in adjacent lines? (The editors of this series in general, but not invariably, assume that words should be spelled in their modern form.) Elizabethan punctuation, too, presents problems. For example in the First Folio, the only text for the play, Macbeth rejects his wife's idea that he can wash the blood from his hand:

> no: this my Hand will rather
> The multitudinous Seas incarnardine,
> Making the Greene one, Red.

Obviously an editor will remove the superfluous capitals, and he will probably alter the spelling to "incarnadine," but will he leave the comma before "red," letting Macbeth speak of the sea as "the green one," or will he (like most modern editors) remove the comma and thus have Macbeth say that his hand will make the ocean *uniformly* red?

An editor will sometimes have to change more than
spelling or punctuation. Macbeth says to his wife:

> I dare do all that may become a man,
> Who dares no more, is none.

For two centuries editors have agreed that the second line
is unsatisfactory, and have emended "no" to "do": "Who
dares do more is none." But when in the same play Ross
says that fearful persons

> floate vpon a wilde and violent Sea
> Each way, and moue,

need "move" be emended to "none," as it often is, on the
hunch that the compositor misread the manuscript? The
editors of the Signet Classic Shakespeare have restrained
themselves from making abundant emendations. In their
minds they hear Dr. Johnson on the dangers of emending:
"I have adopted the Roman sentiment, that it is more
honorable to save a citizen than to kill an enemy." Some
departures (in addition to spelling, punctuation, and linea-
tion) from the copy text have of course been made, but the
original readings are listed in a note following the play, so
that the reader can evaluate them for himself.

The editors of the Signet Classic Shakespeare, following
tradition, have added line numbers and in many cases act
and scene divisions as well as indications of locale at the
beginning of scenes. The Folio divided most of the plays
into acts and some into scenes. Early eighteenth-century
editors increased the divisions. These divisions, which provide a convenient way of referring to passages in the plays,
have been retained, but when not in the text chosen as the
basis for the Signet Classic text they are enclosed in square
brackets [ ] to indicate that they are editorial additions.
Similarly, although no play of Shakespeare's published during his lifetime was equipped with indications of locale at
the heads of scene divisions, locales have here been added
in square brackets for the convenience of the reader, who
lacks the information afforded to spectators by costumes,

properties, and gestures. The spectator can tell at a glance he is in the throne room, but without an editorial indication the reader may be puzzled for a while. It should be mentioned, incidentally, that there are a few authentic stage directions—perhaps Shakespeare's, perhaps a prompter's—that suggest locales: for example, "Enter Brutus in his orchard," and "They go up into the Senate house." It is hoped that the bracketed additions provide the reader with the sort of help provided in these two authentic directions, but it is equally hoped that the reader will remember that the stage was not loaded with scenery.

No editor during the course of his work can fail to recollect some words Heminges and Condell prefixed to the Folio:

> It had been a thing, we confess, worthy to have been wished, that the author himself had lived to have set forth and overseen his own writings. But since it hath been ordained otherwise, and he by death departed from that right, we pray you do not envy his friends the office of their care and pain to have collected and published them.

Nor can an editor, after he has done his best, forget Heminges and Condell's final words: "And so we leave you to other of his friends, whom if you need can be your guides. If you need them not, you can lead yourselves, and others. And such readers we wish him."

SYLVAN BARNET
Tufts University

Introduction

Samuel Johnson found the story of *As You Like It* "wild and pleasing," the dialogue "sprightly," but regretted Shakespeare's "hastening to the end of his work," especially because it meant suppressing the "dialogue between the usurper and the hermit" and thereby losing "an opportunity of exhibiting a moral lesson." From the eighteenth century on, critics have often said that Shakespeare's craftsmanship in *As You Like It* is poor. G. B. Shaw, perhaps with tongue in cheek, in *The Dark Lady of the Sonnets* has Will Shakespear say to Queen Elizabeth: "I have also stole from a book of idle wanton tales two of the most damnable foolishnesses in the world, in the one of which a woman goeth in man's attire and maketh impudent love to her swain, who pleaseth the groundlings by overthrowing a wrestler. . . . I have writ these to save my friends from penury, yet shewing my scorn for such follies and for them that praise them by calling the one As You Like It, meaning that it is not as *I* like it."

Some critics have complained of inconsistencies in the plotting. From several speeches in the play, it would appear that Duke Senior has been banished to the Forest of Arden for a long time, but other speeches suggest that his banishment is recent. In the first scene of the play Shakespeare gives the name Jaques to the middle son of Sir Rowland de Boys, but this Jaques does not appear until the close of the play and his speeches are simply marked "Second Brother." In the meantime we have heard much from another Jaques, the melancholy Jaques, who is one of Duke Senior's retainers. Two characters called by the same name can make for some confusion. These bits of carelessness, if that is what they are, are not unusual in Shakespeare and not peculiar to this play. What is unusual is the extraordinary dispatch with which the plot unfolds. Almost everything that is to happen, happens in the first act; murders are attempted, ribs are cracked, and several major characters are packed off to the Forest of Arden. In the ensuing acts Shakespeare scarcely concerns himself with the troubles that were introduced in the first act. Except for three short scenes we are always in Arden, where the dangers we are chiefly aware of are falling in love or being worsted in a discussion. So that the audience may go home, the two villains are reported to have been converted and four pairs of lovers are lined up to be wed.

Shakespeare has certainly handled the narrative expeditiously. It is very much as if he were eager to be in Arden to "fleet the time carelessly as they did in the golden world." We cannot regret that he missed the "opportunity of exhibiting a moral lesson." Nor can we regret that he gave himself a holiday from the intricate plotting that marks what seems to be the play anterior to *As You Like It*, *Much Ado About Nothing*. Who has not looked at his watch during the last act of a well-made plot and sighed to think of the knots still to be untied? We had rather be in Arden where the wicked are converted by fiat and lovers marry in half-dozen lots.

The plot moves swiftly in the beginning of *As You Like It* (and then stands almost still until the fifth act) because the interest of the play is not intended to arise out of the action or situation. And, as William Hazlitt has remarked, it does not. The play is chiefly concerned with two enduring human illusions—the pastoral ideal, or the dream of a simple life, and the ideal of romantic love. These are given an extremely complex representation through dialogue and contrasting relationships. The plot creates the conditions for this representation. The characters are given reason to wander in the woodland, the proper setting in which to develop the theme of pastoralism. Four diverse pairs are caused to fall in love and their contrasting romances will exemplify the varieties of love. Rosalind, given a double identity, can spoof love and yet be a lover. The plot does very well what it is designed to do.

The motives of the chief characters in *As You Like It* are as simple and abrupt as the action of the play, and they could surely be put in evidence by those who think the play a piece of indifferent craftsmanship. Oliver would see an end to his brother Orlando. Why? "For my soul, yet I know not why, hates nothing more than he." Duke Frederick, the usurper who has banished Duke Senior, would now banish Rosalind. The reason? "Grounded upon no other argument/ But that the people praise her for her virtues." In her scenes with Orlando, Rosalind is in no danger; thus her original reason for pretending to be a man does not apply. Yet she does pretend, and it is only her disguise that prevents their immediate marriage. How is so crucial a decision motivated? "I will speak to him like a saucy lackey, and under that habit play the knave with him." Which is to say that she did it because she would do it.

In *As You Like It* each action follows directly from the uncomplicated nature of the person acting. It is his natural wickedness that impels Oliver to hate Orlando, and it is wickedness that causes Frederick to banish Rosalind. Antonio, in Shakespeare's *The Tempest*, is another younger brother who banishes his elder brother (Prospero) and usurps the dukedom. But Antonio's case is more complex than Frederick's, since, while the usurpation is not justified, there is the excuse that Prospero had neglected his duties as a ruler, and Antonio, Prospero's delegate, through the exercise of ducal power, came to believe (as a liar may come to believe his lie) that he was in fact the Duke. But neither Rosalind nor Duke Senior is culpable, and Duke Frederick's usurpation is not said to result from any such interesting state of mind as Antonio's. Duke Frederick's crimes derive from his nature alone. In *As You Like It* a good nature is as unfailingly manifest as a bad one. Because their hearts are blithe, Celia and Rosalind are able to go into exile saying: "Now go in we content/ To liberty, and not to banishment." Because his nature is noble, Duke Senior can say "Sweet are the uses of adversity" and can find "good in everything." The good in this play will be good whatever the occasion seems to warrant and the evil, at first, will be evil. Of Shakespeare's comedies only *The Comedy of Errors* makes so simple a connection between temperament and action. *The Comedy of Errors* is a farce, but *As You Like It* is not.

Englishmen in the Renaissance liked to construe life as an interaction of Fortune and Nature, and in *As You Like It* there is some talk of these two goddesses. Rosalind, for instance, instructs Celia: "Fortune reigns in gifts of the world, not in the lineaments of Nature." The only tension in the plot of *As You Like It*, set up in the first act, derives from Fortune's unjust distribution of the gifts of the world. The nobler natures, Duke Senior, Rosalind, Celia, and Orlando, are made to suffer by Fortune while the wicked, Oliver and Duke Frederick, thrive. This imbalance between Fortune and Nature requires resolution. The resolution provided is exceptionally good-humored, far more so than in either *Much Ado About Nothing* or *Twelfth Night*, the two plays with which *As You Like It* is conventionally grouped. The wicked are not punished or left rancorous but are converted and, now as virtuous men, Frederick and Oliver bring the fortunes of Duke Senior, Rosalind, and Orlando into harmony with their natures. Frederick's conversion is accomplished by contact with an old religious man, Oliver's by Orlando's generosity in saving his life. Fortunes are adjusted and dark natures are brightened by the simple impact of virtue. All of this makes a tidy package if Fortune and Nature are conceived as the major forces in life and if these forces are thought to work toward human happiness. Shakespeare's world view was ordinarily more complex.

It is, after all, a kind of innocence to believe that evil is certain men and that goodness is certain other men. And it is the sunniest optimism to believe that the evil are converted by contact with the good. In other plays of Shakespeare, even in the other comedies, temperaments are not so consistently agreeable or disagreeable and resolutions are not so sweet. Orsino, in *Twelfth Night*, is as romantic as Orlando but, where Orlando is vigorous and sensible, Orsino is passive and self-indulgent. Orsino is a generally sympathetic character, but there is something in him which dissatisfies us. Beatrice, in *Much Ado About Nothing*, is as witty as Rosalind but lacks her self-knowledge and is sometimes near to shrewishness. Beatrice is an attractive figure, but she has traits that threaten her happiness. The unsympathetic Malvolio, in *Twelfth Night*, is not transformed by contact with goodness; his last line is: "I'll be revenged on the whole pack of you." Shakespeare's characters ordinarily mix good with evil. His dramatic tension often derives from irreconcilable desires within each nature rather than from an easily corrected malallocation of Fortune's gifts. The exercise of virtue in some of his plays only stimulates the wicked to further wickedness. Why are these darker principles suspended in *As You Like It?*

The play is intended to suggest that human life can be harmoniously lived; that good sense, love, humor, and a generous disposition will produce happiness. Such a view requires not suppression of, but inattention to, those aspects of motivation and of human relationship that, in life, continually postpone a general harmony. A world that includes irreconcilable personal conflict and unrepenting evil can achieve justice, but not universal happiness.

As You Like It causes us to entertain seriously an illusion —a view of life in which a human wish plays a greater role than reality. Yet the play is far from being continuously idyllic. It is filled with sharp comment and disillusioning fact, particularly in connection with its chief subjects—the simple life and romantic love. These subjects are themselves illusions, conventional illusions, sentimental and foolish. Shakespeare laughs at their conventional treatment, threatens them with contrary views and conflicting facts, but in the end preserves them. The play reconciles the ideal with the actual. But not all of the actual. Shakespeare has looked away from the uglier facts, the ultimate ironies that cannot be integrated into a vision of harmony and happiness. Perhaps it is only *The Tempest* and *The Winter's Tale*, plays written after the great tragedies, that make happiness seem to be generally possible and yet also offer powerful representations of evil and suffering.

If *As You Like It* offered a completely one-sided presentation of harmony, we might be armed against it. But it does not. It presents numerous contrary arguments, and the tension they bring to the debate in Arden lends credence to the resolution. For as long as the play lasts we do not notice that the case against the ideal has not been as strong as it could be; that matters that cannot be reconciled with the ideal have been passed over. It is an illusion that *As You Like It* creates, but an illusion that admits so much of life as to seem possible.

What is the nature of the contrarieties that are reconciled with the pastoral ideal and the ideal of romantic love? Arrived in Arden, Touchstone is asked how he likes the shepherd's life and he replies:

> In respect that it is solitary, I like it very well; but in respect that it is private, it is a very vile life. Now in respect it is in the fields, it pleaseth me well; but in respect it is not in the court, it is tedious. As it is a spare life, look you, it fits my humor well; but as there is no more plenty in it, it goes much against my stomach.

The expression of one idea stimulates Touchstone to the expression of its contrary. But the ideas are not contraries of objective fact. To be solitary is to be private; to be in the fields is to be not in the court; to lead a spare life is to lead a life that has no more plenty in it. The objective facts are the same and the opposition is one of sentiment. A life spent apart from others can be agreeable or it can be disagreeable. When it is agreeable Touchstone would call it solitary and when it is disagreeable he would call it private. What can cause the same objective condition to change its nature?

Rosalind, who stands in the center of all things in this play, answers our question, but with reference to time rather than life in the forest. "Time," she says, "travels in divers paces with divers persons." She goes on to particularize. For a young maid "between the contract of her marriage and the day it is solemnized" time trots too slowly. For a rich man who "hath not the gout" time ambles most agreeably. For a thief on his way to the gallows time goes too swiftly. To generalize Rosalind's remarks: time and life in the forest are apprehended differently by different persons and differently by one person according to his condition of life and state of appetite. Life in the forest and romantic love are ideal in their season but they are not for all seasons. Like a holiday, the Greenwood and true love offer refreshment and regeneration. Prolonged beyond their season they become absurd and distasteful.

Touchstone concludes the speech quoted above by asking Corin: "Hast any philosophy in thee, shepherd?" Corin's response begins: "No more, but that I know the more one sickens, the worse at ease he is." At first this reply seems a simple extension of Touchstone's list of on-the-one-hand-this, but-on-the-other-hand-that. Then one realizes that the contrast between Corin's two terms, "the more one sickens" and "the worse at ease," does not follow Touchstone's principle. Corin's terms are objective synonyms as are Touchstone's, but Corin's are also subjective synonyms; to be sick and to be ill at ease are both disagreeable. It seems then that simple Corin has missed the point. Except that sickness is one of the things in life that is not psychologically relative; we never have an appetite for it. It is an absolute evil. Without knowing just how much philosophy the old shepherd had in him, we can take his line as the text for another proposition about *As You Like It.* The relativism of the play's discourse is bounded by a set of moral absolutes that cannot be taken as you like it.

Touchstone's speech concerns the pastoral life and this is a major subject of the conversations in Arden through Act III, Scene ii. Pastoralism is a place and time apart. It is the restorative Greenwood, where men live in the simplicity of nature. It is a remote Golden Age of harmony and innocence. The modern time and the corrupt court are its antithesis.

Duke Senior realizes the pastoral dream in Arden, finding "books in the running brooks" and "sermons in stones." Amiens sings sweetly of pastoralism in "Under the Greenwood Tree." But Jaques, who is of another humor, adds a jaundiced verse calling that man a fool who leaves wealth and ease for the wilderness. In course of time it develops that the winds are cold in Arden and the ground is hard, that the deer, "native burghers of this desert city," can be as indifferent to the misery of one of their kind as human beings can be, and that at least one lion and one snake are among the animal life. Life in the forest is not a fixed reality. It is able to produce happiness and able to produce misery. Love has potentialities that are more complex.

Love is revealed directly in the romance of Rosalind and Orlando and, by contrast, in the matching of Silvius with Phebe, and the mating of Audrey with Touchstone. The former pair disenchants us with certain aspects of both pastoralism and love. Silvius at first appears as the lovelorn shepherd of pastoral romance and Phebe as his pouting shepherdess. The sighing and spurning that are so graceful in the classical picture are distasteful when we see a little more of them. Silvius is an abject figure with his "Sweet Phebe, pity me." He shows what love can descend to when it is not combined with good sense. Phebe shows the response such love will inspire in a petulant nature:

> But since that thou canst talk of love so well,
> Thy company, which erst was irksome to me,
> I will endure; and I'll employ thee too.
> But do not look for further recompense
> Than thine own gladness that thou art employed.

We delight in Rosalind's pungent advice to Phebe: "Sell when you can, you are not for all markets."

For Touchstone love is a ubiquitous human need that seeks an object; it is very like a need that in animals is seasonal. Audrey, falling within his tolerance limits, is taken as an object. Romantic love does not have an object; it has an incomparable inspiration. Orlando, with Rosalind for inspiration, hangs love poems on trees and cries her name throughout the forest. Rosalind, hearing that Celia has seen Orlando, excitedly asks: "What did he when thou saw'st him? What said he? How looked he? Wherein went he? What makes he here?"

The several aspects of love are revealed by the three unlike love affairs. They are revealed also in the running discourse in Arden. There is no scene in which the nature of love is debated. No one keeps to the subject for long; Rosalind ends her catechism of love, in which Orlando and Phebe echo Silvius' exalted sentiments, with: "Pray you, no more of this; 'tis like the howling of Irish wolves against the moon." The discourse is composed of an ironic remark from Touchstone in one scene, something extravagantly amorous from Orlando in another, a joke from Celia in still another. The touches of color, the shading, the points of light, are distributed in time, but they come together to make a rather complex representation.

The disillusioned remarks on love, as on pastoralism, come chiefly from Jaques and Touchstone. Jaques is a man who has traveled and come back a weary malcontent; he stands somewhat detached from life. He is a variation on a familiar kind of stage figure in Shakespeare's day, a type first found in the snarling verse satires written by John Marston and Joseph Hall in the 1590's. After 1599 the type appears in the drama: the bitter critic who defends his railing and abusive language by saying that such attacks as his are the only way to purge the world of its vices. In Act II, Scene vii, Duke Senior attacks Jaques as if he were a perfect instance of this type, and Jaques responds with the critic's familiar defense. In fact, however, Shakespeare has departed from the type.

Jaques ridicules human ideals, but his attacks are not corrosive and they are entertainingly expressed. Seeing Touchstone and Audrey press in among the country copulatives, Jaques remarks: "There is, sure, another flood toward, and these couples are coming to the ark." That he enjoys hearing Amiens sing argues a certain sweetness of nature, sweeter at any rate than the nature of Shylock, to whom music is the "vile squeaking of the wry-necked fife." The other characters appear to enjoy the company of Jaques as they would not the company of so vicious a satirist as Thersites in *Troilus and Cressida*. Duke Senior loves to be with him in his "sullen fits," for then Jaques is "full of matter," and at the end the Duke urges Jaques to return with him to the court.

The darker potentialities of Jaques are hinted at, but on the whole he is an entertaining fellow and much that he says about love is true—when one is not in love. However, those who are most in love do not envy Jaques' detachment and knowledge of life. Rosalind gives her opinion that those who are either too sad or too merry are "abominable fellows," but between the two she would rather "have a fool to make me merry than experience to make me sad."

In Touchstone we have the fool Rosalind asks for. He sees as little in life to make one sad as Jaques sees to make one merry. Jaques is perhaps a disappointed idealist; but Touchstone is a realist who believes that happiness derives from the satisfactions of the body and from a wit that is quick to see the absurdity and folly in life. As Miss Gardner and Professor Goldsmith point out, Touchstone is the great parodist of the play (see, for instance, his love poem to Rosalind following those of Orlando). Touchstone's marriage to Audrey, the simple-minded shepherdess, who in fact is a goatherd, is itself a parody, but one of Shakespeare's making rather than Touchstone's. It is a parody on romance and pastoralism; but it is also the author's comment on the limitations of Touchstone's view of life.

Touchstone and Jaques are alike in their rejection of the ideal and alike therefore in their incompleteness. They show us the ideal as absurdity and sentimentality. Orlando and Rosalind show us romantic love as the best part of life so long as it is understood to be only a part, something that is here and now and should be enjoyed in its time. The play as a whole presents this view, but it is fully articulated by Rosalind alone.

Many romantic lines come from Orlando and Rosalind, and if they were to follow one upon another it would be "to have honey a sauce to sugar." Between sweets, however, there is always something sharp to taste. Sometimes it is provided by Jaques or Touchstone or Celia but most often perhaps by Rosalind as Ganymede. The contrast preserves the flavor. When Orlando swears that he will die of love if he cannot have Rosalind, she gives him her answer: "Men have died from time to time, and worms have eaten them, but not for love."

To speak of contrast is to suggest that one aspect is

subordinate to the others; in the extreme case, that it exists only to set off the others. This is not the case with Rosalind's statements about love. Rosalind's line is comically matter-of-fact, very flat, but, after all, true. It checks Orlando just as he is about to move into absurdity. He loves her and it seems to him now that he cannot live without her, but if, in fact, he could not have her he would find reason to live.

Romantic love strains toward eternity. Memory and observation and the foresight they give are its enemies. When Orlando swears that he will love forever and a day, Rosalind responds: "Say 'a day' without the 'ever.' No, no, Orlando. Men are April when they woo, December when they wed. Maids are May when they are maids, but the sky changes when they are wives."

On another occasion Rosalind as Ganymede teases Orlando by insisting that he has not the look of the distracted lover. "You are rather point-device in your accouterments, as loving yourself than seeming the lover of any other." Here again she is ridiculing the extremities of romantic love. At times she makes jokes that are bawdy and so reveal a facet of love. Orlando brings his destiny with him, she says. "What's that?" he asks. "Why horns; which such as you are fain to be beholding to your wives for." And when Orlando asks if she will love him—"Ay, and twenty such."

Yet Rosalind is unquestionably in love. To Celia she confides "that thou didst know how many fathom deep I am in love. But it cannot be sounded. My affection hath an unknown bottom, like the Bay of Portugal." Rosalind's disguise as Ganymede and her game with Orlando in which she is supposed to try to cure him of love provide an excuse for the expression of her many unromantic sentiments. But they are not to be understood as ideas invented for Ganymede with no validity for Rosalind. While in love she is able to realize what love may become in time and how it can appear to those who are not in love. She sees all around her subject, combining perspectives in the manner of certain Picasso portraits. In Rosalind's conversation we see love's two eyes and also its profile and the back of its neck.

Rosalind integrates the ideal and the working-day world;

love is a good time of life, it is youth and springtime. It is not everything, but in its season it would be folly not to enjoy it. "Come, woo me, woo me," she says, "for now I am in a holiday humor and like enough to consent." Rosalind, whose nature unites ardor and intelligence, synthesizes the ideas of the play.

When so much has been said about cuckoldry and about April turning to December, it may be a little difficult to accept the four marriages of the last scene as a happy ending. But the jokes and the irony and the mockery have been directed primarily at love, not at marriage. Marriage belongs to the institutions of a stable society, and these are never questioned in the play. The responsibility of an elder brother for a younger is the institutional frame that immediately establishes Oliver's villainy. The respect a younger brother owes an elder is the standard that marks Frederick a scoundrel. And the last words about love, the words that assign it to its proper place in an orderly society and prepare for the festive dance at the end, are delivered by Hymen:

> Wedding is great Juno's crown,
> O blessed bond of board and bed!
> 'Tis Hymen peoples every town;
> High wedlock then be honorèd.

Note on the date:

On August 4, 1600, the Lord Chamberlain's Men entered *As You Like It* and three other plays in the Stationers' Register "to be staied" as a way of preventing their unauthorized publication. This entry sets the later limit for the date of *As You Like It*. An earlier limit is set by its absence from the list of Shakespeare's plays given by Francis Meres in *Palladis Tamia* (1598). In one of her speeches Celia says: "Since the little wit that fools have was silenced, the little foolery that wise men have makes a great show" (I.ii.). This remark may be a reference to an official order of June 1, 1599, whereby the published writings of a number of satirists were burnt and the future printing of satires prohibited. In view of this possibility and the two limiting dates, the best supposition is that the play was written in the latter half of 1599 or early in 1600.

ALBERT GILMAN
Boston University

As You Like It

As You Like It

ACT I

Scene I. [*Orchard of Oliver's house.*]

Enter Orlando and Adam.

Orlando. As I remember, Adam, it was upon this fashion
bequeathed me by will but poor a°¹ thousand crowns,
and, as thou say'st, charged my brother on his blessing
to breed me well; and there begins my sadness. My
brother Jaques he keeps at school, and report speaks   5
goldenly of his profit.° For my part, he keeps me
rustically° at home or, to speak more properly, stays
me here at home unkept;° for call you that keeping
for a gentleman of my birth that differs not from the
stalling of an ox? His horses are bred better, for,   10
besides that they are fair° with their feeding, they are
taught their manage,° and to that end riders dearly
hired; but I, his brother, gain nothing under him but
growth, for the which his animals on his dunghills
are as much bound to him as I. Besides this nothing   15
that he so plentifully gives me, the something that

---

¹ The degree sign (°) indicates a footnote, which is keyed to the
text by line number. Text references are printed in *italic* type;
the annotation follows in roman type.
I.i.2 *poor a* a mere   6 *goldenly of his profit* glowingly of his progress
6–7 *keeps me rustically* supports me like a peasant   8 *unkept* uncared
for   11 *fair* handsome   12 *manage* paces

nature gave me his countenance° seems to take from
me. He lets me feed with his hinds,° bars me the place
of a brother, and, as much as in him lies, mines my
20 gentility° with my education. This is it, Adam, that
grieves me; and the spirit of my father, which I think
is within me, begins to mutiny against this servitude.
I will no longer endure it, though yet I know no wise
remedy how to avoid it.

Enter Oliver.

25 *Adam.* Yonder comes my master, your brother.

Orlando. Go apart, Adam, and thou shalt hear how he
will shake me up.°

Oliver. Now, sir, what make you° here?

Orlando. Nothing. I am not taught to make anything.

30 *Oliver.* What mar you then, sir?

Orlando. Marry,° sir, I am helping you to mar that
which God made, a poor unworthy brother of yours,
with idleness.

Oliver. Marry, sir, be better employed, and be naught
35 awhile.°

Orlando. Shall I keep your hogs and eat husks with
them? What prodigal portion have I spent° that I
should come to such penury?

Oliver. Know you where° you are, sir?

40 *Orlando.* O, sir, very well. Here in your orchard.

Oliver. Know you before whom, sir?

Orlando. Ay, better than him I am before knows me. I

17 *countenance* behavior 18 *hinds* farm hands 19-20 *mines my gentility* undermines my good birth 27 *shake me up* berate me 28 *make you* are you doing (in the next line Orlando pretends to take the phrase to mean "accomplish") 31 *Marry* (an expletive, from "By the Virgin Mary") 34-35 *be naught awhile* i.e., don't bother me 36-37 *Shall I . . . spent* (an allusion to the story of the Prodigal Son. See Luke 15:11-32) 39 *where* i.e., in whose presence (Orlando pretends to take it literally)

know you are my eldest brother, and in the gentle
condition of blood° you should so know me. The
courtesy of nations° allows you my better in that you   45
are the first born, but the same tradition takes not
away my blood were there twenty brothers betwixt
us. I have as much of my father in me as you, albeit
I confess your coming before me is nearer to his
reverence.°   50

Oliver. What, boy!   [*Strikes him.*]

Orlando. Come, come, elder brother, you are too young
    in this.   [*Seizes him.*]

Oliver. Wilt thou lay hands on me, villain?°

Orlando. I am no villain. I am the youngest son of Sir   55
    Rowland de Boys; he was my father, and he is thrice
    a villain that says such a father begot villains. Wert
    thou not my brother, I would not take this hand from
    thy throat till this other had pulled out thy tongue
    for saying so. Thou hast railed on thyself.   60

Adam. Sweet masters, be patient. For your father's
    remembrance, be at accord.

Oliver. Let me go, I say.

Orlando. I will not till I please. You shall hear me. My
    father charged you in his will to give me good educa-   65
    tion. You have trained me like a peasant, obscuring
    and hiding from me all gentlemanlike qualities.° The
    spirit of my father grows strong in me, and I will no
    longer endure it. Therefore allow me such exercises°
    as may become a gentleman, or give me the poor   70
    allottery° my father left me by testament; with that I
    will go buy my fortunes.

43–44 *in the gentle condition of blood* i.e., of the same good blood
45 *courtesy of nations* i.e., sanctioned custom of primogeniture
49–50 *your coming . . . reverence* i.e., as the eldest son you are head of
the family and therefore entitled to respect   54 *villain* (Oliver uses it
in the sense of "wicked person," but Orlando plays on its other
meaning, "low-born person")   67 *qualities* accomplishments   69 *exercises* occupations   71 *allottery* share

Oliver. And what wilt thou do? Beg when that is spent?
Well, sir, get you in. I will not long be troubled with
75   you. You shall have some part of your will. I pray
you leave me.

Orlando. I will no further offend you than becomes me
for my good.

Oliver. Get you with him, you old dog.

80   *Adam.* Is "old dog" my reward? Most true, I have lost
my teeth in your service. God be with my old master;
he would not have spoke such a word.
                                        Exeunt Orlando, Adam.

Oliver. Is it even so? Begin you to grow upon me?° I
will physic your rankness° and yet give no thousand
85   crowns neither. Holla, Dennis!

                          Enter Dennis.

Dennis. Calls your worship?

Oliver. Was not Charles, the Duke's wrestler, here to
speak with me?

Dennis. So please you, he is here at the door and impor-
90   tunes access to you.

Oliver. Call him in. [*Exit Dennis.*] 'Twill be a good way;
and tomorrow the wrestling is.

                          Enter Charles.

Charles. Good morrow to your worship.

Oliver. Good Monsieur Charles, what's the new news
95   at the new court?

Charles. There's no news at the court, sir, but the old
news. That is, the old Duke° is banished by his
younger brother the new Duke, and three or four
loving lords have put themselves into voluntary exile
100   with him, whose lands and revenues enrich the new

---

83 *grow upon me* i.e., usurp my place   84 *physic your rankness* purge
your overgrowth   97 *old Duke* i.e., Duke Senior

Duke; therefore he gives them good leave to wander.

Oliver. Can you tell if Rosalind, the Duke's daughter,
be banished with her father?

Charles. O, no; for the Duke's daughter, her cousin, so
loves her, being ever from their cradles bred together, *105*
that she would have followed her exile, or have died
to stay behind her. She is at the court, and no less
beloved of her uncle than his own daughter, and never
two ladies loved as they do.

Oliver. Where will the old Duke live? *110*

Charles. They say he is already in the Forest of Arden,°
and a many merry men with him; and there they live
like the old Robin Hood of England. They say many
young gentlemen flock to him every day, and fleet
the time carelessly° as they did in the golden world.° *115*

Oliver. What, you wrestle tomorrow before the new
Duke?

Charles. Marry, do I, sir; and I came to acquaint you
with a matter. I am given, sir, secretly to understand
that your younger brother, Orlando, hath a disposi- *120*
tion to come in disguised against me to try a fall.°
Tomorrow, sir, I wrestle for my credit, and he that
escapes me without some broken limb shall acquit
him well. Your brother is but young and tender, and
for your love I would be loath to foil° him, as I must *125*
for my own honor if he come in. Therefore, out of
my love to you, I came hither to acquaint you withal,
that either you might stay him from his intendment,
or brook° such disgrace well as he shall run into, in
that it is a thing of his own search and altogether *130*
against my will.

---

111 *Forest of Arden* Ardennes (in France; though Shakespeare may
also have had in mind the Forest of Arden near his birthplace)
114–115 *fleet the time carelessly* pass the time at ease   115 *golden
world* (the Golden Age of classical mythology, when men were free
of sin, want, and care)   121 *fall* bout   125 *foil* throw, defeat
129 *brook* endure

Oliver. Charles, I thank thee for thy love to me, which
thou shalt find I will most kindly requite. I had myself notice of my brother's purpose herein and have
135   by underhand means° labored to dissuade him from
it; but he is resolute. I'll tell thee, Charles, it is the
stubbornest young fellow of France; full of ambition,
an envious emulator° of every man's good parts,° a
secret and villainous contriver against me his natural°
140   brother. Therefore use thy discretion. I had as lief°
thou didst break his neck as his finger. And thou
wert best look to't; for if thou dost him any slight
disgrace, or if he do not mightily grace himself on
thee,° he will practice° against thee by poison, entrap
145   thee by some treacherous device, and never leave thee
till he hath ta'en thy life by some indirect means or
other; for, I assure thee, and almost with tears I
speak it, there is not one so young and so villainous
this day living. I speak but brotherly of him, but
150   should I anatomize° him to thee as he is, I must
blush and weep, and thou must look pale and wonder.

Charles. I am heartily glad I came hither to you. If he
come tomorrow, I'll give him his payment. If ever he
go alone° again, I'll never wrestle for prize more. And
155   so God keep your worship.   *Exit.*

Oliver. Farewell, good Charles. Now will I stir this
gamester.° I hope I shall see an end of him; for my
soul, yet I know not why, hates nothing more than
he. Yet he's gentle,° never schooled and yet learned,
160   full of noble device,° of all sorts° enchantingly beloved; and indeed so much in the heart of the world,
and especially of my own people, who best know him,
that I am altogether misprized.° But it shall not be so

cp. Oth.   "he was a ~~kind of daily beauty~~ etc "

135 *by underhand means* indirectly   138 *envious emulator* malicious
rival   138 *parts* abilities   139 *natural* blood   140 *lief* soon   143–
144 *grace himself on thee* gain credit at your expense   144 *practice* plot   150 *anatomize* fully describe   154 *go alone* i.e., walk
without crutches   157 *gamester* athlete, sportsman   159 *gentle* en-
dowed with the qualities of a gentleman   160 *noble device* gentleman-
like purposes   160 *all sorts* all kinds of people   163 *misprized* scorned

long; this wrestler shall clear all.° Nothing remains
but that I kindle the boy thither, which now I'll go   165
about.   *Exit.*

Scene II. [*The Duke's palace.*]

Enter Rosalind and Celia.

Celia. I pray thee, Rosalind, sweet my coz,° be merry.

Rosalind. Dear Celia, I show more mirth than I am
mistress of, and would you yet I were merrier? Unless
you could teach me to forget a banished father, you
must not learn° me how to remember any extraordi-   5
nary pleasure.

Celia. Herein I see thou lov'st me not with the full
weight that I love thee. If my uncle, thy banished
father, had banished thy uncle, the Duke my father,
so° thou hadst been still with me, I could have taught   10
my love to take thy father for mine. So wouldst thou,
if the truth of thy love to me were so righteously
tempered° as mine is to thee.

Rosalind. Well, I will forget the condition of my estate°
to rejoice in yours.   15

Celia. You know my father hath no child but I, nor
none is like to have; and truly, when he dies, thou
shalt be his heir; for what he hath taken away from
thy father perforce,° I will render thee again in affection. By mine honor, I will, and when I break that   20
oath, let me turn monster. Therefore, my sweet Rose,
my dear Rose, be merry.

---

164 *clear all* settle matters   I.ii.1 *sweet my coz* my sweet cousin
5 *learn* teach   10 *so* provided that   12–13 *righteously tempered* perfectly composed   14 *estate* fortune   19 *perforce* forcibly

Rosalind. From henceforth I will, coz, and devise sports.
Let me see, what think you of falling in love?

25 *Celia.* Marry, I prithee, do, to make sport withal; but
love no man in good earnest, nor no further in sport
neither than with safety of a pure° blush thou mayst
in honor come off° again.

Rosalind. What shall be our sport then?

30 *Celia.* Let us sit and mock the good housewife° Fortune
from her wheel,° that her gifts may henceforth be
bestowed equally.

Rosalind. I would we could do so, for her benefits are
mightily misplaced, and the bountiful blind woman
35 doth most mistake in her gifts to women.

Celia. 'Tis true, for those that she makes fair,° she scarce
makes honest,° and those that she makes honest, she
makes very ill-favoredly.°

Rosalind. Nay, now thou goest from Fortune's office°
40 to Nature's. Fortune reigns in gifts of the world,° not
in the lineaments of Nature.°

Enter [Touchstone, the] Clown.

Celia. No; when Nature hath made a fair creature, may
she not by Fortune fall into the fire? Though Nature
hath given us wit to flout at Fortune, hath not For-
45 tune sent in this fool to cut off the argument?

Rosalind. Indeed, there is Fortune too hard for Nature
when Fortune makes Nature's natural° the cutter-off
of Nature's wit.

Celia. Peradventure° this is not Fortune's work neither,
50 but Nature's, who perceiveth our natural wits too

27 *pure* mere   28 *come off* get away   30 *housewife* (1) woman of the
house (with a spinning wheel) (2) inconstant hussy   31 *wheel*(the
wheel turned by Fortune, blind goddess who distributed her favors at ran-
dom, elevated some men and hurled others down)   36 *fair* beautiful
37 *honest* chaste   38 *ill-favoredly* ugly   39 *office* function   40 *gifts
of the world* e.g., wealth, power   41 *lineaments of Nature* e.g., virtue,
intelligence   47 *natural* born fool, halfwit   49 *Peradventure* perhaps

dull to reason of such goddesses and hath sent this
natural for our whetstone. For always the dullness of
the fool is the whetstone of the wits. How now, wit;
whither wander you?

Touchstone. Mistress, you must come away to your   55
father.

Celia. Were you made the messenger?

Touchstone. No, by mine honor, but I was bid to come
for you.

Rosalind. Where learned you that oath, fool?   60

Touchstone. Of a certain knight that swore by his honor
they were good pancakes, and swore by his honor the
mustard was naught.° Now I'll stand to it,° the pancakes were naught, and the mustard was good, and   65
yet was not the knight forsworn.°

Celia. How prove you that in the great heap of your
knowledge?

Rosalind. Ay, marry, now unmuzzle your wisdom.

Touchstone. Stand you both forth now. Stroke your
chins, and swear by your beards that I am a knave.   70

Celia. By our beards, if we had them, thou art.

Touchstone. By my knavery, if I had it, then I were;
but if you swear by that that is not, you are not forsworn; no more was this knight, swearing by his
honor, for he never had any; or if he had, he had   75
sworn it away before ever he saw those pancakes or
that mustard.

Celia. Prithee, who is't that thou mean'st?

Touchstone. One that old Frederick, your father, loves.

Celia. My father's love is enough to honor him enough.   80

---

63 *naught* worthless   63 *stand to it* swear   65 *forsworn* perjured

Speak no more of him; you'll be whipped for taxa-
tion° one of these days.

Touchstone. The more pity that fools may not speak
wisely what wise men do foolishly.

85 *Celia.* By my troth,° thou sayest true, for since the little
wit that fools have was silenced, the little foolery that
wise men have makes a great show. Here comes
Monsieur Le Beau.

Enter Le Beau.

Rosalind. With his mouth full of news.

90 *Celia.* Which he will put° on us as pigeons feed their
young.

Rosalind. Then shall we be news-crammed.

Celia. All the better; we shall be the more marketable.
Bon jour, Monsieur Le Beau, what's the news?

95 *Le Beau.* Fair princess, you have lost much good sport.

Celia. Sport? Of what color?°

Le Beau. What color, madam? How shall I answer you?

Rosalind. As wit and fortune° will.

Touchstone. Or as the Destinies decrees.°

100 *Celia.* Well said; that was laid on with a trowel.

Touchstone. Nay, if I keep not my rank—

Rosalind. Thou losest thy old smell.

Le Beau. You amaze° me, ladies. I would have told you
of good wrestling, which you have lost the sight of.°

105 *Rosalind.* Yet tell us the manner of the wrestling.

Le Beau. I will tell you the beginning; and if it please
your ladyships, you may see the end, for the best is

82 *taxation* slander 85 *troth* faith 90 *put* force 96 *color* sort
98 *fortune* good luck 99 *decrees* (the ending *s* was a common variant
in the third person plural) 103 *amaze* confuse 104 *lost the sight
of* missed

yet to do,° and here, where you are, they are coming
to perform it.

Celia. Well, the beginning that is dead and buried.   110

Le Beau. There comes an old man and his three sons—

Celia. I could match this beginning with an old tale.°

Le Beau. Three proper° young men, of excellent growth
and presence.

Rosalind. With bills° on their necks, "Be it known unto   115
all men by these presents."°

Le Beau. The eldest of the three wrestled with Charles,
the Duke's wrestler; which Charles in a moment
threw him and broke three of his ribs, that there is
little hope of life in him. So he served the second, and   120
so the third. Yonder they lie, the poor old man, their
father, making such pitiful dole° over them that all
the beholders take his part with weeping.

Rosalind. Alas!

Touchstone. But what is the sport, monsieur, that the   125
ladies have lost?

Le Beau. Why, this that I speak of.

Touchstone. Thus men may grow wiser every day. It is
the first time that ever I heard breaking of ribs was
sport for ladies.   130

Celia. Or I, I promise thee.

Rosalind. But is there any° else longs to see this broken
music° in his sides? Is there yet another dotes upon
rib-breaking? Shall we see this wrestling, cousin?

Le Beau. You must, if you stay here, for here is the   135

---

108 *do* be done   112 *old tale* (Le Beau's story has a "Once upon a
time" beginning)   113 *proper* fine   115 *bills* notices   116 *by these
presents* (part of the opening formula of many legal documents. Rosalind puns on Le Beau's use of "presence," meaning "bearing")
122 *dole* lamentation   132 *any* anyone   132–133 *broken music* music
arranged in parts for different instruments

place appointed for the wrestling, and they are ready
to perform it.

Celia. Yonder sure they are coming. Let us now stay
and see it.

*Flourish.° Enter Duke [Frederick], Lords, Orlando,
Charles, and Attendants.*

140 *Duke Frederick.* Come on. Since the youth will not be
entreated, his own peril on his forwardness.

Rosalind. Is yonder the man?

Le Beau. Even he, madam.

Celia. Alas, he is too young; yet he looks successfully.°

145 *Duke Frederick.* How now, daughter and cousin; are
you crept hither to see the wrestling?

Rosalind. Ay, my liege, so please you give us leave.

Duke Frederick. You will take little delight in it, I can
tell you, there is such odds in the man.° In pity of the
150 challenger's youth I would fain° dissuade him, but he
will not be entreated. Speak to him, ladies; see if you
can move him.

Celia. Call him hither, good Monsieur Le Beau.

Duke Frederick. Do so. I'll not be by.

155 *Le Beau.* Monsieur the challenger, the princess calls for
you.

Orlando. I attend them with all respect and duty.

Rosalind. Young man, have you challenged Charles the
wrestler?

160 *Orlando.* No, fair princess. He is the general challenger;
I come but in as others do, to try with him the strength
of my youth.

Celia. Young gentleman, your spirits are too bold for

139 *s.d. Flourish* trumpet fanfare   144 *successfully* able to succeed
149 *such odds in the man* i.e., the odds are all in Charles' favor
150 *fain* like to

your years. You have seen cruel proof of this man's
strength; if you saw yourself with your eyes or knew   165
yourself with your judgment, the fear of your adventure would counsel you to a more equal enterprise.
We pray you for your own sake to embrace your own
safety and give over this attempt.

Rosalind. Do, young sir. Your reputation shall not   170
therefore be misprized;° we will make it our suit to
the Duke that the wrestling might not go forward.

Orlando. I beseech you, punish me not with your hard
thoughts, wherein I confess me much guilty to deny
so fair and excellent ladies anything. But let your fair   175
eyes and gentle wishes go with me to my trial; wherein
if I be foiled,° there is but one shamed that was never
gracious;° if killed, but one dead that is willing to be
so. I shall do my friends no wrong, for I have none
to lament me; the world no injury, for in it I have   180
nothing. Only in the world I° fill up a place, which
may be better supplied when I have made it empty.

Rosalind. The little strength that I have, I would it were
with you.

Celia. And mine to eke° out hers.   185

Rosalind. Fare you well. Pray heaven I be deceived in
you!°

Celia. Your heart's desires be with you!

Charles. Come, where is this young gallant that is so
desirous to lie with his mother earth?   190

Orlando. Ready, sir; but his will hath in it a more
modest working.°

Duke Frederick. You shall try but one fall.

Charles. No, I warrant your Grace you shall not entreat

---

171 *misprized* despised   **177** *foiled* thrown   **178** *gracious* graced by
Fortune   **181** *Only in the world I* in the world I only   **185** *eke* stretch
186–187 *deceived in you* i.e., wrong in my estimation of your strength
192 *modest working* humble aim

195   him to a second that have so mightily persuaded him
from a first.

Orlando. You mean to mock me after. You should not
have mocked me before. But come your ways.°

Rosalind. Now Hercules be thy speed,° young man!

200 *Celia.* I would I were invisible, to catch the strong
fellow by the leg.   *Wrestle.*

Rosalind. O excellent young man!

Celia. If I had a thunderbolt in mine eye, I can tell who
should down.   [*Charles is thrown.*] *Shout.*

205 *Duke Frederick.* No more, no more.

Orlando. Yes, I beseech your Grace; I am not yet well
breathed.°

Duke Frederick. How dost thou, Charles?

Le Beau. He cannot speak, my lord.

210 *Duke Frederick.* Bear him away. What is thy name,
young man?

Orlando. Orlando, my liege, the youngest son of Sir
Rowland de Boys.

Duke Frederick. I would thou hadst been son to some
man else.
215 The world esteemed thy father honorable,
But I did find him still° mine enemy.
Thou shouldst have better pleased me with this deed
Hadst thou descended from another house.
But fare thee well; thou art a gallant youth;
220 I would thou hadst told me of another father.
                                    Exit Duke, [with Train].

Celia. Were I my father, coz, would I do this?

Orlando. I am more proud to be Sir Rowland's son,

---

198 *come your ways* i.e., let's get started   199 *Hercules be thy speed*
may Hercules help you   206–207 *well breathed* fully warmed up
216 *still* always

His youngest son, and would not change that calling°
To be adopted heir to Frederick.

Rosalind. My father loved Sir Rowland as his soul,   225
And all the world was of my father's mind.
Had I before known this young man his son,
I should have given him tears unto° entreaties
Ere he should thus have ventured.

Celia.   Gentle cousin,
Let us go thank him and encourage him.   230
My father's rough and envious disposition
Sticks° me at heart. Sir, you have well deserved;
If you do keep your promises in love
But justly° as you have exceeded all promise,
Your mistress shall be happy.

Rosalind.   Gentleman, [*gives chain*] 235
Wear this for me, one out of suits° with fortune,
That could° give more but that her hand lacks means.
Shall we go, coz?

Celia.   Ay. Fare you well, fair gentleman.

Orlando. Can I not say "I thank you"? My better parts°
Are all thrown down, and that which here stands up 240
Is but a quintain,° a mere lifeless block.

Rosalind. He calls us back. My pride fell with my
        fortunes;
I'll ask him what he would. Did you call, sir?
Sir, you have wrestled well, and overthrown
More than your enemies.

Celia.   Will you go, coz?   245

Rosalind. Have with you.° Fare you well.
                              Exit [*with Celia*].

Orlando. What passion° hangs these weights upon my
        tongue?

223 *calling* name   228 *unto* as well as   232 *Sticks* pains   234 *justly*
exactly   236 *out of suits* in disfavor   237 *could* would   239 *parts*
qualities   241 *quintain* wooden post (used for tilting practice)
246 *Have with you* I'm coming   247 *passion* strong feeling

I cannot speak to her, yet she urged conference.°

Enter Le Beau.

250 O poor Orlando, thou art overthrown!
Or Charles or something weaker masters thee.

Le Beau. Good sir, I do in friendship counsel you
To leave this place. Albeit you have deserved
High commendation, true applause, and love,
255 Yet such is now the Duke's condition
That he misconsters° all that you have done.
The Duke is humorous.° What he is, indeed,
More suits you to conceive° than I to speak of.

Orlando. I thank you, sir; and pray you, tell me this:
Which of the two was daughter of the Duke,
260 That here was at the wrestling?

Le Beau. Neither his daughter, if we judge by manners,
But yet indeed the taller° is his daughter,
The other is daughter to the banished Duke,
And here detained by her usurping uncle
265 To keep his daughter company, whose loves
Are dearer than the natural bond of sisters.
But I can tell you that of late this Duke
Hath ta'en displeasure 'gainst his gentle niece,
Grounded upon no other argument°
270 But that the people praise her for her virtues
And pity her for her good father's sake;
And, on my life, his malice 'gainst the lady
Will suddenly break forth. Sir, fare you well.
Hereafter, in a better world° than this,
275 I shall desire more love and knowledge of you.

Orlando. I rest much bounden° to you. Fare you well.
[*Exit Le Beau.*]
Thus must I from the smoke into the smother,°

248 *conference* conversation   255 *misconsters* misinterprets   256 *humorous* moody   257 *conceive* understand   262 *taller* (unless "taller" is a printer's slip for "smaller," Shakespeare here erred. Rosalind is later said to be taller)   269 *argument* basis   274 *a better world* better times   276 *bounden* indebted   277 *smother* smothering smoke (the idea is: "Out of the frying pan into the fire")

From tyrant Duke unto a tyrant brother.
But heavenly Rosalind!   *Exit.*

Scene III. [*The palace.*]

Enter Celia and Rosalind.

Celia. Why, cousin, why, Rosalind! Cupid have mercy, not a word?

Rosalind. Not one to throw at a dog.

Celia. No, thy words are too precious to be cast away upon curs; throw some of them at me; come, lame 5
me with reasons.

Rosalind. Then there were two cousins laid up, when the one should be lamed with reasons and the other mad° without any.

Celia. But is all this for your father? 10

Rosalind. No, some of it is for my child's father.° O, how full of briers is this working-day world!

Celia. They are but burrs, cousin, thrown upon thee in holiday foolery; if we walk not in the trodden paths, our very petticoats will catch them. 15

Rosalind. I could shake them off my coat; these burrs are in my heart.

Celia. Hem° them away.

Rosalind. I would try, if I could cry "hem,"° and have him. 20

Celia. Come, come, wrestle with thy affections.°

I.iii.9 *mad* melancholy   11 *child's father* i.e., future husband, Orlando
18 *Hem* (1) cough (2) tuck   19 *cry* "*Hem*" clear my throat (with a pun on "him")   21 *affections* feelings

Rosalind. O, they take the part of a better wrestler than
myself!

Celia. O, a good wish upon you! You will try° in time,
in despite of a fall. But turning these jests out of
service,° let us talk in good earnest. Is it possible on
such a sudden you should fall into so strong a liking
with old Sir Rowland's youngest son?

Rosalind. The Duke my father loved his father dearly.

Celia. Doth it therefore ensue that you should love his
son dearly? By this kind of chase,° I should hate him,
for my father hated his father dearly; yet I hate not
Orlando.

Rosalind. No, faith, hate him not, for my sake.

Celia. Why should I not? Doth he not deserve well?°

Enter Duke [Frederick], with Lords.

Rosalind. Let me love him for that,° and do you love
him because I do. Look, here comes the Duke.

Celia. With his eyes full of anger.

Duke Frederick. Mistress, dispatch you with your safest
haste
And get you from our court.

Rosalind.   Me, uncle?

Duke Frederick.   You, cousin.°
Within these ten days if that thou beest found
So near our public court as twenty miles,
Thou diest for it.

Rosalind.   I do beseech your Grace
Let me the knowledge of my fault bear with me.
If with myself I hold intelligence°

24 *try* i.e., chance a bout   25–26 *turning . . . service* to stop joking
31 *chase* pursuit (of the argument)   35 *deserve well* i.e., deserve to be
hated (if Rosalind's reasoning is valid, it follows that Celia should hate
Orlando)   36 *for that* i.e., for his virtues (Rosalind takes "deserve
well" in its usual sense)   40 *cousin* kinsman   45 *hold intelligence*
communicate

Or have acquaintance with mine own desires,
If that I do not dream or be not frantic,°
As I do trust I am not; then, dear uncle,
Never so much as in a thought unborn
Did I offend your Highness.

Duke Frederick.   Thus do all traitors.   50
If their purgation° did consist in words,
They are as innocent as grace° itself.
Let it suffice thee that I trust thee not.

Rosalind. Yet your mistrust cannot make me a traitor.
Tell me whereon the likelihoods° depends.   55

Duke Frederick. Thou art thy father's daughter, there's
    enough.

Rosalind. So was I when your Highness took his duke-
    dom;
So was I when your Highness banished him.
Treason is not inherited, my lord,
Or if we did derive it from our friends,°   60
What's that to me? My father was no traitor.
Then, good my liege, mistake me not so much
To think my poverty is treacherous.

Celia. Dear sovereign, hear me speak.

Duke Frederick. Ay, Celia. We stayed° her for your sake,   65
Else had she with her father ranged° along.

Celia. I did not then entreat to have her stay;
It was your pleasure and your own remorse.°
I was too young that time to value her,
But now I know her. If she be a traitor,   70
Why, so am I. We still° have slept together,
Rose at an instant, learned, played, eat° together;
And wheresoe'er we went, like Juno's swans,
Still we went coupled and inseparable.

47 *frantic* insane   51 *purgation* clearance   52 *grace* virtue   55 *likeli-hoods* possibilities   60 *friends* relatives   65 *stayed* kept   66 *ranged* wandered   68 *remorse* pity   71 *still* always   72 *eat* eaten

Duke Frederick. She is too subtile° for thee; and her
75   smoothness,
    Her very silence and her patience,
    Speak to the people, and they pity her.
    Thou art a fool. She robs thee of thy name,
    And thou wilt show more bright and seem more
        virtuous°
80 When she is gone. Then open not thy lips.
    Firm and irrevocable is my doom°
    Which I have passed upon her; she is banished.

Celia. Pronounce that sentence then on me, my liege;
    I cannot live out of her company.

Duke Frederick. You are a fool. You, niece, provide
85   yourself;
    If you outstay the time, upon mine honor,
    And in the greatness° of my word, you die.

                                Exit Duke, &c.

Celia. O my poor Rosalind, whither wilt thou go?
    Wilt thou change fathers? I will give thee mine.
90 I charge thee be not thou more grieved than I am.

Rosalind. I have more cause.

Celia.   Thou hast not, cousin.
    Prithee be cheerful. Know'st thou not the Duke
    Hath banished me, his daughter?

Rosalind.   That he hath not.

Celia. No? Hath not? Rosalind lacks then the love
95 Which teacheth thee that thou and I am one.
    Shall we be sund'red, shall we part, sweet girl?
    No, let my father seek another heir.
    Therefore devise with me how we may fly,
    Whither to go, and what to bear with us;
100 And do not seek to take your change° upon you,
    To bear your griefs yourself and leave me out;

---

75 *subtile* crafty   79 *virtuous* full of good qualities   81 *doom* sentence
87 *greatness* power   100 *change* i.e., change of fortune

For, by this heaven, now at our sorrows pale,°
Say what thou canst, I'll go along with thee.

Rosalind. Why, whither shall we go?

Celia. To seek my uncle in the Forest of Arden.   105

Rosalind. Alas, what danger will it be to us,
  Maids as we are, to travel forth so far!
  Beauty provoketh thieves sooner than gold.

Celia. I'll put myself in poor and mean° attire
  And with a kind of umber° smirch my face;   110
  The like do you; so shall we pass along
  And never stir assailants.

Rosalind.   Were it not better,
  Because that I am more than common° tall,
  That I did suit me all points° like a man?
  A gallant curtle-ax° upon my thigh,   115
  A boar-spear in my hand; and, in my heart
  Lie there what hidden woman's fear there will,
  We'll have a swashing° and a martial outside,
  As many other mannish cowards have
  That do outface° it with their semblances.°   120

Celia. What shall I call thee when thou art a man?

Rosalind. I'll have no worse a name than Jove's own
      page,
  And therefore look you call me Ganymede.
  But what will you be called?

Celia. Something that hath a reference to my state: 125
  No longer Celia, but Aliena.°

Rosalind. But, cousin, what if we assayed° to steal
  The clownish fool out of your father's court;
  Would he not be a comfort to our travel?

---

102 *now at our sorrows pale* now pale at our sorrows   109 *mean* lowly
110 *umber* reddish-brown color   113 *common* usually   114 *suit me at
all points* dress myself entirely   115 *curtle-ax* cutlass   118 *swashing*
blustering   120 *outface* bluff   120 *semblances* appearances (of bravery)   126 *Aliena* (Latin: the estranged one)   127 *assayed* attempted

130 *Celia.* He'll go along o'er the wide world with me;
        Leave me alone to woo° him. Let's away
        And get our jewels and our wealth together,
        Devise the fittest time and safest way
        To hide us from pursuit that will be made
135   After my flight. Now go in we content
        To liberty, and not to banishment.   *Exeunt.*

131 *woo* coax

ACT II

Scene I. [*The Forest of Arden.*]

Enter Duke Senior, Amiens, and two or three
Lords, like Foresters.

Duke Senior. Now, my co-mates and brothers in exile,°
 Hath not old custom made this life more sweet
 Than that of painted pomp? Are not these woods
 More free from peril than the envious court?
 Here feel we not° the penalty of Adam;°   5
 The seasons' difference, as° the icy fang
 And churlish° chiding of the winter's wind,
 Which, when it bites and blows upon my body
 Even till I shrink with cold, I smile and say
 "This is no flattery; these are counselors   10
 That feelingly° persuade me what I am."
 Sweet are the uses of adversity,
 Which, like the toad, ugly and venomous,
 Wears yet a precious jewel° in his head;
 And this our life, exempt from public haunt,°   15
 Finds tongues in trees, books in the running brooks,
 Sermons in stones, and good in everything.

II.i.1 *exile* (accent on second syllable)   5 *feel we not* we do not feel
(some editors emend "not" to "but")   5 *penalty of Adam* loss of Eden
6 *as* for example   7 *churlish* harsh   11 *feelingly* (1) through the senses
(2) with intensity   14 *a precious jewel* (the fabled toadstone)   15 *public haunt* society

59

Amiens. I would not change it; happy is your Grace
That can translate the stubbornness° of fortune
20 Into so quiet and so sweet a style.

Duke Senior. Come, shall we go and kill us venison?
And yet it irks me the poor dappled fools,°
Being native burghers° of this desert° city,
Should, in their own confines, with forkèd heads°
Have their round haunches gored.

25 *First Lord.*   Indeed, my lord,
The melancholy Jaques° grieves at that,
And in that kind° swears you do more usurp
Than doth your brother that hath banished you.
Today my Lord of Amiens and myself
30 Did steal behind him as he lay along°
Under an oak, whose antique root peeps out
Upon the brook that brawls° along this wood;
To the which place a poor sequest'red° stag
That from the hunter's aim had ta'en a hurt
35 Did come to languish; and indeed, my lord,
The wretched animal heaved forth such groans
That their discharge did stretch his leathern coat
Almost to bursting, and the big round tears
Coursed one another down his innocent nose
40 In piteous chase; and thus the hairy fool,
Much markèd of° the melancholy Jaques,
Stood on th' extremest verge of the swift brook,
Augmenting it with tears.

Duke Senior.   But what said Jaques?
Did he not moralize° this spectacle?

45 *First Lord.* O, yes, into a thousand similes.
First, for his weeping into the needless° stream:
"Poor deer," quoth he, "thou mak'st a testament
As worldlings do, giving thy sum of more

---

19 *stubbornness* hardness 22 *fools* simple creatures 23 *burghers* citizens 23 *desert* deserted 24 *forkèd heads* arrows 26 *Jaques* (dissyl-abic, pronounced "Jā′ kis") 27 *kind* way 30 *along* stretched out
32 *brawls* makes noise 33 *sequest'red* separated 41 *markèd of* noted
by 44 *moralize* sermonize 46 *needless* i.e., needing no more water

    To that which had too much." Then, being there
        alone,
    Left and abandoned of his velvet° friend: *50*
    " 'Tis right," quoth he, "thus misery doth part
    The flux° of company." Anon a careless° herd,
    Full of the pasture, jumps along by him
    And never stays to greet him; "Ay," quoth Jaques,
    "Sweep on, you fat and greasy citizens,   *55*
    'Tis just the fashion; wherefore do you look°
    Upon that poor and broken bankrupt there?"
    Thus most invectively he pierceth through
    The body of the country, city, court,
    Yea, and of this our life, swearing that we   *60*
    Are mere usurpers, tyrants, and what's worse,
    To fright the animals and to kill them up
    In their assigned° and native dwelling place.

Duke Senior. And did you leave him in this contempla-
    tion?

Second Lord. We did, my lord, weeping and commenting   *65*
    Upon the sobbing deer.

Duke Senior.   Show me the place.
    I love to cope° him in these sullen fits,
    For then he's full of matter.

First Lord. I'll bring you to him straight.°   *Exeunt.*

---

50 *velvet* i.e., courtierlike (the furry skin on the antlers, or the sleek hide,
makes the deer resemble a velvet-clad courtier)   52 *flux* stream
52 *Anon a careless* soon an untroubled   56 *wherefore do you look* why
should you bother looking   63 *assigned* allotted (by nature)   67 *cope*
encounter   69 *straight* at once

Scene II. [*The palace.*]

Enter Duke [Frederick], with Lords.

Duke Frederick. Can it be possible that no man saw
  them?
It cannot be; some villains of my court
Are of consent and sufferance° in this.

First Lord. I cannot hear of any that did see her.
5 The ladies, her attendants of her chamber,
Saw her abed, and in the morning early
They found the bed untreasured of their mistress.

Second Lord. My lord, the roynish° clown at whom so
  oft
Your Grace was wont to laugh is also missing.
10 Hisperia, the princess' gentlewoman,
Confesses that she secretly o'erheard
Your daughter and her cousin much commend
The parts and graces° of the wrestler
That did but lately foil the sinewy Charles,
15 And she believes, wherever they are gone,
That youth is surely in their company.

Duke Frederick. Send to his brother, fetch that gallant
  hither;
If he be absent, bring his brother to me;
I'll make him find him. Do this suddenly,°
20 And let not search and inquisition quail°
To bring again these foolish runaways.   *Exeunt.*

II.ii.3 *Are of consent and sufferance* approved and helped   8 *roynish*
scurvy   13 *parts and graces* good qualities and manner   19 *suddenly*
immediately   20 *quail* fail

Scene III. [*Oliver's house.*]

Enter Orlando and Adam.

Orlando. Who's there?

Adam. What, my young master, O my gentle master,
O my sweet master, O you memory
Of old Sir Rowland, why, what make you° here?
Why are you virtuous? Why do people love you?
And wherefore are you gentle, strong, and valiant?   5
Why would you be so fond° to overcome
The bonny prizer° of the humorous° Duke?
Your praise is come too swiftly home before you.
Know you not, master, to some kind of men
Their graces serve them but as enemies?
No more° do yours. Your virtues, gentle master,   10
Are sanctified and holy traitors to you.°
O, what a world is this, when what is comely
Envenoms him that bears it!

Orlando. Why, what's the matter?   15

Adam.   O unhappy youth,
Come not within these doors; within this roof
The enemy of all your graces lives.
Your brother—no, no brother, yet the son—
Yet not the son, I will not call him son,
Of him I was about to call his father—
Hath heard your praises, and this night he means   20
To burn the lodging where you use° to lie
And you within it. If he fail of that,

II.iii.4 *make you* are you doing   7 *fond* foolish   8 *bonny prizer* stout
fighter   8 *humorous* moody, temperamental   12 *No more* no better
12–13 *Your virtues . . . traitors to you* i.e., Orlando's blessed virtues have
worked against him   23 *use* are accustomed

25 He will have other means to cut you off.
I overheard him, and his practices;°
This is no place, this house is but a butchery;°
Abhor it, fear it, do not enter it!

Orlando. Why, whither, Adam, wouldst thou have me
go?

30 *Adam.* No matter whither, so you come not here.

Orlando. What, wouldst thou have me go and beg my
food,
Or with a base and boist'rous° sword enforce
A thievish living on the common road?°
This I must do, or know not what to do;
35 Yet this I will not do, do how I can.
I rather will subject me to the malice
Of a diverted° blood and bloody brother.

Adam. But do not so. I have five hundred crowns,
The thrifty hire I saved° under your father,
40 Which I did store to be my foster nurse
When service should in my old limbs lie lame
And unregarded age in corners thrown.
Take that, and he that doth the ravens feed,
Yea, providently caters for the sparrow,°
45 Be comfort to my age. Here is the gold;
All this I give you. Let me be your servant;
Though I look old, yet I am strong and lusty,
For in my youth I never did apply
Hot and rebellious° liquors in my blood,
50 Nor did not with unbashful forehead° woo
The means of weakness and debility;
Therefore my age is as a lusty winter,
Frosty, but kindly. Let me go with you;
I'll do the service of a younger man
55 In all your business and necessities.

26 *practices* plots   27 *butchery* slaughterhouse   32 *base and boist'-rous* low and swaggering   33 *common road* highway   37 *diverted* estranged   39 *thrifty hire I saved* wages I carefully saved   43–44 *he that . . . the sparrow* (see Psalms 147:9, Luke 12:6)   49 *rebellious* i.e., causing the flesh to rebel   50 *unbashful forehead* bold face

Orlando. O good old man, how well in thee appears
  The constant° service of the antique world,°
  When service sweat for duty, not for meed!°
  Thou art not for the fashion of these times,
  Where none will sweat but for promotion,   60
  And having that, do choke their service up
  Even with the having; it is not so with thee.
  But, poor old man, thou prun'st a rotten tree
  That cannot so much as a blossom yield
  In lieu of° all thy pains and husbandry.   65
  But come thy ways, we'll go along together,
  And ere we have thy youthful wages spent,
  We'll light upon some settled low content.°

Adam. Master, go on, and I will follow thee
  To the last gasp with truth and loyalty.   70
  From seventeen years till now almost fourscore
  Here livèd I, but now live here no more;
  At seventeen years many their fortunes seek,
  But at fourscore it is too late a week:°
  Yet fortune cannot recompense me better   75
  Than to die well and not my master's debtor. *Exeunt.*

Scene IV. [*The Forest of Arden.*]

*Enter Rosalind for Ganymede, Celia for Aliena, and
        Clown, alias Touchstone.*

Rosalind. O Jupiter, how weary are my spirits!

Touchstone. I care not for my spirits if my legs were
  not weary.

Rosalind. I could find in my heart to disgrace my man's

57 *constant* faithful   57 *the antique world* the past   58 *meed* reward
65 *In lieu of* in return for   68 *low content* humble way of life
74 *week* time

⁵ apparel and to cry like a woman; but I must comfort
the weaker vessel, as doublet and hose° ought to
show itself courageous to petticoat. Therefore, courage, good Aliena!

Celia. I pray you bear with me; I cannot go no further.

¹⁰ *Touchstone.* For my part, I had rather bear with you
than bear you; yet I should bear no cross° if I did
bear you, for I think you have no money in your
purse.

Rosalind. Well, this is the Forest of Arden.

¹⁵ *Touchstone.* Ay, now am I in Arden, the more fool I.
When I was at home, I was in a better place, but
travelers must be content.

Enter Corin and Silvius.

Rosalind. Ay, be so, good Touchstone. Look you, who
comes here, a young man and an old in solemn talk.

²⁰ *Corin.* That is the way to make her scorn you still.

Silvius. O Corin, that thou knew'st how I do love her!

Corin. I partly guess, for I have loved ere now.

Silvius. No, Corin, being old, thou canst not guess,
Though in thy youth thou wast as true a lover
²⁵ As ever sighed upon a midnight pillow.
But if thy love were ever like to mine,
As sure I think did never man love so,
How many actions most ridiculous
Hast thou been drawn to by thy fantasy?°

³⁰ *Corin.* Into a thousand that I have forgotten.

Silvius. O, thou didst then never love so heartily!
If thou rememb'rest not the slightest folly
That ever love did make thee run into,
Thou hast not loved.

II.iv.6 *doublet and hose* jacket and breeches   11 *cross* (1) trouble (2)
coin stamped with a cross   29 *fantasy* love (and all its fancies)

    Or if thou hast not sat as I do now,   35
    Wearing° thy hearer in thy mistress' praise,
    Thou hast not loved.
    Or if thou hast not broke from company
    Abruptly, as my passion now makes me,
    Thou has not loved.   40
    O Phebe, Phebe, Phebe!   *Exit.*

Rosalind. Alas, poor shepherd! Searching of° thy wound,
    I have by hard adventure° found mine own.

Touchstone. And I mine. I remember, when I was in love
I broke my sword upon a stone and bid him take that   45
for coming a-night to Jane Smile; and I remember
the kissing of her batler,° and the cow's dugs that her
pretty chopt° hands had milked; and I remember the
wooing of a peascod° instead of her, from whom I
took two cods, and giving her them again, said with   50
weeping tears, "Wear these for my sake." We that
are true lovers run into strange capers; but as all is
mortal in nature, so is all nature in love mortal in
folly.°

Rosalind. Thou speak'st wiser than thou art ware° of.   55

Touchstone. Nay, I shall ne'er be ware of mine own wit°
till I break my shins against it.

Rosalind. Jove, Jove! This shepherd's passion
    Is much upon my fashion.

Touchstone. And mine, but it grows something stale   60
with me.

Celia. I pray you, one of you question yond man
    If he for gold will give us any food.
    I faint almost to death.

Touchstone. Holla, you clown!°   65

36 *Wearing* exhausting   42 *Searching of* probing   43 *hard adventure* bad luck   47 *batler* wooden paddle (used in washing clothes)   48 *chopt* chapped   49 *peascod* peapod   52–54 *as all is mortal ... folly* just as everything that lives must die, so all who love inevitably do foolish things   55 *art ware* know   56 *wit* wisdom   65 *clown* (1) rustic (2) fool

Rosalind. Peace, fool! He's not thy kinsman.

Corin. Who calls?

Touchstone. Your betters, sir.

Corin.   Else are they very wretched.

Rosalind. Peace, I say! Good even to you, friend.

70 *Corin.* And to you, gentle sir, and to you all.

Rosalind. I prithee, shepherd, if that love or gold
   Can in this desert place buy entertainment,°
   Bring us where we may rest ourselves and feed.
   Here's a young maid with travel much oppressed,
   And faints for succor.

75 *Corin.*   Fair sir, I pity her
   And wish, for her sake more than for mine own,
   My fortunes were more able to relieve her;
   But I am shepherd to another man
   And do not shear the fleeces that I graze.
80 My master is of churlish° disposition
   And little recks° to find the way to heaven
   By doing deeds of hospitality.
   Besides, his cote,° his flocks, and bounds of feed°
   Are now on sale, and at our sheepcote now,
85 By reason of his absence, there is nothing
   That you will feed on; but what is, come see,
   And in my voice° most welcome shall you be.

Rosalind. What is he that shall buy his flock and pasture?

Corin. That young swain that you saw here but ere-
      while,°
90 That little cares for buying anything.

Rosalind. I pray thee, if it stand° with honesty,
   Buy thou the cottage, pasture, and the flock,
   And thou shalt have° to pay for it of us.

___

72 *entertainment* food and shelter   80 *churlish* miserly   81 *recks*
thinks   83 *cote* cottage   83 *bounds of feed* pastures   87 *in my voice*
as far as my position allows   89 *erewhile* a short while ago   91 *stand*
be consistent   93 *have* i.e., have the money

Celia. And we will mend° thy wages. I like this place
  And willingly could waste° my time in it.   95

Corin. Assuredly the thing is to be sold.
  Go with me; if you like upon report
  The soil, the profit, and this kind of life,
  I will your very faithful feeder° be
  And buy it with your gold right suddenly.   *Exeunt.* 100

Scene V. [*The forest.*]

Enter Amiens, Jaques, and others.

Song.

Amiens. Under the greenwood tree
      Who loves to lie with me,
    And turn° his merry note
      Unto the sweet bird's throat,
  Come hither, come hither, come hither.   5
      Here shall he see no enemy
    But winter and rough weather.

Jaques. More, more, I prithee more!

Amiens. It will make you melancholy, Monsieur Jaques.

Jaques. I thank it. More, I prithee more! I can suck   10
  melancholy out of a song as a weasel sucks eggs.
  More, I prithee more!

Amiens. My voice is ragged. I know I cannot please you.

Jaques. I do not desire you to please me; I do desire you
  to sing. Come, more, another stanzo! Call you 'em   15
  stanzos?

94 *mend* improve   95 *waste* spend   99 *feeder* servant   II.v.3 *turn*
attune, adapt

Amiens. What you will, Monsieur Jaques.

Jaques. Nay, I care not for their names; they owe me
nothing.° Will you sing?

20 *Amiens.* More at your request than to please myself.

Jaques. Well then, if ever I thank any man, I'll thank
you. But that they call compliment° is like th' encounter of two dog-apes,° and when a man thanks
me heartily, methinks I have given him a penny and
25 he renders me the beggarly thanks.° Come, sing; and
you that will not, hold your tongues.

Amiens. Well, I'll end the song. Sirs, cover the while;°
the Duke will drink under this tree. He hath been all
this day to look you.

30 *Jaques.* And I have been all this day to avoid him. He
is too disputable for my company. I think of as many
matters as he, but I give heaven thanks and make no
boast of them. Come, warble, come.

Song.

All together here.

Who doth ambition shun
35   And loves to live i' th' sun,
Seeking the food he eats,
        And pleased with what he gets,
Come hither, come hither, come hither.
        Here shall he see no enemy
40   But winter and rough weather.

Jaques. I'll give you a verse to this note° that I made
yesterday in despite of my invention.°

18-19 *names . . . nothing* (Jaques plays on the word "name," a term
for the borrower's signature on a loan)   22 *compliment* politeness
23 *dog-apes* baboons   23-25 *and when . . . beggarly thanks* i.e., the
hearty thanks of polite society are no more sincere than the extravagant
gratitude of a beggar given a small coin   27 *cover the while* lay the
table in the meantime   41 *note* tune   42 *in despite of my invention*
without using my imagination

Amiens. And I'll sing it.

Jaques. Thus it goes.

> If it do come to pass   45
>   That any man turn ass,
> Leaving his wealth and ease
>   A stubborn will to please,
> Ducdame,° ducdame, ducdame.
> Here shall he see gross fools as he,   50
>   An if° he will come to me.

Amiens. What's that "ducdame"?

Jaques. 'Tis a Greek° invocation to call fools into a
circle. I'll go sleep, if I can; if I cannot, I'll rail against
all the first-born of Egypt.°   55

Amiens. And I'll go seek the Duke. His banquet° is
prepared.   *Exeunt.*

Scene VI. [*The forest.*]

Enter Orlando and Adam.

Adam. Dear master, I can go no further. O, I die for
food. Here lie I down and measure out my grave.
Farewell, kind master.

Orlando. Why, how now, Adam? No greater heart in
thee? Live a little, comfort° a little, cheer thyself a   5

---

49 *Ducdame* (various derivations have been suggested: Romany *dukrà
mè* ["I tell fortunes"]; Welsh *dewch 'da mi* ["come with me"]; Latin *duc
ad me* ["bring (him) to me"]; Italian *Duc' da mè* ["duke by myself" or
"duke without a dukedom"]. Probably the word is nonsense)   51 *An
if* if only   53 *Greek* unintelligible   55 *first-born of Egypt* (perhaps
"persons of high rank," but perhaps an allusion to life in the Forest of
Arden. Exodus 11,12 reports that when the first-born of Egypt died, the
Israelites were sent into the wilderness)   56 *banquet* light meal
II.vi.5 *comfort* take comfort

little. If this uncouth° forest yield anything savage, I
will either be food for it or bring it for food to thee.
Thy conceit° is nearer death than thy powers. For my
sake be comfortable; hold death awhile at the arm's
10   end. I will here be with thee presently,° and if I bring
thee not something to eat, I will give thee leave to
die; but if thou diest before I come, thou art a mocker
of my labor. Well said; thou look'st cheerly, and I'll
be with thee quickly. Yet thou liest in the bleak air.
15   Come, I will bear thee to some shelter, and thou
shalt not die for lack of a dinner if there live anything
in this desert. Cheerly, good Adam.   *Exeunt.*

Scene VII. [*The forest.*]

Enter Duke Senior, and Lords, like Outlaws.

Duke Senior. I think he be transformed into a beast,
   For I can nowhere find him like a man.

First Lord. My lord, he is but even now gone hence;
   Here was he merry, hearing of a song.

5   *Duke Senior.* If he, compact of jars,° grow musical,
   We shall have shortly discord in the spheres.°
   Go seek him; tell him I would speak with him.

Enter Jaques.

First Lord. He saves my labor by his own approach.

Duke Senior. Why, how now, monsieur, what a life is
      this,
10   That your poor friends must woo your company?
   What, you look merrily.

6 *uncouth* wild   8 *conceit* thought   10 *presently* at once   II.vii.5 *compact of jars* made up of discord   6 *discord in the spheres* (Ptolemaic astronomy taught that the planetary spheres produced a ravishing harmony as they revolved)

Jaques. A fool, a fool! I met a fool i' th' forest,
   A motley° fool! A miserable world!
   As I do live by food, I met a fool
   Who laid him down and basked him in the sun   15
   And railed on Lady Fortune in good terms,
   In good set terms,° and yet a motley fool.
   "Good morrow, fool," quoth I. "No, sir," quoth he,
   "Call me not fool till heaven hath sent me fortune."°
   And then he drew a dial from his poke,°   20
   And looking on it with lack-luster eye,
   Says very wisely, "It is ten o'clock.
   Thus we may see," quoth he, "how the world wags.°
   'Tis but an hour ago since it was nine,
   And after one hour more 'twill be eleven;   25
   And so, from hour to hour,° we ripe and ripe,
   And then, from hour to hour, we rot and rot;
   And thereby hangs a tale." When I did hear
   The motley fool thus moral° on the time,
   My lungs began to crow like chanticleer°   30
   That fools should be so deep contemplative;
   And I did laugh sans intermission°
   An hour by his dial. O noble fool,
   A worthy fool! Motley's the only wear.

Duke Senior. What fool is this?   35

Jaques. O worthy fool! One that hath been a courtier,
   And says, if ladies be but young and fair,
   They have the gift to know it. And in his brain,
   Which is as dry as the remainder biscuit°
   After a voyage, he hath strange places crammed   40
   With observation, the which he vents°

13 *motley* garbed in the multicolored costume of the court fool (a motley costume is commonly thought to be checkered or patched; Leslie Hotson, in *Shakespeare's Motley*, argues it was of varicolored threads but drab, like a tweed)   17 *set terms* precise phrases   19 *Call me ... fortune* (fortune proverbially favors fools)   20 *dial from his poke* sundial from his pocket   23 *wags* goes   26 *hour to hour* (perhaps with a pun on "whore")   29 *moral* moralize   30 *chanticleer* (traditional name for a rooster)   32 *sans intermission* without stop   39 *remainder biscuit* leftover hardtack   41 *vents* gives forth

In mangled forms. O that I were a fool!
I am ambitious for a motley coat.

Duke Senior. Thou shalt have one.

Jaques.   It is my only suit,°
45   Provided that you weed your better judgments
Of all opinion that grows rank° in them
That I am wise. I must have liberty
Withal, as large a charter° as the wind,
To blow on whom I please, for so fools have.
50   And they that are most gallèd° with my folly,
They most must laugh. And why, sir, must they so?
The why is plain as way to parish church:
He that a fool doth very wisely hit
Doth very foolishly, although he smart,
55   Not to seem senseless of the bob.° If not,
The wise man's folly is anatomized°
Even by the squand'ring glances° of the fool.
Invest° me in my motley, give me leave
To speak my mind, and I will through and through
60   Cleanse the foul body of th' infected world,
If they will patiently receive my medicine.

Duke Senior. Fie on thee! I can tell what thou wouldst
   do.

Jaques. What, for a counter,° would I do but good?

Duke Senior. Most mischievous foul sin, in chiding sin.
65   For thou thyself hast been a libertine,
As sensual as the brutish sting° itself;
And all th' embossèd° sores and headed evils
That thou with license of free foot° hast caught,
Wouldst thou disgorge into the general world.

70 *Jaques.* Why, who cries out on pride

---

44 *suit* (1) garment (2) petition   46 *rank* luxuriant   48 *large a charter* liberal license   50 *gallèd* chafed   55 *senseless of the bob* unaware of the hit   56 *anatomized* revealed   57 *squand'ring glances* chance hits   58 *Invest* clothe   63 *counter* worthless coin   66 *the brutish sting* lust   67 *embossèd* swollen   68 *license of free foot* complete freedom

That can therein tax any private party?°
Doth it not flow as hugely as the sea
Till that the weary very.means do ebb?°
What woman in the city do I name
When that I say the city woman bears   75
The cost° of princes on unworthy shoulders?
Who can come in and say that I mean her,
When such a one as she, such is her neighbor?
Or what is he of basest function°
That says his bravery is not on my cost,°   80
Thinking that I mean him, but therein suits
His folly to the mettle of my speech?°
There then, how then, what then? Let me see wherein
My tongue hath wronged him. If it do him right,
Then he hath wronged himself. If he be free,°   85
Why, then my taxing like a wild goose flies
Unclaimed of any man. But who comes here?

    Enter Orlando [with his sword drawn].

Orlando. Forbear, and eat no more!

Jaques.   Why, I have eat none yet.

Orlando. Nor shalt not, till necessity be served.

Jaques. Of what kind° should this cock come of?   90

Duke Senior. Art thou thus boldened, man, by thy
    distress,
  Or else a rude despiser of good manners,
  That in civility thou seem'st so empty?

Orlando. You touched my vein at first.° The thorny
    point
  Of bare distress hath ta'en from me the show   95

71 *tax any private party* criticize any particular person   73 *weary very
means do ebb* (perhaps: "ostentation eventually exhausts the wealth
that makes it possible." Some editors emend "weary" to "wearer's")
76 *cost* wealth   79 *function* position   80 *his bravery ... cost* his
fine dress is not paid for by me (and therefore is not my business)
81–82 *suits ... my speech* matches his folly to the substance of my
words   85 *free* innocent   90 *kind* breed   94 *You touched ... first*
i.e., the Duke's first supposition is correct

Of smooth civility; yet am I inland bred°
And know some nurture.° But forbear, I say!
He dies that touches any of this fruit
Till I and my affairs are answerèd.°

100 *Jaques.* An° you will not be answered with reason,° I
     must die.

Duke Senior. What would you have? Your gentleness
     shall force
More than your force move us to gentleness.

Orlando. I almost die for food, and let me have it!

Duke Senior. Sit down and feed, and welcome to our
105   table.

Orlando. Speak you so gently? Pardon me, I pray you.
I thought that all things had been savage here,
And therefore put I on the countenance
Of stern commandment. But whate'er you are
110 That in this desert inaccessible,
Under the shade of melancholy boughs,
Lose and neglect the creeping hours of time;
If ever you have looked on better days,
If ever been where bells have knolled° to church,
115 If ever sat at any good man's feast,
If ever from your eyelids wiped a tear
And know what 'tis to pity and be pitied,
Let gentleness my strong enforcement° be;
In the which hope I blush, and hide my sword.

120 *Duke Senior.* True is it that we have seen better days,
And have with holy bell been knolled to church,
And sat at good men's feasts, and wiped our eyes
Of drops that sacred pity hath engend'red;
And therefore sit you down in gentleness,
125 And take upon command° what help we have
That to your wanting° may be minist'red.

---

96 *inland bred* brought up in civilized society   97 *nurture* good breeding   99 *answerèd* provided for   100 *An* if   100 *reason* (perhaps Jaques
puns, eating a raisin [grape])   114 *knolled* rung   118 *enforcement*
support   125 *upon command* as you wish   126 *wanting* need

Orlando. Then but forbear your food a little while,
    Whiles, like a doe, I go to find my fawn
    And give it food. There is an old poor man
    Who after me hath many a weary step   *130*
    Limped in pure love. Till he be first sufficed,
    Oppressed with two weak evils,° age and hunger,
    I will not touch a bit.

Duke Senior.   Go find him out,
    And we will nothing waste° till you return.

Orlando. I thank ye, and be blest for your good comfort! *135*
                                [Exit.]

Duke Senior. Thou seest we are not all alone unhappy:
    This wide and universal theater
    Presents more woeful pageants° than the scene
    Wherein we play in.

Jaques.   All the world's a stage,
    And all the men and women merely players;   *140*
    They have their exits and their entrances,
    And one man in his time plays many parts,
    His acts being seven ages.° At first, the infant,
    Mewling° and puking in the nurse's arms.
    Then the whining schoolboy, with his satchel   *145*
    And shining morning face, creeping like snail
    Unwillingly to school. And then the lover,
    Sighing like furnace, with a woeful ballad
    Made to his mistress' eyebrow. Then a soldier,
    Full of strange oaths and bearded like the pard,°   *150*
    Jealous° in honor, sudden° and quick in quarrel,
    Seeking the bubble reputation
    Even in the cannon's mouth. And then the justice,
    In fair round belly with good capon lined,°

---

132 *weak evils* evils causing weakness   134 *waste* consume   138 *pageants* scenes   143 *seven ages* (for a survey in art and literature of the image of man's life divided into ages, see Samuel C. Chew, "'This Strange Eventful History,'" in *Joseph Quincy Adams Memorial Studies,* ed. James G. McManaway *et al.*)   144 *Mewling* bawling   150 *pard* leopard   151 *Jealous* touchy   151 *sudden* rash   154 *capon lined* (perhaps an allusion to the practice of bribing a judge with a capon)

155 With eyes severe and beard of formal cut,
     Full of wise saws° and modern instances;°
     And so he plays his part. The sixth age shifts
     Into the lean and slippered pantaloon,°
     With spectacles on nose and pouch on side;
160 His youthful hose,° well saved, a world too wide
     For his shrunk shank, and his big manly voice,
     Turning again toward childish treble, pipes
     And whistles in his° sound. Last scene of all,
     That ends this strange eventful history,
165 Is second childishness and mere° oblivion,
     Sans teeth, sans eyes, sans taste, sans everything.

Enter Orlando, with Adam.

Duke Senior. Welcome. Set down your venerable burden
     And let him feed.

Orlando. I thank you most for him.

Adam.   So had you need.
170 I scarce can speak to thank you for myself.

Duke Senior. Welcome, fall to. I will not trouble you
     As yet to question you about your fortunes.
     Give us some music; and, good cousin, sing.

Song.

Amiens.
     Blow, blow, thou winter wind,
175 Thou art not so unkind°
       As man's ingratitude:
     Thy tooth is not so keen,
     Because thou art not seen,
       Although thy breath be rude.
180 Heigh-ho, sing heigh-ho, unto the green holly.
     Most friendship is faining,° most loving mere folly:

156 *saws* sayings 156 *modern instances* commonplace examples
158 *pantaloon* ridiculous old man (from Pantalone, a stock figure in
Italian comedy) 160 *hose* breeches 163 *his* its 165 *mere* utter
175 *unkind* unnatural 181 *faining* longing (perhaps with a pun on
"feigning" [pretending])

   Then, heigh-ho, the holly.
   This life is most jolly.

   Freeze, freeze, thou bitter sky
   That dost not bite so nigh   185
      As benefits forgot:
   Though thou the waters warp,°
   Thy sting is not so sharp
      As friend rememb'red not
Heigh-ho, sing, &c.   190

Duke Senior. If that you were the good Sir Rowland's
      son,
   As you have whispered faithfully you were,
   And as mine eye doth his effigies° witness
   Most truly limned° and living in your face,
   Be truly welcome hither. I am the Duke   195
   That loved your father. The residue of your fortune
   Go to my cave and tell me. Good old man,
   Thou art right welcome, as thy master is.
   Support him by the arm. Give me your hand,
   And let me all your fortunes understand.   *Exeunt.*   200

187 *warp* turn (into ice)   193 *effigies* likeness (accent on second syllable)   194 *limned* depicted

ACT III

Scene I. [*The palace.*]

Enter Duke [Frederick], Lords, and Oliver.

Duke Frederick. Not see him since? Sir, sir, that cannot
    be.
    But were I not the better part made mercy,°
    I should not seek an absent argument°
    Of my revenge, thou present. But look to it:
5   Find out thy brother, wheresoe'er he is;
    Seek him with candle; bring him dead or living
    Within this twelvemonth, or turn° thou no more
    To seek a living in our territory.
    Thy lands, and all things that thou dost call thine
10   Worth seizure, do we seize into our hands
    Till thou canst quit° thee by thy brother's mouth°
    Of what we think against thee.

Oliver. O that your Highness knew my heart in this!
    I never loved my brother in my life.

Duke Frederick. More villain thou. Well, push him out
15   of doors,
    And let my officers of such a nature°

III.i.2 *the better part made mercy* so merciful   3 *argument* object (i.e.,
Orlando)   7 *turn* return   11 *quit* acquit   11 *mouth* testimony   16 *of
such a nature* i.e., appropriate

Make an extent upon° his house and lands.
Do this expediently° and turn him going.   *Exeunt.*

Scene II. [*The forest.*]

Enter Orlando, [with a paper].

Orlando. Hang there, my verse, in witness of my love;
      And thou, thrice-crownèd Queen of Night,° survey
With thy chaste eye, from thy pale sphere above,
      Thy huntress' name° that my full life doth sway.
O Rosalind! These trees shall be my books,   5
      And in their barks my thoughts I'll character,°
That every eye which in this forest looks
      Shall see thy virtue witnessed° everywhere.
Run, run, Orlando, carve on every tree
The fair, the chaste, and unexpressive she.°   *Exit.*   10

Enter Corin and [Touchstone, the] Clown.

Corin. And how like you this shepherd's life, Master
Touchstone?

Touchstone. Truly, shepherd, in respect of itself, it is a
good life; but in respect that it is a shepherd's life, it
is naught.° In respect that it is solitary, I like it very   15
well; but in respect that it is private,° it is a very vile
life. Now in respect it is in the fields, it pleaseth me
well; but in respect it is not in the court, it is tedious.
As it is a spare° life, look you, it fits my humor° well;
but as there is no more plenty in it, it goes much   20

---

17 *Make an extent upon* seize by writ 18 *expediently* speedily
III.ii.2 *thrice-crownèd Queen of Night* Diana (goddess of the moon, the
hunt, and of chastity)   4 *Thy huntress' name* i.e., Rosalind, who, because she is chaste, serves Diana   6 *character* write   8 *virtue witnessed*
power attested to   10 *unexpressive she* i.e., woman beyond description
15 *naught* worthless 16 *private* lonely 19 *spare* frugal 19 *humor*
disposition

against my stomach. Hast any philosophy° in thee,
shepherd?

Corin, No more, but that I know the more one sickens,
the worse at ease he is; and that he that wants°
money, means, and content is without three good
friends; that the property of rain is to wet and fire
to burn; that good pasture makes fat sheep, and that
a great cause of the night is lack of the sun; that he
that hath learned no wit by nature nor art° may
complain° of good breeding, or comes of a very dull
kindred.

Touchstone. Such a one is a natural philosopher.° Wast
ever in court, shepherd?

Corin. No, truly.

Touchstone. Then thou art damned.

Corin. Nay, I hope.

Touchstone. Truly thou art damned, like an ill-roasted
egg, all on one side.

Corin. For not being at court? Your reason.

Touchstone. Why, if thou never wast at court, thou
never saw'st good manners;° if thou never saw'st
good manners, then thy manners must be wicked;
and wickedness is sin, and sin is damnation. Thou
art in a parlous° state, shepherd.

Corin. Not a whit, Touchstone. Those that are good
manners at the court are as ridiculous in the country
as the behavior of the country is most mockable at
the court. You told me you salute not at the court
but you kiss° your hands. That courtesy would be
uncleanly if courtiers were shepherds.

Touchstone. Instance,° briefly. Come, instance.

21 *philosophy* learning   24 *wants* lacks   29 *by nature nor art* by birth or
education   30 *complain* cry the lack   32 *a natural philosopher* (1) wise
by nature (2) a wise idiot   41 *manners* (1) behavior (2) morals   44 *par-
lous* dangerous   49 *but you kiss* without kissing   51 *Instance* proof

Corin. Why, we are still° handling our ewes, and their
   fells° you know are greasy.

Touchstone. Why, do not your courtier's hands sweat?
   And is not the grease of a mutton as wholesome as   55
   the sweat of a man? Shallow, shallow. A better
   instance, I say. Come.

Corin. Besides, our hands are hard.

Touchstone. Your lips will feel them the sooner. Shallow
   again. A more sounder instance, come.   60

Corin. And they are often tarred over with the surgery°
   of our sheep, and would you have us kiss tar? The
   courtier's hands are perfumed with civet.°

Touchstone. Most shallow man! Thou worms' meat° in
   respect of° a good piece of flesh indeed! Learn of the   65
   wise, and perpend.° Civet is of a baser birth than tar,
   the very uncleanly flux° of a cat. Mend the instance,°
   shepherd.

Corin. You have too courtly a wit for me; I'll rest.

Touchstone. Wilt thou rest damned? God help thee,   70
   shallow man! God make incision in thee!° Thou art
   raw.°

Corin. Sir, I am a true laborer; I earn that° I eat, get
   that I wear, owe no man hate, envy no man's happiness, glad of other men's good, content with my   75
   harm;° and the greatest of my pride is to see my ewes
   graze and my lambs suck.

Touchstone. That is another simple sin in you: to bring
   the ewes and the rams together and to offer to get
   your living by the copulation of cattle, to be bawd to   80

52 *still* always   53 *fells* fleeces   61 *tarred . . . surgery* (shepherds used
tar as an ointment)   63 *civet* perfume obtained from the civet cat
64 *worms' meat* food for worms   65 *respect of* comparison with
66 *perpend* consider   67 *flux* secretion   67 *Mend the instance* give a
better example   71 *make incision in thee* let your blood (a common
cure, here for folly)   72 *raw* (1) inexperienced (2) sore   73 *that* what
75–76 *content with my harm* bear with my troubles

a bell-wether° and to betray a she-lamb of a twelvemonth to a crookèd-pated° old cuckoldly° ram, out
of all reasonable match. If thou beest not damned for
this, the devil himself will have no shepherds; I can-
85   not see else how thou shouldst 'scape.

Corin. Here comes young Master Ganymede, my new
mistress' brother.

Enter Rosalind, [reading a paper].

Rosalind.
      "From the east to western Ind,
          No jewel is like Rosalind.
90   Her worth, being mounted on the wind,
          Through all the world bears Rosalind.
          All the pictures fairest lined°
          Are but black to Rosalind.
          Let no face be kept in mind
95   But the fair° of Rosalind."

Touchstone. I'll rhyme you so eight years together,
dinners and suppers and sleeping hours excepted. It
is the right butterwomen's rank to market.°

Rosalind. Out, fool!

100 *Touchstone.* For a taste:
          If a hart do lack a hind,
          Let him seek out Rosalind.
          If the cat will after kind,°
          So be sure will Rosalind.
105   Wintred° garments must be lined,°
          So must slender Rosalind.
          They that reap must sheaf and bind,
          Then to cart° with Rosalind.

---

81 *bell-wether* (the leading sheep of a flock carries a bell)   82 *crookèd-pated* i.e., with crooked horns   82 *cuckoldy* (because horned)   92 *lined* drawn   95 *fair* lovely face   98 *right butterwomen's rank to market* i.e., the verses jog along exactly like a procession of women riding to market   103 *kind* its own kind   105 *Wintred* i.e., prepared for winter   105 *lined* stuffed   108 *to cart* (perhaps an allusion not only to the harvest but to the custom of transporting prostitutes to jail in a cart)

Sweetest nut hath sourest rind,
Such a nut is Rosalind.   110
He that sweetest rose will find
Must find love's prick, and Rosalind.

This is the very false gallop of verses. Why do you
infect yourself with them?

Rosalind. Peace, you dull fool! I found them on a tree. 115

Touchstone. Truly the tree yields bad fruit.

Rosalind. I'll graff° it with you and then I shall graff it
with a medlar.° Then it will be the earliest fruit i' th'
country; for you'll be rotten ere you be half ripe, and
that's the right virtue° of the medlar.   120

Touchstone. You have said; but whether wisely or no,
let the forest judge.

Enter Celia, with a writing.

Rosalind. Peace! Here comes my sister reading; stand
aside.

Celia. "Why should this a desert be?   125
        For° it is unpeopled? No.
    Tongues I'll hang on every tree
        That shall civil sayings° show:
    Some, how brief the life of man
        Runs his erring pilgrimage,   130
    That the stretching of a span°
        Buckles in° his sum of age;
    Some, of violated vows
        'Twixt the souls of friend and friend;
    But upon the fairest boughs,   135
        Or at every sentence end,
    Will I 'Rosalinda' write,
        Teaching all that read to know
    The quintessence of every sprite°

---

117 *graff* graft   118 *medlar* (1) an applelike fruit, not ready to eat
until it is almost rotten (2) interferer   120 *right virtue* true quality
126 *For* because   128 *civil sayings* civilized maxims   131 *stretching
of a span* span of an open hand   132 *Buckles in* limits   139 *sprite* soul

140   Heaven would in little° show.
         Therefore heaven Nature charged
            That one body should be filled
         With all graces wide-enlarged.
            Nature presently° distilled
145   Helen's cheek, but not her heart,°
            Cleopatra's majesty,
         Atalanta's better part,°
            Sad° Lucretia's° modesty.
         Thus Rosalind of many parts
150   By heavenly synod° was devised,
         Of many faces, eyes, and hearts,
            To have the touches° dearest prized.
         Heaven would that she these gifts should have,
         And I to live and die her slave."

155 *Rosalind.* O most gentle pulpiter, what tedious homily
      of love have you wearied your parishioners withal,
      and never cried, "Have patience, good people"!

Celia. How now? Back, friends. Shepherd, go off a
      little. Go with him, sirrah.

160 *Touchstone.* Come, shepherd, let us make an honorable
      retreat; though not with bag and baggage, yet with
      scrip and scrippage.°   *Exit [with Corin].*

Celia. Didst thou hear these verses?

Rosalind. O, yes, I heard them all, and more too; for
165   some of them had in them more feet° than the verses
      would bear.

Celia. That's no matter. The feet might bear the verses.

Rosalind. Ay, but the feet were lame, and could not

---

140 *in little* in miniature (i.e., the microcosm)   144 *presently* thereupon
145 *cheek ... heart* i.e., Helen's beauty but not her false heart
147 *Atalanta's better part* i.e., Rosalind has the gracefulness but not the
cruelty of Atalanta, a huntress famed in Greek mythology for her fleet-
ness   148 *Sad* dignified   148 *Lucretia* (a Roman matron who killed
herself rather than live dishonored)   150 *synod* council   152 *touches*
features   162 *scrip and scrippage* shepherd's pouch and its contents
165 *feet* metrical units

bear themselves without the verse, and therefore
stood lamely in the verse.   170

Celia. But didst thou hear without wondering how thy
name should be hanged and carved upon these trees?

Rosalind. I was seven of the nine days° out of the
wonder before you came; for look here what I found
on a palm tree. I was never so berhymed since   175
Pythagoras'° time that° I was an Irish rat,° which I
can hardly remember.

Celia. Trow° you who hath done this?

Rosalind. Is it a man?

Celia. And a chain that you once wore, about his neck.   180
Change you color?

Rosalind. I prithee who?

Celia. O Lord, Lord, it is a hard matter for friends to
meet; but mountains may be removed with earth-
quakes, and so encounter.   185

Rosalind. Nay, but who is it?

Celia. Is it possible?

Rosalind. Nay, I prithee now with most petitionary
vehemence,° tell me who it is.

Celia. O wonderful, wonderful, and most wonderful   190
wonderful, and yet again wonderful, and after that,
out of all hooping!°

Rosalind. Good my complexion!° Dost thou think,
though I am caparisoned° like a man, I have a doublet
and hose in my disposition? One inch of delay more   195

---

173 *seven of the nine days* (cf. the phrase "nine days' wonder")
176 *Pythagoras* (Greek philosopher who taught the doctrine of the
transmigration of souls)   176 *that* when   176 *Irish rat* (it was believed
that Irish sorcerers could kill rats with rhymed spells)   178 *Trow*
know   188–189 *with most petitionary vehemence* i.e., I beg you
192 *out of all hooping* beyond all measure   193 *Good my complexion*
(a mild expletive)   194 *caparisoned* dressed

is a South Sea of discovery.° I prithee tell me who is
it quickly, and speak apace.° I would thou couldst
stammer, that thou mightst pour this concealed man
out of thy mouth as wine comes out of a narrow-
200 mouthed bottle; either too much at once, or none at
all. I prithee take the cork out of thy mouth, that I
may drink thy tidings.

Celia. So you may put a man in your belly.

Rosalind. Is he of God's making? What manner of man?
205 Is his head worth a hat? Or his chin worth a beard?

Celia. Nay, he hath but a little beard.

Rosalind. Why, God will send more, if the man will be
thankful. Let me stay° the growth of his beard, if
thou delay me not the knowledge of his chin.

210 *Celia.* It is young Orlando, that tripped up the wrestler's
heels and your heart both in an instant.

Rosalind. Nay, but the devil take mocking! Speak sad
brow and true maid.°

Celia. I' faith, coz, 'tis he.

215 *Rosalind.* Orlando?

Celia. Orlando.

Rosalind. Alas the day! What shall I do with my
doublet and hose? What did he when thou saw'st
him? What said he? How looked he? Wherein went
220 he?° What makes he here? Did he ask for me? Where
remains he? How parted he with thee? And when
shalt thou see him again? Answer me in one word.

Celia. You must borrow me Gargantua's° mouth first;
'tis a word too great for any mouth of this age's size.
225 To say "ay" and "no" to these particulars is more
than to answer in a catechism.

195–196 *One inch . . . discovery* i.e., another minute more will seem as
long as it takes to voyage to the South Seas   197 *apace* quickly
208 *stay* wait for   212–213 *sad brow and true maid* i.e., seriously and
truthfully   219–220 *Wherein went he* how was he dressed   223 *Gargantua* (a giant in Rabelais and other writers)

Rosalind. But doth he know that I am in this forest, and in man's apparel? Looks he as freshly° as he did the day he wrestled?

Celia. It is as easy to count atomies° as to resolve the propositions° of a lover; but take a taste of my finding him, and relish it with good observance.° I found him under a tree, like a dropped acorn.   230

Rosalind. It may well be called Jove's tree° when it drops forth fruit.   235

Celia. Give me audience,° good madam.

Rosalind. Proceed.

Celia. There lay he stretched along like a wounded knight.

Rosalind. Though it be pity to see such a sight, it well becomes the ground.   240

Celia. Cry "holla"° to the tongue, I prithee; it curvets° unseasonably. He was furnished° like a hunter.

Rosalind. O, ominous! He comes to kill my heart.°

Celia. I would sing my song without a burden.° Thou bring'st me out of tune.   245

Rosalind. Do you not know I am a woman? When I think, I must speak. Sweet, say on.

Enter Orlando and Jaques.

Celia. You bring me out. Soft. Comes he not here?

Rosalind. 'Tis he! Slink by, and note him.   250

Jaques. I thank you for your company; but, good faith, I had as lief have been myself alone.

Orlando. And so had I; but yet for fashion sake I thank you too for your society.

228 *freshly* handsome   230 *atomies* motes   230–231 *resolve the propositions* answer the questions   232 *good observance* close attention
234 *Jove's tree* (the oak, sacred to Jove)   236 *Give me audience* listen
242 *holla* whoa   242 *curvets* frolics   243 *furnished* dressed   244 *heart* (pun on "hart")   245 *burden* refrain

255 *Jaques.* God b' wi' you; let's meet as little as we can.

Orlando. I do desire we may be better strangers.

Jaques. I pray you mar no more trees with writing love songs in their barks.

Orlando. I pray you mar no moe° of my verses with
260   reading them ill-favoredly.°

Jaques. Rosalind is your love's name?

Orlando. Yes, just.

Jaques. I do not like her name.

Orlando. There was no thought of pleasing you when
265   she was christened.

Jaques. What stature is she of?

Orlando. Just as high as my heart.

Jaques. You are full of pretty answers. Have you not been acquainted with goldsmiths' wives, and conned
270   them out of rings?°

Orlando. Not so; but I answer you right painted cloth,° from whence you have studied your questions.

Jaques. You have a nimble wit; I think 'twas made of Atalanta's heels.° Will you sit down with me, and we
275   two will rail against our mistress the world and all our misery.

Orlando. I will chide no breather° in the world but myself, against whom I know most faults.

Jaques. The worst fault you have is to be in love.

280 *Orlando.* 'Tis a fault I will not change for your best virtue. I am weary of you.

---

259 *moe* more   260 *ill-favoredly* badly   269–270 *conned them out of rings* i.e., memorized the sentimental sayings inscribed in rings 271 *painted cloth* (cheap substitute for tapestry, on which were painted pictures with trite sayings)   274 *Atalanta's heels* (Atalanta was a symbol of speed)   277 *breather* creature

Jaques. By my troth, I was seeking for a fool when I
  found you.

Orlando. He is drowned in the brook. Look but in and
  you shall see him.   285

Jaques. There I shall see mine own figure.

Orlando. Which I take to be either a fool or a cipher.°

Jaques. I'll tarry no longer with you. Farewell, good
  Signior Love.

Orlando. I am glad of your departure. Adieu, good   290
  Monsieur Melancholy.   [*Exit Jaques.*]

Rosalind. I will speak to him like a saucy lackey, and
  under that habit° play the knave with him. Do you
  hear, forester?

Orlando. Very well. What would you?   295

Rosalind. I pray you, what is't o'clock?

Orlando. You should ask me, what time o' day. There's
  no clock in the forest.

Rosalind. Then there is no true lover in the forest, else
  sighing every minute and groaning every hour would   300
  detect° the lazy foot of Time as well as a clock.

Orlando. And why not the swift foot of Time? Had not
  that been as proper?

Rosalind. By no means, sir. Time travels in divers paces
  with divers persons. I'll tell you who Time ambles   305
  withal, who Time trots withal, who Time gallops
  withal, and who he stands still withal.

Orlando. I prithee, who doth he trot withal?

Rosalind. Marry, he trots hard with a young maid
  between the contract of her marriage° and the day it 310

---

287 *cipher* zero   293 *habit* guise   301 *detect* show   310 *contract of
her marriage* betrothal

is solemnized. If the interim be but a se'nnight,° Time's pace is so hard that it seems the length of seven year.

Orlando. Who ambles Time withal?

315 *Rosalind.* With a priest that lacks Latin and a rich man that hath not the gout; for the one sleeps easily because he cannot study, and the other lives merrily because he feels no pain; the one lacking the burden of lean and wasteful° learning, the other knowing no 320 burden of heavy tedious penury. These Time ambles withal.

Orlando. Who doth he gallop withal?

Rosalind. With a thief to the gallows; for though he go as softly° as foot can fall, he thinks himself too soon 325 there.

Orlando. Who stays it still withal?

Rosalind. With lawyers in the vacation; for they sleep between term° and term, and then they perceive not how time moves.

330 *Orlando.* Where dwell you, pretty youth?

Rosalind. With this shepherdess, my sister; here in the skirts of the forest, like fringe upon a petticoat.

Orlando. Are you native of this place?

Rosalind. As the cony° that you see dwell where she is 335 kindled.°

Orlando. Your accent is something finer than you could purchase° in so removed° a dwelling.

Rosalind. I have been told so of many. But indeed an old religious° uncle of mine taught me to speak, who 340 was in his youth an inland° man; one that knew

311 *a se'nnight* seven days, a week   319 *wasteful* i.e., causing one to waste away   324 *softly* slowly   328 *term* court session   334 *cony* rabbit   335 *kindled* born   337 *purchase* acquire   337 *removed* remote   339 *religious* i.e., a member of a religious order   340 *inland* city

courtship° too well, for there he fell in love. I have
heard him read many lectures against it; and I thank
God I am not a woman, to be touched° with so many
giddy° offenses as he hath generally taxed their whole
sex withal.   345

Orlando. Can you remember any of the principal evils
that he laid to the charge of women?

Rosalind. There were none principal. They were all like
one another as halfpence are, every one fault seeming
monstrous till his fellow fault came to match it.   350

Orlando. I prithee recount some of them.

Rosalind. No, I will not cast away my physic but on
those that are sick. There is a man haunts the forest
that abuses our young plants with carving "Rosalind"
on their barks, hangs odes upon hawthorns, and   355
elegies on brambles; all, forsooth, deifying the name
of Rosalind. If I could meet that fancy-monger,° I
would give him some good counsel, for he seems to
have the quotidian° of love upon him.

Orlando. I am he that is so love-shaked. I pray you tell   360
me your remedy.

Rosalind. There is none of my uncle's marks upon you.
He taught me how to know a man in love; in which
cage of rushes° I am sure you are not prisoner.

Orlando. What were his marks?   365

Rosalind. A lean cheek, which you have not; a blue eye°
and sunken, which you have not; an unquestionable°
spirit, which you have not; a beard neglected, which
you have not—but I pardon you for that, for simply
your having° in beard is a younger brother's revenue.°   370

---

341 *courtship* (1) court manners (2) wooing   343 *touched* tainted
344 *giddy* frivolous   357 *fancy-monger* dealer in love   359 *quotidian*
daily fever   364 *cage of rushes* i.e., prison easy to escape from   366 *a
blue eye* i.e., dark circles under the eyes   367 *unquestionable* averse to
conversation   369–370 *simply your having* truthfully what you have
370 *a younger brother's revenue* i.e., a small portion

Then your hose should be ungartered, your bonnet unbanded, your sleeve unbuttoned, your shoe untied, and everything about you demonstrating a careless desolation.° But you are no such man: you are rather
375 point-device in your accouterments,° as loving yourself than seeming the lover of any other.

Orlando. Fair youth, I would I could make thee believe I love.

Rosalind. Me believe it? You may as soon make her
380 that you love believe it, which I warrant she is apter to do than to confess she does; that is one of the points in the which women still give the lie to their consciences. But in good sooth, are you he that hangs the verses on the trees wherein Rosalind is so admired?

385 *Orlando.* I swear to thee, youth, by the white hand of Rosalind, I am that he, that unfortunate he.

Rosalind. But are you so much in love as your rhymes speak?

Orlando. Neither rhyme nor reason can express how
390 much.

Rosalind. Love is merely° a madness, and, I tell you, deserves as well a dark house and a whip° as madmen do; and the reason why they are not so punished and cured is that the lunacy is so ordinary that the
395 whippers are in love too. Yet I profess curing it by counsel.

Orlando. Did you ever cure any so?

Rosalind. Yes, one, and in this manner. He was to imagine me his love, his mistress; and I set him every
400 day to woo me. At which time would I, being but a moonish° youth, grieve, be effeminate, changeable, longing and liking, proud, fantastical,° apish, shallow,

373–4 *a careless desolation* indifferent despondency   375 *point-device in your accouterments* precise in your dress   391 *merely* completely 392 *a dark house and a whip* (the usual treatment of the insane in Shakespeare's day)   401 *moonish* changeable   402 *fantastical* capricious

inconstant, full of tears, full of smiles; for every
passion something and for no passion truly anything,
as boys and women are for the most part cattle of   405
this color; would now like him, now loathe him;
then entertain him, then forswear him; now weep
for him, then spit at him; that I drave my suitor from
his mad humor° of love to a living° humor of madness, which was, to forswear the full stream of the   410
world and to live in a nook merely monastic. And
thus I cured him; and this way will I take upon me
to wash your liver° as clean as a sound sheep's heart,
that there shall not be one spot of love in't.

Orlando. I would not be cured, youth.   415

Rosalind. I would cure you, if you would but call me
Rosalind and come every day to my cote and woo me.

Orlando. Now, by the faith of my love, I will. Tell me
where it is.

Rosalind. Go with me to it, and I'll show it you; and   420
by° the way you shall tell me where in the forest you
live. Will you go?

Orlando. With all my heart, good youth.

Rosalind. Nay, you must call me Rosalind. Come, sister,
will you go?   *Exeunt.* 425

Scene III. [*The forest.*]

*Enter [Touchstone, the] Clown, Audrey; and Jaques
[apart].*

Touchstone. Come apace,° good Audrey. I will fetch up
your goats, Audrey. And how, Audrey, am I the man
yet? Doth my simple feature° content you?

409 *humor* condition   409 *living* real   413 *liver* (thought to be the seat
of love)   421 *by* along   III.iii.1 *apace* swiftly   3 *feature* appearance

Audrey. Your features, Lord warrant° us! What features?

Touchstone. I am here with thee and thy goats, as the
most capricious poet, honest Ovid, was among the
Goths.°

Jaques. [*Aside*] O knowledge ill-inhabited,° worse than
Jove in a thatched house!

Touchstone. When a man's verses cannot be understood,
nor a man's good wit seconded with° the forward
child, understanding, it strikes a man more dead than
a great reckoning in a little room.° Truly, I would
the gods had made thee poetical.

Audrey. I do not know what poetical is. Is it honest in
deed and word? Is it a true thing?

Touchstone. No, truly; for the truest poetry is the most
feigning, and lovers are given to poetry, and what
they swear in poetry may be said as lovers they do
feign.°

Audrey. Do you wish then that the gods had made me
poetical?

Touchstone. I do truly; for thou swear'st to me thou
art honest. Now, if thou wert a poet, I might have
some hope thou didst feign.

Audrey. Would you not have me honest?

Touchstone. No, truly, unless thou wert hard-favored;°
for honesty coupled to beauty is to have honey a
sauce to sugar.

Jaques. [*Aside*] A material° fool.

4 *warrant* save   7–8 *capricious . . . Goths* (the Roman poet Ovid was
exiled among the Goths—pronounced in Elizabethan England the
same as "goats"—for the immorality of his verses. Touchstone plays
on the words "honest" [chaste] and "capricious" [derived from Latin
caper, male goat])   9 *ill-inhabited* ill-housed   12 *with* by   14 *great
reckoning . . . room* large bill for poor accommodations   21 *feign* (1)
pretend (2) desire (a pun on "fain")   28 *hard-favored* ugly   31 *material* full of good matter

Audrey. Well, I am not fair, and therefore I pray the gods make me honest.

Touchstone. Truly, and to cast away honesty upon a foul slut were to put good meat into an unclean dish.　35

Audrey. I am not a slut, though I thank the gods I am foul.

Touchstone. Well, praised be the gods for thy foulness! Sluttishness may come hereafter. But be it as it may be, I will marry thee; and to that end I have been　40 with Sir° Oliver Mar-text, the vicar of the next village, who hath promised to meet me in this place of the forest and to couple us.

Jaques. [*Aside*] I would fain see this meeting.

Audrey. Well, the gods give us joy!　45

Touchstone. Amen. A man may, if he were of a fearful heart, stagger° in this attempt; for here we have no temple but the wood, no assembly but horn-beasts.° But what though? Courage! As horns are odious, they are necessary.° It is said, "Many a man knows　50 no end of his goods." Right! Many a man has good horns and knows no end of them. Well, that is the dowry of his wife; 'tis none of his own getting. Horns! Even so, poor men alone. No, no; the noblest deer hath them as huge as the rascal.° Is the single man　55 therefore blessed? No; as a walled town is more worthier than a village, so is the forehead of a married man more honorable than the bare brow of a bachelor; and by how much defense° is better than no skill, by so much is a horn more precious than to　60 want.°

Enter Sir Oliver Mar-text.

Here comes Sir Oliver. Sir Oliver Mar-text, you are

---

41 *Sir* (an old form of address for a priest)　47 *stagger* tremble　48 *horn-beasts* (1) horned animals (2) cuckolds　50 *necessary* inevitable　55 *rascal* inferior deer　59 *defense* the art of defense　61 *want* i.e., lack horns

well met. Will you dispatch us° here under this tree,
or shall we go with you to your chapel?

65 *Oliver Mar-text.* Is there none here to give the woman?

Touchstone. I will not take her on gift of any man.

Oliver Mar-text. Truly, she must be given, or the marriage is not lawful.

Jaques. [*Comes forward*] Proceed, proceed; I'll give her.

70 *Touchstone.* Good even, good Master What-ye-call't.°
How do you, sir? You are very well met. God 'ield
you for your last company;° I am very glad to see
you. Even a toy° in hand here, sir. Nay, pray be
covered.°

75 *Jaques.* Will you be married, motley?

Touchstone. As the ox hath his bow,° sir, the horse his
curb, and the falcon her bells, so man hath his desires; and as pigeons bill, so wedlock would be
nibbling.

80 *Jaques.* And will you, being a man of your breeding, be
married under a bush like a beggar? Get you to
church, and have a good priest that can tell you what
marriage is. This fellow will but join you together as
they join wainscot;° then one of you will prove a
85 shrunk panel, and like green timber warp, warp.

Touchstone. [*Aside*] I am not in the mind but° I were
better to be married of him than of another; for he
is not like to marry me well; and not being well
married,° it will be a good excuse for me hereafter
90 to leave my wife.

---

63 *dispatch us* finish our business   70 *Master What-ye-call't* (Touchstone delicately avoids the name "Jaques," which could be pronounced
"jakes," a privy)   71–72 *God 'ield . . . company* God reward you for
the last time we met   73 *toy* trifle   73–74 *pray be covered* (Jaques has
removed his hat)   76 *bow* yoke   84 *wainscot* wood paneling   86 *I am
not in the mind but* I am not sure but that   88–89 *well married* (1) le-
gally married (2) happily married (3) married into wealth

Jaques. Go thou with me and let me counsel thee.

Touchstone. Come, sweet Audrey.
  We must be married, or we must live in bawdry.
  Farewell, good Master Oliver: not
          O sweet Oliver,   95
          O brave Oliver,
       Leave me not behind thee;
but
          Wind° away,
          Be gone, I say;   100
       I will not to wedding with thee.

Oliver Mar-text. 'Tis no matter. Ne'er a fantastical°
  knave of them all shall flout me out of my calling.
                             Exeunt.

Scene IV. [*The forest.*]

Enter Rosalind and Celia.

Rosalind. Never talk to me; I will weep.

Celia. Do, I prithee; but yet have the grace to consider
  that tears do not become a man.

Rosalind. But have I not cause to weep?

Celia. As good cause as one would desire; therefore   5
  weep.

Rosalind. His very hair is of the dissembling color.°

Celia. Something browner than Judas'. Marry, his kisses
  are Judas' own children.

Rosalind. I' faith, his hair is of a good color.   10

---

99 *Wind* turn   102 *fantastical* odd   III.iv.7 *dissembling color* i.e., red,
like the hair of Judas

Celia. An excellent color. Your chestnut was ever the only color.

Rosalind. And his kissing is as full of sanctity as the touch of holy bread.°

15 *Celia.* He hath bought a pair of cast° lips of Diana.° A nun of winter's sisterhood° kisses not more religiously; the very ice of chastity is in them.

Rosalind. But why did he swear he would come this morning, and comes not?

20 *Celia.* Nay, certainly there is no truth in him.

Rosalind. Do you think so?

Celia. Yes; I think he is not a pickpurse nor a horse-stealer, but for his verity in love, I do think him as concave° as a covered goblet or a worm-eaten nut.

25 *Rosalind.* Not true in love?

Celia. Yes, when he is in, but I think he is not in.

Rosalind. You have heard him swear downright he was.

Celia. "Was" is not "is." Besides, the oath of a lover is no stronger than the word of a tapster;° they are
30   both the confirmer of false reckonings. He attends here in the forest on the Duke your father.

Rosalind. I met the Duke yesterday and had much question° with him. He asked me of what parentage I was. I told him, of as good as he; so he laughed
35   and let me go. But what talk we of fathers when there is such a man as Orlando?

Celia. O, that's a brave° man; he writes brave verses, speaks brave words, swears brave oaths, and breaks them bravely, quite traverse,° athwart the heart of

14 *holy bread* (not the sacramental wafer, but bread brought to church to be blessed and then distributed to the poor)   15 *cast* (1) molded (2) castoff   15 *Diana* goddess of chastity   16 *winter's sisterhood* i.e., the most rigorous chastity   24 *concave* hollow   29 *tapster* waiter in a tavern   33 *question* talk   37 *brave* fine   39 *traverse* at an angle (instead of head-on)

his lover, as a puisny° tilter, that spurs his horse but   40
on one side, breaks his staff like a noble goose. But
all's brave that youth mounts and folly guides. Who
comes here?

Enter Corin.

Corin. Mistress and master, you have oft enquired
  After the shepherd that complained° of love,   45
  Who you saw sitting by me on the turf,
  Praising the proud disdainful shepherdess
  That was his mistress.

Celia.   Well, and what of him?

Corin. If you will see a pageant° truly played
  Between the pale complexion of true love   50
  And the red glow of scorn and proud disdain,
  Go hence a little, and I shall conduct you,
  If you will mark it.

Rosalind.   O, come, let us remove:
  The sight of lovers feedeth those in love.
  Bring us to this sight, and you shall say   55
  I'll prove a busy actor in their play.   *Exeunt.*

Scene V. [*The forest.*]

Enter Silvius and Phebe.

Silvius. Sweet Phebe, do not scorn me; do not, Phebe!
  Say that you love me not, but say not so
  In bitterness. The common executioner,
  Whose heart th' accustomed sight of death makes
      hard,
  Falls° not the ax upon the humbled neck   5

40 *puisny* inexperienced   45 *complained* lamented   49 *pageant* scene,
show   III.v.5 *Falls* lets fall

But first begs pardon. Will you sterner be
Than he that dies and lives° by bloody drops?

Enter [apart] Rosalind, Celia, and Corin.

Phebe. I would not be thy executioner.
   I fly thee, for I would not injure thee.
10   Thou tell'st me there is murder in mine eye:
   'Tis pretty, sure, and very probable
   That eyes, that are the frail'st and softest things,
   Who shut their coward gates on atomies,°
   Should be called tyrants, butchers, murderers.
15   Now I do frown on thee with all my heart,
   And if mine eyes can wound, now let them kill thee.
   Now counterfeit to swound;° why, now fall down;
   Or if thou canst not, O, for shame, for shame,
   Lie not, to say mine eyes are murderers.
20   Now show the wound mine eye hath made in thee;
   Scratch thee but with a pin, and there remains
   Some scar of it; lean upon a rush,
   The cicatrice and capable impressure°
   Thy palm some moment keeps; but now mine eyes,
25   Which I have darted at thee, hurt thee not,
   Nor I am sure there is no force in eyes
   That can do hurt.

Silvius.   O dear Phebe,
   If ever, as that ever may be near,°
   You meet in some fresh cheek the power of fancy,°
30   Then shall you know the wounds invisible
   That love's keen arrows make.

Phebe.   But till that time
   Come thou not near me; and when that time comes,
   Afflict me with thy mocks, pity me not,
   As till that time I shall not pity thee.

---

7 *dies and lives* earns his living   13 *atomies* motes   17 *counterfeit to swound* pretend to swoon   23 *cicatrice and capable impressure* mark and visible impression   28 *as that ever may be near* and may the time be soon   29 *fancy* love

Rosalind. And why, I pray you? Who might be your
    mother,   35
  That you insult, exult, and all at once,
  Over the wretched? What though you have no beauty
  (As, by my faith, I see no more in you
  Than without candle may go dark to bed°)
  Must you be therefore proud and pitiless?   40
  Why, what means this? Why do you look on me?
  I see no more in you than in the ordinary
  Of nature's sale-work.° 'Od's° my little life,
  I think she means to tangle my eyes too!
  No, faith, proud mistress, hope not after it;   45
  'Tis not your inky brows, your black silk hair,
  Your bugle° eyeballs, nor your cheek of cream
  That can entame my spirits to your worship.
  You foolish shepherd, wherefore do you follow her,
  Like foggy south,° puffing with wind and rain?   50
  You are a thousand times a properer° man
  Than she a woman. 'Tis such fools as you
  That makes the world full of ill-favored children.
  'Tis not her glass,° but you, that flatters her,
  And out of you she sees herself more proper   55
  Than any of her lineaments can show her.
  But mistress, know yourself. Down on your knees,
  And thank heaven, fasting, for a good man's love;
  For I must tell you friendly in your ear,
  Sell when you can, you are not for all markets.   60
  Cry the man mercy,° love him, take his offer;
  Foul° is most foul, being foul to be a scoffer;
  So take her to thee, shepherd. Fare you well.

Phebe. Sweet youth, I pray you chide a year together;
  I had rather hear you chide than this man woo.   65

Rosalind. [*Aside*] He's fall'n in love with your foulness,
  and she'll fall in love with my anger. If it be so, as

---

39 *Than . . . to bed* i.e., your beauty is not so dazzling as to light up the
room   42–43 *ordinary/Of nature's sale-work* usual product of nature's
manufacture   43 *'Od's* God save   47 *bugle* black and glassy
50 *south* south wind   51 *properer* more handsome   54 *glass* mirror
61 *Cry the man mercy* ask the man's forgiveness   62 *Foul* (1) ugliness
(2) wickedness

fast as she answers thee with frowning looks, I'll
sauce her with bitter words. [*To Phebe*] Why look
70 you so upon me?

Phebe. For no ill will I bear you.

Rosalind. I pray you do not fall in love with me,
For I am falser than vows made in wine.
Besides, I like you not. If you will know my house,
75 'Tis at the tuft of olives, here hard° by.
Will you go, sister? Shepherd, ply her hard.
Come, sister. Shepherdess, look on him better
And be not proud. Though all the world could see,
None could be so abused° in sight as he.
80 Come, to our flock.   *Exit* [*with Celia and Corin*].

Phebe. Dead shepherd, now I find thy saw° of might,
"Who ever loved that loved not at first sight?"°

Silvius. Sweet Phebe.

Phebe.   Ha! What say'st thou, Silvius?

Silvius. Sweet Phebe, pity me.

85 *Phebe.* Why, I am sorry for thee, gentle Silvius.

Silvius. Wherever sorrow is, relief would be.
If you do sorrow at my grief in love,
By giving love your sorrow and my grief
Were both extermined.°

90 *Phebe.* Thou hast my love. Is not that neighborly?°

Silvius. I would have you.

Phebe.   Why, that were covetousness.
Silvius, the time was that I hated thee;
And yet it is not that I bear thee love,
But since that thou canst talk of love so well,
95 Thy company, which erst° was irksome to me,

75 *hard* near   79 *abused* deceived   81 *saw* saying   82 *Who ever . . .
sight* (a line from Christopher Marlowe's poem *Hero and Leander*, published in 1598. The "Dead shepherd" is Marlowe, who died in 1593)
89 *extermined* ended   90 *neighborly* friendly (perhaps alluding to the
commandment to love one's neighbor)   95 *erst* formerly

I will endure; and I'll employ thee too;
But do not look for further recompense
Than thine own gladness that thou art employed.

Silvius. So holy and so perfect is my love,
And I in such a poverty of grace,°   *100*
That I shall think it a most plenteous crop
To glean the broken ears after the man
That the main harvest reaps. Loose now and then
A scatt'red° smile, and that I'll live upon.

Phebe. Know'st thou the youth that spoke to me ere-
     while?°   *105*

Silvius. Not very well, but I have met him oft,
And he hath bought the cottage and the bounds
That the old carlot° once was master of.

Phebe. Think not I love him, though I ask for him;
'Tis but a peevish boy; yet he talks well.   *110*
But what care I for words? Yet words do well
When he that speaks them pleases those that hear.
It is a pretty youth. Not very pretty.
But sure he's proud. And yet his pride becomes him.
He'll make a proper man. The best thing in him   *115*
Is his complexion. And faster than his tongue
Did make offense, his eye did heal it up.
He is not very tall. Yet for his years he's tall.
His leg is but so so. And yet 'tis well.
There was a pretty redness in his lip,   *120*
A little riper and more lusty red
Than that mixed in his cheek. 'Twas just the difference
Betwixt the constant° red and mingled damask.°
There be some women, Silvius, had they marked him
In parcels° as I did, would have gone near   *125*
To fall in love with him; but, for my part,
I love him not nor hate him not. And yet
I have more cause to hate him than to love him;
For what had he to do to chide at me?

100 *a poverty of grace* small favor   104 *scatt'red* stray   105 *erewhile*
a short time ago   108 *carlot* countryman   123 *constant* uniform
123 *mingled damask* pink and white   125 *In parcels* piece by piece

¹³⁰ He said mine eyes were black and my hair black;
And, now I am rememb'red,° scorned at me.
I marvel why I answered not again.
But that's all one: omittance is no quittance.°
I'll write to him a very taunting letter,
¹³⁵ And thou shalt bear it. Wilt thou, Silvius?

Silvius. Phebe, with all my heart.

Phebe.   I'll write it straight;°
The matter's in my head and in my heart;
I will be bitter with him and passing short.°
Go with me, Silvius.   *Exeunt.*

---

131 *rememb'red* reminded   133 *omittance is no quittance* i.e., the fact
that I did not reply does not mean I will not do so later   136 *straight*
at once   138 *passing short* very curt

ACT IV

Scene I. [*The forest.*]

Enter Rosalind and Celia and Jaques.

Jaques. I prithee, pretty youth, let me be better acquainted with thee.

Rosalind. They say you are a melancholy fellow.

Jaques. I am so; I do love it better than laughing.

Rosalind. Those that are in extremity of° either are   5
abominable fellows, and betray themselves to every
modern censure° worse than drunkards.

Jaques. Why, 'tis good to be sad and say nothing.

Rosalind. Why then, 'tis good to be a post.

Jaques. I have neither the scholar's melancholy, which   10
is emulation;° nor the musician's, which is fantastical;
nor the courtier's, which is proud; nor the soldier's,
which is ambitious; nor the lawyer's, which is politic;°
nor the lady's, which is nice;° nor the lover's, which
is all these: but it is a melancholy of mine own, com-   15
pounded of many simples,° extracted from many
objects, and indeed the sundry contemplation of my

IV.i.5 *are in extremity of* go to extremes in   6–7 *every modern censure*
i.e., the average man's disapproval   11 *emulation* envy   13 *politic* i.e.,
put on to seem grave   14 *nice* fastidious   16 *simples* ingredients

travels, in which my often rumination° wraps me in
a most humorous sadness.

20 *Rosalind.* A traveler! By my faith, you have great reason
to be sad. I fear you have sold your own lands to see
other men's. Then to have seen much and to have
nothing is to have rich eyes and poor hands.

Jaques. Yes, I have gained my experience.

Enter Orlando.

25 *Rosalind.* And your experience makes you sad. I had
rather have a fool to make me merry than experience
to make me sad—and to travel° for it too.

Orlando. Good day and happiness, dear Rosalind.

Jaques. Nay then, God b'wi'you, an° you talk in
30 blank verse.   [*Exit.*]

Rosalind. Farewell, Monsieur Traveler. Look you lisp°
and wear strange suits, disable° all the benefits of
your own country, be out of love with your nativity,°
and almost chide God for making you that counte-
35 nance you are; or I will scarce think you have swam
in a gundello.° Why, how now, Orlando, where have
you been all this while? You a lover? An you serve
me such another trick, never come in my sight more.

Orlando. My fair Rosalind, I come within an hour of
40 my promise.

Rosalind. Break an hour's promise in love? He that
will divide a minute into a thousand parts and break
but a part of the thousand part of a minute in the
affairs of love, it may be said of him that Cupid hath
45 clapped° him o' th' shoulder, but I'll warrant him
heart-whole.

Orlando. Pardon me, dear Rosalind.

---

18 *often rumination* constant reflection   27 *travel* (pun on "travail")
29 *an* if   31 *lisp* speak affectedly   32 *disable* disparage   33 *nativity*
birthplace   36 *gundello* gondola   45 *clapped* touched

Rosalind. Nay, an you be so tardy, come no more in my sight. I had as lief be wooed of a snail.

Orlando. Of a snail?   50

Rosalind. Ay, of a snail; for though he comes slowly, he carries his house on his head; a better jointure,° I think, than you make a woman. Besides, he brings his destiny with him.

Orlando. What's that?   55

Rosalind. Why, horns; which such as you are fain to be beholding to your wives for; but he comes armed° in his fortune and prevents° the slander of his wife.

Orlando. Virtue is no horn-maker, and my Rosalind is virtuous.   60

Rosalind. And I am your Rosalind.

Celia. It pleases him to call you so; but he hath a Rosalind of a better leer° than you.

Rosalind. Come, woo me, woo me; for now I am in a holiday humor and like enough to consent. What   65
would you say to me now, an I were your very very Rosalind?

Orlando. I would kiss before I spoke.

Rosalind. Nay, you were better speak first, and when you were graveled for lack of matter,° you might take   70
occasion to kiss. Very good orators, when they are out,° they will spit; and for lovers, lacking—God warn° us!—matter, the cleanliest shift is to kiss.

Orlando. How if the kiss be denied?

Rosalind. Then she puts you to entreaty, and there   75
begins new matter.

---

52 *jointure* marriage settlement   57 *armed* i.e., with horns   58 *prevents* (1) forestalls (2) anticipates (?)   63 *leer* face   70 *graveled for lack of matter* hard put for something to say   72 *out* i.e., out of material   73 *warn* protect (warrant)

Orlando. Who could be out, being before his beloved mistress?

Rosalind. Marry, that should you, if I were your mis-
80   tress, or I should think my honesty ranker° than my wit.

Orlando. What, of my suit?

Rosalind. Not out of your apparel, and yet out of your suit.° Am not I your Rosalind?

85 *Orlando.* I take some joy to say you are, because I would be talking of her.

Rosalind. Well, in her person, I say I will not have you.

Orlando. Then, in mine own person, I die.

Rosalind. No, faith, die by attorney.° The poor world
90 is almost six thousand years old, and in all this time there was not any man died in his own person,° videlicet,° in a love cause. Troilus° had his brains dashed out with a Grecian club; yet he did what he could to die before, and he is one of the patterns of
95 love. Leander,° he would have lived many a fair year though Hero had turned nun, if it had not been for a hot midsummer night; for, good youth, he went but forth to wash him in the Hellespont, and being taken with the cramp, was drowned; and the foolish
100 chroniclers of that age found° it was "Hero of Sestos." But these are all lies. Men have died from time to time, and worms have eaten them, but not for love.

Orlando. I would not have my right Rosalind of this mind, for I protest her frown might kill me.

---

80 *honesty ranker* virtue fouler   84 *suit* (1) apparel (2) entreaty   89 *attorney* proxy   91 *in his own person* in real life (as opposed to fiction)
92 *videlicet* that is to say   92 *Troilus* (Priam's son, betrayed in love by Cressida and killed by the spear of Achilles.   "As true as Troilus" became a proverbial expression)   95 *Leander* (a prototype of dedicated love, who swam the Hellespont nightly to see his mistress, Hero of Sestos)   100 *found* gave the verdict

Rosalind. By this hand, it will not kill a fly. But come, 105
now I will be your Rosalind in a more coming-on
disposition; and ask me what you will, I will grant it.

Orlando. Then love me, Rosalind.

Rosalind. Yes, faith, will I, Fridays and Saturdays and
all. 110

Orlando. And wilt thou have me?

Rosalind. Ay, and twenty such.

Orlando. What sayest thou?

Rosalind. Are you not good?

Orlando. I hope so. 115

Rosalind. Why then, can one desire too much of a good
thing? Come, sister, you shall be the priest and marry
us. Give me your hand, Orlando. What do you say,
sister?

Orlando. Pray thee marry us. 120

Celia. I cannot say the words.

Rosalind. You must begin, "Will you, Orlando—"

Celia. Go to.° Will you, Orlando, have to wife this
Rosalind?

Orlando. I will. 125

Rosalind. Ay, but when?

Orlando. Why now, as fast as she can marry us.

Rosalind. Then you must say, "I take thee, Rosalind,
for wife."

Orlando. I take thee, Rosalind, for wife. 130

Rosalind. I might ask you for your commission;° but I
do take thee, Orlando, for my husband. There's a

123 *Go to* that's enough　　131 *commission* license

girl goes before° the priest, and certainly a woman's
thought runs before her actions.

135 *Orlando.* So do all thoughts; they are winged.

Rosalind. Now tell me how long you would have her
after you have possessed her.

Orlando. For ever and a day.

Rosalind. Say "a day," without the "ever." No, no,
140 Orlando. Men are April when they woo, December
when they wed. Maids are May when they are maids,
but the sky changes when they are wives. I will be
more jealous of thee than a Barbary cock-pigeon°
over his hen, more clamorous than a parrot against°
145 rain, more newfangled° than an ape, more giddy° in
my desires than a monkey. I will weep for nothing,
like Diana in the fountain,° and I will do that when
you are disposed to be merry; I will laugh like a hyen,
and that when thou art inclined to sleep.

150 *Orlando.* But will my Rosalind do so?

Rosalind. By my life, she will do as I do.

Orlando. O, but she is wise.

Rosalind. Or else she could not have the wit to do this;
the wiser, the waywarder. Make° the doors upon a
155 woman's wit, and it will out at the casement; shut
that, and 'twill out at the keyhole; stop that,'twill fly
with the smoke out at the chimney.

Orlando. A man that had a wife with such a wit, he
might say, "Wit, whither wilt?"°

160 *Rosalind.* Nay, you might keep that check° for it till you
met your wife's wit going to your neighbor's bed.

133 *goes before* runs ahead (Rosalind has not waited for Celia to say,
"Will you, Rosalind, have to husband")   143 *Barbary cock-pigeon*
Barb pigeon ("Barbary" suggests jealousy)   144 *against* before
145 *newfangled* given to novelty   145 *giddy* changeable   147 *like Diana in the fountain* i.e., steadily (Diana was a popular subject for fountain statuary)   154 *Make* shut   159 *Wit, whither wilt* i.e., where are
your senses   160 *check* rebuke

Orlando. And what wit could wit have to excuse that?

Rosalind. Marry, to say she came to seek you there. You
shall never take her without her answer unless you
take her without her tongue. O, that woman that   *165*
cannot make her fault her husband's occasion,° let
her never nurse her child herself, for she will breed
it like a fool.

Orlando. For these two hours, Rosalind, I will leave thee.

Rosalind. Alas, dear love, I cannot lack thee two hours!   *170*

Orlando. I must attend the Duke at dinner. By two
o'clock I will be with thee again.

Rosalind. Ay, go your ways, go your ways; I knew
what you would prove. My friends told me as much,
and I thought no less. That flattering tongue of yours   *175*
won me. 'Tis but one cast away,° and so, come
death! Two o'clock is your hour?

Orlando. Ay, sweet Rosalind.

Rosalind. By my troth, and in good earnest, and so
God mend me, and by all pretty oaths that are not   *180*
dangerous, if you break one jot of your promise or
come one minute behind your hour, I will think you
the most pathetical° break-promise, and the most
hollow lover, and the most unworthy of her you call
Rosalind, that may be chosen out of the gross° band   *185*
of the unfaithful. Therefore beware my censure and
keep your promise.

Orlando. With no less religion° than if thou wert indeed
my Rosalind. So adieu.

Rosalind. Well, Time is the old justice that examines all   *190*
such offenders, and let Time try. Adieu.

                              Exit [Orlando].

166 *make . . . occasion* i.e., turn defense of her own actions into an accusation of her husband's   176 *one cast away* i.e., one girl deserted
183 *pathetical* (1) pitiful (2) passionate (?)   185 *gross* large   188 *religion* faith

Celia. You have simply misused° our sex in your love-
prate. We must have your doublet and hose plucked
over your head, and show the world what the bird
195   hath done to her own nest.

Rosalind. O coz, coz, coz, my pretty little coz, that thou
didst know how many fathom deep I am in love! But
it cannot be sounded. My affection hath an unknown
bottom, like the Bay of Portugal.

200   *Celia.* Or rather, bottomless, that as fast as you pour
affection in, it runs out.

Rosalind. No, that same wicked bastard of Venus° that
was begot of thought,° conceived of spleen,° and born
of madness, that blind rascally boy that abuses every
205   one's eyes because his own are out, let him be judge
how deep I am in love. I'll tell thee, Aliena, I cannot
be out of the sight of Orlando. I'll go find a shadow,
and sigh till he come.

Celia. And I'll sleep.   *Exeunt.*

Scene II. [*The forest.*]

Enter Jaques; and Lords, [like] Foresters.

Jaques. Which is he that killed the deer?

Lord. Sir, it was I.

Jaques. Let's present him to the Duke like a Roman
conqueror; and it would do well to set the deer's
5   horns upon his head for a branch of victory. Have
you no song, forester, for this purpose?

Another Lord. Yes, sir.

---

192 *simply misused* completely abused   202 *bastard of Venus* Cupid
203 *thought* despondency   203 *spleen* sheer impulse

Jaques. Sing it. 'Tis no matter how it be in tune, so it
make noise enough.   *Music.*

Song.

What shall he have that killed the deer?   10
His leather skin and horns to wear:
    Then sing him home. The rest shall bear
        This burden.°

Take thou no scorn° to wear the horn,
It was a crest ere thou wast born,   15
    Thy father's father wore it,
    And thy father bore it.
The horn, the horn, the lusty horn,
Is not a thing to laugh to scorn.°   *Exeunt.*

Scene III. [*The forest.*]

Enter Rosalind and Celia.

Rosalind. How say you now, is it not past two o'clock?
    And here much° Orlando!

Celia. I warrant you, with pure love and troubled brain,
    he hath ta'en his bow and arrows and is gone forth
    to sleep.   5

IV.ii.12–13 *The rest shall bear This burden* i.e., not only the forester who
killed the deer but all men will wear the horns of cuckoldry (many editors read the line as a stage direction: the other foresters ["the rest"]
are to join in the refrain ["burden"] after one forester has sung the first
three lines of the song. If the Folio version—here followed—is correct,
it is likely that all sing the song from the beginning)   14 *Take thou no
scorn* do not be ashamed   19 *laugh to scorn* ridicule   IV.iii.2 *much* i.e.,
not much

Enter Silvius.

Look who comes here.

Silvius. My errand is to you, fair youth.
My gentle Phebe bid me give you this.
I know not the contents, but, as I guess
10   By the stern brow and waspish action
Which she did use as she was writing of it,
It bears an angry tenor. Pardon me;
I am but as a guiltless messenger.

Rosalind. Patience herself would startle at this letter
15   And play the swaggerer. Bear this, bear all!
She says I am not fair, that I lack manners;
She calls me proud, and that she could not love me,
Were man as rare as phoenix.° 'Od's my will!
Her love is not the hare that I do hunt.
20   Why writes she so to me? Well, shepherd, well,
This is a letter of your own device.

Silvius. No, I protest, I know not the contents.
Phebe did write it.

Rosalind.   Come, come, you are a fool,
And turned into the extremity° of love.
25   I saw her hand. She has a leathern hand,
A freestone-colored° hand. I verily did think
That her old gloves were on, but 'twas her hands.
She has a housewife's hand; but that's no matter:
I say she never did invent° this letter;
30   This is a man's invention and his hand.

Silvius. Sure it is hers.

Rosalind. Why, 'tis a boisterous and a cruel style,
A style for challengers. Why, she defies me
Like Turk to Christian. Women's gentle brain
35   Could not drop forth such giant-rude° invention,

18 *phoenix* (a legendary bird, of which there was only one in the world
at any time)   24 *turned into the extremity* became the very essence
26 *freestone-colored* i.e., yellowish-brown   29 *invent* compose   35 *gi-
ant-rude* incredibly rude

Such Ethiop words, blacker in their effect
Than in their countenance. Will you hear the letter?

Silvius. So please you, for I never heard it yet;
Yet heard too much of Phebe's cruelty.

Rosalind. She Phebes me.° Mark how the tyrant writes.   40
   (*Read.*) "Art thou god, to shepherd turned,
        That a maiden's heart hath burned?"
Can a woman rail thus?

Silvius. Call you this railing?

Rosalind.
   (*Read.*) "Why, thy godhead laid apart,°   45
        Warr'st thou with a woman's heart?"
Did you ever hear such railing?
       "Whiles the eye of man did woo me,
        That could do no vengeance° to me."
Meaning me a beast.   50
       "If the scorn of your bright eyne°
       Have power to raise such love in mine,
       Alack, in me what strange effect
       Would they work in mild aspect!°
       Whiles you chid me, I did love;   55
       How then might your prayers move!
       He that brings this love to thee
       Little knows this love in me;
       And by him seal up thy mind,°
       Whether that thy youth and kind°   60
       Will the faithful offer take
       Of me and all that I can make,°
       Or else by him my love deny,
       And then I'll study how to die."

Silvius. Call you this chiding?   65

Celia. Alas, poor shepherd!

---

40 *She Phebes me* i.e., she writes with her customary disdain   45 *thy godhead laid apart* i.e., having assumed human form   49 *vengeance* harm   51 *eyne* eyes   54 *aspect* (1) look (2) planetary influence   59 *seal up thy mind* i.e., tell your feelings in a letter   60 *youth and kind* youthful nature   62 *make* give

Rosalind. Do you pity him? No, he deserves no pity.
Wilt thou love such a woman? What, to make thee
an instrument,° and play false strains upon thee? Not
70 to be endured! Well, go your way to her, for I see
love hath made thee a tame snake,° and say this to
her: that if she love me, I charge her to love thee; if
she will not, I will never have her unless thou entreat
for her. If you be a true lover, hence, and not a word;
75 for here comes more company.   *Exit Silvius.*

Enter Oliver.

Oliver. Good morrow, fair ones. Pray you, if you know,
Where in the purlieus° of this forest stands
A sheepcote, fenced about with olive trees?

Celia. West of this place, down in the neighbor bottom.°
80 The rank of osiers° by the murmuring stream
Left on your right hand brings you to the place.
But at this hour the house doth keep itself;
There's none within.

Oliver. If that an eye may profit by a tongue,
85 Then should I know you by description,
Such garments and such years: "The boy is fair,
Of female favor,° and bestows° himself
Like a ripe sister;° the woman low,°
And browner than her brother." Are not you
90 The owner of the house I did enquire for?

Celia. It is no boast, being asked, to say we are.

Oliver. Orlando doth commend him to you both,
And to that youth he calls his Rosalind
He sends this bloody napkin.° Are you he?

95 *Rosalind.* I am. What must we understand by this?

Oliver. Some of my shame, if you will know of me

68–69 *make thee an instrument* use you   71 *tame snake* poor worm
77 *purlieus* borders   79 *neighbor bottom* nearby valley   80 *rank of
osiers* row of willows   87 *favor* features   87 *bestows* carries   88 *ripe
sister* grown-up woman (some editors emend "sister" to "forester")
88 *low* short   94 *napkin* handkerchief

What man I am, and how and why and where
This handkercher was stained.

Celia.   I pray you tell it.

Oliver. When last the young Orlando parted from you,
He left a promise to return again   *100*
Within an hour; and pacing through the forest,
Chewing the food of sweet and bitter fancy,°
Lo, what befell. He threw his eye aside,
And mark what object did present itself:
Under an old oak, whose boughs were mossed with
   age   *105*
And high top bald with dry antiquity,
A wretched ragged man, o'ergrown with hair,
Lay sleeping on his back; about his neck
A green and gilded snake had wreathed itself,
Who with her head, nimble in threats, approached   *110*
The opening of his mouth; but suddenly,
Seeing Orlando, it unlinked itself
And with indented° glides did slip away
Into a bush, under which bush's shade
A lioness, with udders all drawn dry,   *115*
Lay couching,° head on ground, with catlike watch
When that the sleeping man should stir; for 'tis
The royal disposition of that beast
To prey on nothing that doth seem as dead.
This seen, Orlando did approach the man   *120*
And found it was his brother, his elder brother.

Celia. O, I have heard him speak of that same brother,
And he did render° him the most unnatural
That lived amongst men.

Oliver.   And well he might so do,
For well I know he was unnatural.   *125*

Rosalind. But, to Orlando: did he leave him there,
Food to the sucked and hungry lioness?

Oliver. Twice did he turn his back and purposed so;

102 *fancy* love   113 *indented* serpentine   116 *couching* crouching
123 *render* describe

But kindness,° nobler ever than revenge,
130 And nature, stronger than his just occasion,°
Made him give battle to the lioness,
Who quickly fell before him; in which hurtling
From miserable slumber I awaked.

Celia. Are you his brother?

Rosalind.   Was't you he rescued?

135 *Celia.* Was't you that did so oft contrive° to kill him?

Oliver. 'Twas I. But 'tis not I. I do not shame
    To tell you what I was, since my conversion
    So sweetly tastes, being the thing I am.

Rosalind. But, for the bloody napkin?

Oliver.   By and by.°
140 When from the first to last, betwixt us two,
    Tears our recountments° had most kindly bathed,
    As how I came into that desert place:
    In brief, he led me to the gentle Duke,
    Who gave me fresh array and entertainment,°
145 Committing me unto my brother's love,
    Who led me instantly unto his cave,
    There stripped himself, and here upon his arm
    The lioness had torn some flesh away,
    Which all this while had bled; and now he fainted,
150 And cried, in fainting, upon Rosalind.
    Brief, I recovered° him, bound up his wound;
    And after some small space, being strong at heart,
    He sent me hither, stranger as I am,
    To tell this story, that you might excuse
155 His broken promise, and to give this napkin,
    Dyed in his blood, unto the shepherd youth
    That he in sport doth call his Rosalind.
                                [*Rosalind swoons.*]

Celia. Why, how now, Ganymede, sweet Ganymede!

129 *kindness* familial affection   130 *occasion* opportunity   135 *con-trive* plot   139 *By and by* soon   141 *recountments* recital (of our adventures since we last met)   144 *entertainment* hospitality   151 *recovered* revived

Oliver. Many will swoon when they do look on blood.

Celia. There is more in it. Cousin Ganymede!   *160*

Oliver. Look, he recovers.

Rosalind. I would I were at home.

Celia.   We'll lead you thither.
    I pray you, will you take him by the arm?

Oliver. Be of good cheer, youth. You a man! You lack
    a man's heart.   *165*

Rosalind. I do so, I confess it. Ah, sirrah, a body would
    think this was well counterfeited.° I pray you tell
    your brother how well I counterfeited. Heigh-ho!

Oliver. This was not counterfeit. There is too great
    testimony in your complexion that it was a passion   *170*
    of earnest.°

Rosalind. Counterfeit, I assure you.

Oliver. Well then, take a good heart and counterfeit to
    be a man.

Rosalind. So I do; but, i' faith, I should have been a   *175*
    woman by right.

Celia. Come, you look paler and paler. Pray you draw
    homewards. Good sir, go with us.

Oliver. That will I, for I must bear answer back
    How you excuse my brother, Rosalind.   *180*

Rosalind. I shall devise something. But I pray you
    commend my counterfeiting to him. Will you go?
                          Exeunt.

---

167 *counterfeited* pretended   170–171 *passion of earnest* real emotion

ACT V

Scene I. [*The forest.*]

Enter [Touchstone, the] Clown and Audrey.

Touchstone. We shall find a time, Audrey. Patience,
gentle Audrey.

Audrey. Faith, the priest was good enough, for all the
old gentleman's saying.

5   *Touchstone.* A most wicked Sir Oliver, Audrey, a most
vile Mar-text. But, Audrey, there is a youth here in
the forest lays claim to you.

Audrey. Ay, I know who 'tis. He hath no interest in me
in the world. Here comes the man you mean.

Enter William.

10   *Touchstone.* It is meat and drink to me to see a clown;°
by my troth, we that have good wits have much to
answer for. We shall be flouting;° we cannot hold.°

William. Good ev'n, Audrey.

Audrey. God ye° good ev'n, William.

15   *William.* And good ev'n to you, sir.

V.i.10 *clown* yokel   12 *flouting* mocking   12 *hold* i.e., keep from
mocking   14 *God ye* God give you

Touchstone. Good ev'n, gentle friend. Cover thy head,° cover thy head. Nay, prithee be covered. How old are you, friend?

William. Five-and-twenty, sir.

Touchstone. A ripe° age. Is thy name William?   *20*

William. William, sir.

Touchstone. A fair name. Wast born i' th' forest here?

William. Ay, sir, I thank God.

Touchstone. "Thank God." A good answer. Art rich?

William. Faith, sir, so so.   *25*

Touchstone. "So so" is good, very good, very excellent good; and yet it is not, it is but so so. Art thou wise?

William. Ay, sir, I have a pretty wit.

Touchstone. Why, thou say'st well. I do now remember a saying, "The fool doth think he is wise, but the wise   *30* man knows himself to be a fool." The heathen philosopher, when he had a desire to eat a grape, would open his lips when he put it into his mouth, meaning thereby that grapes were made to eat and lips to open. You do love this maid?   *35*

William. I do, sir.

Touchstone. Give me your hand. Art thou learned?

William. No, sir.

Touchstone. Then learn this of me: to have is to have; for it is a figure° in rhetoric that drink, being poured   *40* out of a cup into a glass, by filling the one doth empty the other; for all your writers do consent that *ipse*° is he. Now, you are not *ipse*, for I am he.

William. Which he, sir?

Touchstone. He, sir, that must marry this woman. There-   *45*

16 *Cover thy head* (William has removed his hat)   20 *ripe* fine   40 *figure* figure of speech   43 *ipse* he himself (Latin)

fore, you clown, abandon—which is in the vulgar,
leave—the society—which in the boorish is, company
—of this female—which in the common is, woman.
Which together is, abandon the society of this female,
or, clown, thou perishest; or, to thy better understanding, diest; or, to wit, I kill thee, make thee away,
translate thy life into death, thy liberty into bondage.
I will deal in poison with thee, or in bastinado,° or
in steel; I will bandy with thee in faction;° I will
o'errun thee with policy;° I will kill thee a hundred
and fifty ways. Therefore tremble and depart.

Audrey. Do, good William.

William. God rest you merry, sir.   *Exit.*

Enter Corin.

Corin. Our master and mistress seeks you. Come away,
away!

Touchstone. Trip, Audrey, trip, Audrey. I attend,° I
attend.   *Exeunt.*

Scene II. [*The forest.*]

Enter Orlando and Oliver.

Orlando. Is't possible that on so little acquaintance you
should like her? That but seeing, you should love
her? And loving, woo? And wooing, she should
grant? And will you persever to enjoy her?

Oliver. Neither call the giddiness° of it in question, the
poverty of her, the small acquaintance, my sudden
wooing, nor her sudden consenting; but say with me,

53 *bastinado* cudgeling   54 *bandy with thee in faction* i.e., argue with
you as do politicians   55 *o'errun thee with policy* overwhelm you with
craft   61 *attend* come   V.ii.5 *giddiness* suddenness

I love Aliena; say with her that she loves me; consent
with both that we may enjoy each other. It shall be
to your good; for my father's house, and all the   10
revenue that was old Sir Rowland's, will I estate°
upon you, and here live and die a shepherd.

Enter Rosalind.

Orlando. You have my consent. Let your wedding be
tomorrow: thither will I invite the Duke and all's
contented followers. Go you and prepare Aliena; for   15
look you, here comes my Rosalind.

Rosalind. God save you, brother.

Oliver. And you, fair sister.   [*Exit.*]

Rosalind. O my dear Orlando, how it grieves me to see
thee wear thy heart in a scarf!°   20

Orlando. It is my arm.

Rosalind. I thought thy heart had been wounded with
the claws of a lion.

Orlando. Wounded it is, but with the eyes of a lady.

Rosalind. Did your brother tell you how I counterfeited 25
to sound° when he showed me your handkercher?

Orlando. Ay, and greater wonders than that.

Rosalind. O, I know where you are! Nay, 'tis true.
There was never anything so sudden but the fight of
two rams and Caesar's thrasonical° brag of "I came,   30
saw, and overcame"; for your brother and my sister
no sooner met but they looked; no sooner looked
but they loved; no sooner loved but they sighed; no
sooner sighed but they asked one another the reason;
no sooner knew the reason but they sought the   35
remedy: and in these degrees° have they made a pair
of stairs to marriage, which they will climb incon-

11 *estate* settle   20 *scarf* sling   26 *sound* swoon   30 *thrasonical*
boastful (after the braggart soldier Thraso in Terence's comedy
Eunuchus)   36 *degrees* (a pun on the literal meaning, "steps")

tinent, or else be incontinent° before marriage: they
are in the very wrath of love, and they will together;
40   clubs cannot part them.

Orlando. They shall be married tomorrow, and I will
bid the Duke to the nuptial. But, O, how bitter a
thing it is to look into happiness through another
man's eyes! By so much the more shall I tomorrow
45   be at the height of heart-heaviness, by how much I
shall think my brother happy in having what he
wishes for.

Rosalind. Why then, tomorrow I cannot serve your
turn for Rosalind?

50 *Orlando.* I can live no longer by thinking.

Rosalind. I will weary you then no longer with idle
talking. Know of me then, for now I speak to some
purpose, that I know you are a gentleman of good
conceit.° I speak not this that you should bear a good
55   opinion of my knowledge, insomuch I say I know
you are; neither do I labor for a greater esteem than
may in some little measure draw a belief from you,
to do yourself good, and not to grace me.° Believe
then, if you please, that I can do strange things. I
60   have, since I was three year old, conversed° with a
magician, most profound in his art and yet not
damnable.° If you do love Rosalind so near the heart
as your gesture° cries it out, when your brother
marries Aliena shall you marry her. I know into what
65   straits of fortune she is driven; and it is not impossible to me, if it appear not inconvenient° to you, to
set her before your eyes tomorrow, human as she is,°
and without any danger.

Orlando. Speak'st thou in sober meanings?

37–38 *incontinent . . . incontinent* with all haste . . . unchaste   54 *conceit* understanding   58 *to grace me* to do credit to myself   60 *con-
versed* spent time   61–62 *and yet not damnable* (because he practices
white, not black, magic)   63 *gesture* conduct   66 *inconvenient* un-
fitting   67 *human as she is* i.e., Rosalind herself, not a spirit

Rosalind. By my life, I do, which I tender dearly,°   70
  though I say I am a magician.° Therefore put you in
  your best array, bid your friends; for if you will be
  married tomorrow, you shall; and to Rosalind, if
  you will.

Enter Silvius and Phebe.

  Look, here comes a lover of mine and a lover of hers.   75

Phebe. Youth, you have done me much ungentleness
  To show the letter that I writ to you.

Rosalind. I care not if I have. It is my study°
  To seem despiteful° and ungentle to you.
  You are there followed by a faithful shepherd: 80
  Look upon him, love him; he worships you.

Phebe. Good shepherd, tell this youth what 'tis to love.

Silvius. It is to be all made of sighs and tears;
  And so am I for Phebe.

Phebe. And I for Ganymede.   85

Orlando. And I for Rosalind.

Rosalind. And I for no woman.

Silvius. It is to be all made of faith and service;
  And so am I for Phebe.

Phebe. And I for Ganymede.   90

Orlando. And I for Rosalind.

Rosalind. And I for no woman.

Silvius. It is to be all made of fantasy,°
  All made of passion, and all made of wishes,
  All adoration, duty, and observance,°   95
  All humbleness, all patience, and impatience,

---

70 *tender dearly* hold precious   71 *though . . . magician* (a magician
could be punished with death)   78 *study* intention   79 *despiteful* scorn-
ful   93 *fantasy* fancy   95 *observance* devoted attention

All purity, all trial, all observance;°
And so am I for Phebe.

Phebe. And so am I for Ganymede.

100 *Orlando.* And so am I for Rosalind.

Rosalind. And so am I for no woman.

Phebe. If this be so, why blame you me to love you?

Silvius. If this be so, why blame you me to love you?

Orlando. If this be so, why blame you me to love you?

Rosalind. Why do you speak too,° "Why blame you me
105   to love you?"

Orlando. To her that is not here, nor doth not hear.

Rosalind. Pray you, no more of this; 'tis like the howling
of Irish wolves against the moon. [*To Silvius*] I will
help you if I can. [*To Phebe*] I would love you if I
110   could. Tomorrow meet me all together. [*To Phebe*] I
will marry you if ever I marry woman, and I'll be
married tomorrow. [*To Orlando*] I will satisfy you if
ever I satisfied man, and you shall be married tomorrow. [*To Silvius*] I will content you if what pleases
115   you contents you, and you shall be married tomorrow. [*To Orlando*] As you love Rosalind, meet. [*To
Silvius*] As you love Phebe, meet. And as I love no
woman, I'll meet. So fare you well. I have left you
commands.

120 *Silvius.* I'll not fail if I live.

Phebe. Nor I.

Orlando. Nor I.   *Exeunt.*

---

97 *observance* (some editors emend to "obedience")   105 *Why do you
speak too* (some editors emend to "Who do you speak to")

Scene III. [*The forest.*]

Enter [Touchstone, the] Clown and Audrey.

Touchstone. Tomorrow is the joyful day, Audrey; tomorrow will we be married.

Audrey. I do desire it with all my heart; and I hope it
is no dishonest desire to desire to be a woman of the
world.° Here come two of the banished Duke's pages.

Enter two Pages.   5

First Page. Well met, honest° gentleman.

Touchstone. By my troth, well met. Come, sit, sit, and
a song!

Second Page. We are for you. Sit i'th'middle.

First Page. Shall we clap into't roundly,° without hawk-
ing or spitting or saying we are hoarse, which are the
only° prologues to a bad voice?   10

Second Page. I'faith, i'faith! and both in a tune,° like
two gypsies on a horse.

Song.

It was a lover and his lass,
    With a hey, and a ho, and a hey nonino,
That o'er the green cornfield° did pass   15
    In springtime, the only pretty ringtime,°

V.iii.4–5 *a woman of the world* i.e., (1) married (2) fashionable   6 *honest* honorable   10 *clap into't roundly* begin directly   11–12 *the only*
merely the   13 *in a tune* in unison   17 *cornfield* wheatfield   18 *ring-
time* i.e., the time for giving marriage rings

When birds do sing, hey ding a ding, ding.
20   Sweet lovers love the spring.

Between the acres° of the rye,
    With a hey, and a ho, and a hey nonino,
These pretty country folks would lie
    In springtime, &c.

25   This carol they began that hour,
    With a hey, and a ho, and a hey nonino,
How that a life was but a flower
    In springtime, &c.

And therefore take° the present time,
30   With a hey, and a ho, and a hey nonino,
For love is crownèd with the prime°
    In springtime, &c.

Touchstone. Truly, young gentlemen, though there was
    no great matter in the ditty,° yet the note° was very
35 untuneable.

First Page. You are deceived, sir. We kept time, we lost
    not our time.

Touchstone. By my troth, yes; I count it but time lost
    to hear such a foolish song. God b' wi' you, and God
40 mend your voices. Come, Audrey.   *Exeunt.*

Scene IV. [*The forest.*]

*Enter Duke Senior, Amiens, Jaques, Orlando, Oliver,
Celia.*

Duke Senior. Dost thou believe, Orlando, that the boy
    Can do all this that he hath promisèd?

21 *Between the acres* i.e., in the strips of unploughed land   29 *take*
seize   31 *prime* spring   34 *ditty* words of the song   34 *note* melody

Orlando. I sometimes do believe, and sometimes do not,
  As those that fear they hope,° and know they fear.

> *Enter Rosalind, Silvius, and Phebe.*

Rosalind. Patience once more, whiles our compact is
    urged.°   5
  You say, if I bring in your Rosalind,
  You will bestow her on Orlando here?

Duke Senior. That would I, had I kingdoms to give
  with her.

Rosalind. And you say you will have her when I bring
  her?

Orlando. That would I, were I of all kingdoms king.   10

Rosalind. You say you'll marry me, if I be willing?

Phebe. That will I, should I die the hour after.

Rosalind. But if you do refuse to marry me,
  You'll give yourself to this most faithful shepherd?

Phebe. So is the bargain.   15

Rosalind. You say that you'll have Phebe, if she will?

Silvius. Though to have her and death were both one
    thing.

Rosalind. I have promised to make all this matter even.°
  Keep you your word, O Duke, to give your daughter;
  You yours, Orlando, to receive his daughter;   20
  Keep you your word, Phebe, that you'll marry me,
  Or else, refusing me, to wed this shepherd;
  Keep your word, Silvius, that you'll marry her
  If she refuse me; and from hence I go,
  To make these doubts all even.   25

> *Exit Rosalind and Celia.*

Duke Senior. I do remember in this shepherd boy
  Some lively° touches of my daughter's favor.°

V.iv.4 *hope* i.e., hope in vain   5 *compact is urged* agreement is restated
18 *make all this matter even* straighten out everything   27 *lively* living
27 *favor* features

Orlando. My lord, the first time that I ever saw him
   Methought he was a brother to your daughter.
30   But, my good lord, this boy is forest-born,
   And hath been tutored in the rudiments
   Of many desperate° studies by his uncle,
   Whom he reports to be a great magician,
   Obscured° in the circle of this forest.

Enter [Touchstone, the] Clown and Audrey.

35 *Jaques.* There is, sure, another flood toward,° and
   these couples are coming to the ark.° Here comes a
   pair of very strange beasts, which in all tongues are
   called fools.

Touchstone. Salutation and greeting to you all!

40 *Jaques.* Good my lord, bid him welcome. This is the
   motley-minded gentleman that I have so often met
   in the forest. He hath been a courtier, he swears.

Touchstone. If any man doubt that, let him put me to
   my purgation.° I have trod a measure;° I have flat-
45   tered a lady; I have been politic° with my friend,
   smooth with mine enemy; I have undone° three tail-
   ors; I have had four quarrels, and like to have fought
   one.°

Jaques. And how was that ta'en up?°

50 *Touchstone.* Faith, we met, and found the quarrel was
   upon the seventh cause.

Jaques. How seventh cause? Good my lord, like this
   fellow.

Duke Senior. I like him very well.

55 *Touchstone.* God 'ield° you, sir; I desire you of the like.°

32 *desperate* dangerous 34 *Obscurèd* hidden 35 *toward* approaching
36 *couples are coming to the ark* (cf. Genesis 7:2, "and of beasts
that are not clean by two, the male and his female") 43–44 *put me
to my purgation* test me 44 *measure* stately dance 45 *politic* crafty
46 *undone* ruined (by not paying his bills) 47–48 *like to have
fought one* almost fought over one 49 *ta'en up* settled 55 *God 'ield*
God reward 55 *I desire you of the like* may I return the compliment

I press in here, sir, amongst the rest of the country copulatives,° to swear and to forswear, according as marriage binds and blood breaks.° A poor virgin, sir, an ill-favored thing, sir, but mine own; a poor humor° of mine, sir, to take that that no man else will. Rich 60 honesty° dwells like a miser, sir, in a poor house, as your pearl in your foul oyster.

Duke Senior. By my faith, he is very swift and sententious.°

Touchstone. According to the fool's bolt,° sir, and such 65 dulcet diseases.°

Jaques. But, for the seventh cause. How did you find the quarrel on the seventh cause?

Touchstone. Upon a lie seven times removed—bear your body more seeming,° Audrey—as thus, sir. I did dis- 70 like the cut of a certain courtier's beard. He sent me word, if I said his beard was not cut well, he was in the mind it was: this is called the Retort Courteous. If I sent him word again it was not well cut, he would send me word he cut it to please himself: this is called 75 the Quip Modest.° If again, it was not well cut, he disabled° my judgment: this is called the Reply Churlish. If again, it was not well cut, he would answer I spake not true: this is called the Reproof Valiant. If again, it was not well cut, he would say I lie: this is 80 called the Countercheck° Quarrelsome: and so to the Lie Circumstantial° and the Lie Direct.

Jaques. And how oft did you say his beard was not well cut?

Touchstone. I durst go no further than the Lie Circum- 85

---

57 *copulatives* couples soon to be wed   58 *blood breaks* sexual interest wanes   59 *humor* whim   61 *honesty* virtue   63–64 *swift and sententious* quick-witted and pithy   65 *According to the fool's bolt* (cf. the proverb "A fool's bolt [arrow] is soon shot")   66 *dulcet diseases* pleasing weaknesses   70 *seeming* becomingly   76 *Modest* moderate   77 *disabled* did not value   81 *Countercheck* contradiction   82 *Circumstantial* indirect

stantial, nor he durst not give me the Lie Direct; and
so we measured swords° and parted.

Jaques. Can you nominate° in order now the degrees
of the lie?

90 *Touchstone.* O sir, we quarrel in print, by the book,° as
you have books for good manners. I will name you
the degrees. The first, the Retort Courteous; the
second, the Quip Modest; the third, the Reply Churlish; the fourth, the Reproof Valiant; the fifth, the
95 Countercheck Quarrelsome; the sixth, the Lie with
Circumstance; the seventh, the Lie Direct. All these
you may avoid but the Lie Direct, and you may avoid
that too, with an If. I knew when seven justices could
not take up° a quarrel, but when the parties were
100 met themselves, one of them thought but of an If:
as, "If you said so, then I said so"; and they shook
hands and swore brothers. Your If is the only peace-
maker. Much virtue in If.

Jaques. Is not this a rare fellow, my lord? He's as good
105 at anything, and yet a fool.

Duke Senior. He uses his folly like a stalking horse,°
and under the presentation° of that he shoots his wit.

Enter Hymen,° Rosalind, and Celia. Still° music.

Hymen. Then is there mirth in heaven
    When earthly things made even°
110   Atone together.°
    Good Duke, receive thy daughter;
    Hymen from heaven brought her,
       Yea, brought her hither,
    That thou mightst join her hand with his
115   Whose heart within his bosom is.

---

87 *measured swords* (swords were measured before a duel)   88 *nom-
inate* name   90 *by the book* according to the rules   99 *take up* settle
106 *stalking horse* (any object under cover of which a hunter pursues
his game)   107 *presentation* protection   107 s.d. *Hymen* god of marriage   107 s.d. *Still* soft   109 *made even* i.e., reconciled   110 *Atone
together* are set at one

Rosalind. [*To Duke*] To you I give myself, for I am yours.
   [*To Orlando*] To you I give myself, for I am yours.

Duke Senior. If there be truth in sight, you are my
   daughter.

Orlando. If there be truth in sight, you are my Rosalind.

Phebe. If sight and shape be true,   120
   Why then, my love adieu!

Rosalind. [*To Duke*] I'll have no father, if you be not he.
   [*To Orlando*] I'll have no husband, if you be not he.
   [*To Phebe*] Nor ne'er wed woman, if you be not she.

Hymen. Peace ho! I bar confusion: 125
    'Tis I must make conclusion
      Of these most strange events.
    Here's eight that must take hands
    To join in Hymen's bands,
      If truth holds true contents.°   130
[*To Orlando and Rosalind*]
    You and you no cross° shall part.
[*To Oliver and Celia*]
    You and you are heart in heart.
[*To Phebe*]
    You to his love must accord,°
    Or have a woman to your lord.
[*To Touchstone and Audrey*]
    You and you are sure together°   135
    As the winter to foul weather.
[*To all*]
    Whiles a wedlock hymn we sing,
    Feed yourselves with questioning,
    That reason wonder may diminish
    How thus we met, and these things finish.   140

Song.

Wedding is great Juno's crown,
   O blessed bond of board and bed!

130 *If truth . . . contents* if the truth is true   131 *cross* quarrel   133 *ac-cord* agree   135 *sure together* securely bound

'Tis Hymen peoples every town;
   High° wedlock then be honorèd.
145   Honor, high honor, and renown
       To Hymen, god of every town!

Duke Senior. O my dear niece, welcome thou art to me,
  Even daughter,° welcome, in no less degree!

Phebe. [*To Silvius*] I will not eat my word, now thou
    art mine;
150   Thy faith my fancy to thee doth combine.°

       Enter Second Brother [*Jaques de Boys*].

Second Brother. Let me have audience for a word or two.
  I am the second son of old Sir Rowland
  That bring these tidings to this fair assembly.
  Duke Frederick, hearing how that every day
155 Men of great worth resorted to this forest,
  Addressed a mighty power,° which were on foot
  In his own conduct,° purposely to take
  His brother here and put him to the sword;
  And to the skirts of this wild wood he came,
160 Where, meeting with an old religious man,°
  After some question° with him, was converted
  Both from his enterprise and from the world,
  His crown bequeathing to his banished brother,
  And all their lands restored to them again
165 That were with him exiled. This to be true
  I do engage° my life.

Duke Senior.   Welcome, young man.
  Thou offer'st fairly° to thy brothers' wedding:
  To one, his lands withheld; and to the other,
  A land itself at large, a potent° dukedom.
170 First, in this forest let us do those ends°
  That here were well begun and well begot;
  And after, every° of this happy number

144 *High* solemn   148 *Even daughter* i.e., even as a daughter   150 *combine* unite   156 *Addressed a mighty power* prepared a mighty army   157 *conduct* leadership   160 *old religious man* (a hermit?)   161 *question* talk   166 *engage* pledge   167 *offer'st fairly* bring a good gift   169 *potent* powerful   170 *do those ends* complete those purposes   172 *every* each one

That have endured shrewd° days and nights with us
Shall share the good of our returnèd fortune,
According to the measure° of their states.   175
Meantime forget this new-fall'n° dignity
And fall into our rustic revelry.
Play, music, and you brides and bridegrooms all,
With measure heaped in joy, to th' measures° fall.

Jaques. Sir, by your patience. If I heard you rightly,   180
The Duke hath put on a religious life
And thrown into neglect the pompous court.°

Second Brother. He hath.

Jaques. To him will I. Out of these convertites°
There is much matter to be heard and learned.   185
[*To Duke*] You to your former honor I bequeath;
Your patience and your virtue well deserves it.
[*To Orlando*] You to a love that your true faith doth
    merit;
[*To Oliver*] You to your land and love and great allies;
[*To Silvius*] You to a long and well-deservèd bed;   190
[*To Touchstone*] And you to wrangling, for thy loving
    voyage
Is but for two months victualled. So, to your pleas-
    ures:
I am for other than for dancing measures.

Duke Senior. Stay, Jaques, stay.

Jaques. To see no pastime I. What you would have   195
I'll stay to know at your abandoned cave.   *Exit.*
Duke Senior. Proceed, proceed. We will begin these
    rites,
As we do trust they'll end, in true delights.
                                   Exit [after the dance].

[EPILOGUE]

Rosalind. It is not the fashion to see the lady the epilogue, but it is no more unhandsome° than to see the

173 *shrewd* hard   175 *measure* rank   176 *new-fall'n* newly acquired
179 *measures* dance steps   182 *thrown into ... court* given up the cere-
monious life of the court   184 *convertites* converts   Epilogue
2 *unhandsome* unbecoming

lord the prologue. If it be true that good wine needs
no bush,° 'tis true that a good play needs no epilogue;
yet to good wine they do use good bushes, and good
plays prove the better by the help of good epilogues.
What a case am I in then, that am neither a good
epilogue, nor cannot insinuate with you° in the behalf
of a good play! I am not furnished° like a beggar;
therefore to beg will not become me. My way is to
conjure° you, and I'll begin with the women. I charge
you, O women, for the love you bear to men, to like
as much of this play as please you; and I charge you,
O men, for the love you bear to women—as I perceive by your simpering none of you hates them—
that between you and the women the play may please.
If I were a woman,° I would kiss as many of you as
had beards that pleased me, complexions that liked°
me, and breaths that I defied° not; and I am sure, as
many as have good beards, or good faces, or sweet
breaths, will, for my kind offer, when I make curtsy,
bid me farewell.°   *Exit.*

FINIS

4 *no bush* no advertisement (in Shakespeare's time vintners used an ivy
bush as a sign)   8 *insinuate with you* slyly get your approval   9 *furnished* dressed   11 *conjure* (1) solemnly entreat (2) charm (by magic)
17 *If I were a woman* (Rosalind, of course, was played by a boy)
18 *liked* pleased   19 *defied* disliked   22 *bid me farewell* i.e., applaud

Textual Note

As You Like It did not appear in print until the First Folio of 1623. The text is a good one and may represent a carefully prepared promptbook. Act and scene division is intelligent; exits and entrances are for the most part correctly indicated; and the stage directions are brief but generally adequate. The present edition follows the Folio text closely, admitting only those emendations that seem clearly necessary. A few directions not in the Folio but helpful in clarifying the action are placed in square brackets. Spelling and punctuation are modernized, speech prefixes are extended from abbreviations, obvious typographical errors and mislineation are corrected, and the Latin divisions into act and scene are translated. Other significant departures from the Folio (F) are listed below, the present reading in italics followed by F's reading in roman.

I.i.106 *she* hee   156 *Oliver* [F omits]

I.ii.3 *yet I were* yet were   51 *goddesses and hath* god lesses, hath
80 *Celia* Ros   88 *Le·Beau* the Beu   279 *Rosalind* Rosaline [from here on, F uses either form]

I.iii.76 *her patience* per patience

II.i.49 *much* must   59 *of the country* of Countrie

II.iii.10 *some* seeme   16 *Orlando* [F omits]   29 *Orlando* Ad[am]
71 *seventeen* seauentie

II.iv.1 *weary* merry   42 *thy wound* they would   69 *you, friend* your friend

II.v.1 *Amiens* [F omits]   39–40 *no enemy . . . weather* &c   44 *Jaques* Amy [i.e., Amiens]

II.vii.55 *Not to seem* Seeme   87 *comes* come   174 *Amiens* [F omits] 182 *Then* the

III.ii.125 *this a desert* this Desert   145 *her* his   155 *pulpiter* Iupiter 255 *b' wi'* buy   356 *deifying* defying

III.iv.28 *of a lover* of Louer

III.v.127–128 *yet I have* yet Haue

IV.i.1 *me be better* me better   18 *my* by   29 *b' wi'* buy   201 *in, it* in, in

IV.ii.7 *Another Lord* Lord

IV.iii.5s.d. *Enter Silvius* [F places after "brain"]   8 *Phebe bid* Phebe, did bid   143 *In* I   156 *his blood* this bloud

V.ii.7 *nor her sudden* nor sodaine

V.iii.18 *In spring time* In the spring time   15–32 [the fourth stanza here appears as the second in F]   39 *b' wi'* buy

V.iv.34s.d. *Enter . . . Audrey* [F prints after line 33]   81 *so to the* so ro 114 *her hand* his hand   164 *them* him   197 *we will* wee'l

The Source of
"As You Like It"

Shakespeare's source for *As You Like It* is Thomas Lodge's pastoral romance, *Rosalynde or Euphues' Golden Legacy*, printed in 1590. This romance in turn is based in part on a short narrative poem of the fourteenth century, "The Tale of Gamelyn," telling of the unjust treatment of Gamelyn by his older brother, the bloody fights between them, Gamelyn's flight to the greenwood, where he becomes the leader of a happy band of outlaws, and the eventual recovery of his land after his brother has been hanged. The only reference to love comes in the last lines, where we are told that Gamelyn took a "wyf bothe good and feyr."

To this rapid and brutally humorous narrative, Lodge added the story of a banished king, Gerismond, and three love stories: one of these concerns Rosader (Gamelyn of the early poem and Shakespeare's Orlando) and Rosalynde; the others, Alinda and Saladyne (Shakespeare's Celia and Oliver) and Phoebe and Montanus (Shakespeare's Phebe and Silvius). Interspersed throughout *Rosalynde* are elegant love poems. The whole, a medley of folk tale, pastoral love eclogue, and pastoral romance, is predominantly written in the highly mannered style known as Euphuism, a style made popular by John Lyly in the 1570's, but it is enlivened by homely phrases and proverbs.

Although there is no evidence that Shakespeare drew directly upon any work other than Lodge's, it is possible that three plays were in Shakespeare's mind when he came to write *As You Like It*. Two Robin Hood plays performed in 1598 by the Admiral's Company, *The Downfall of Robert*

Earl of Huntingdon and *The Death of Robert Earl of Huntingdon*, may have inspired Shakespeare's treatment of the singing outlaws, and *Sir Clyomon and Clamydes* (printed in 1599) may have suggested the rustics, Audrey and William. (In *Sir Clyomon* a princess disguised as a man meets a crude but amusing shepherd named Corin who describes in plain language the love-making of real shepherds and country girls.)

To return from conjecture to fact: *As You Like It* owes a great deal to *Rosalynde*. Shakespeare follows the outline of Lodge's plot closely and develops many of its situations, such as the enmity of two sets of characters, the wrestling match, the flight to the Forest, Orlando's desperate demand for food, the momentary hesitation of Orlando to save his brother from the lioness, the wooing of Rosalind disguised as Ganymede, the marriage of Celia and Oliver, the disdain of Phebe and her use of Silvius as messenger, and the return to the court. The title too may come from Lodge, who in a note to his "gentlemen readers," says, "If you like it, so."

It is not only in plot and situation that Shakespeare is indebted to Lodge. Lodge's two princesses possess in embryo almost all the characteristics of their counterparts, but compared to Shakespeare's heroine Lodge's Rosalynde is wooden. She does not master events as does Rosalind, and as a woman in love she is scarcely differentiated from Alinda (Shakespeare's Celia) or, at some points, from Phebe.

The differences are as striking as the resemblances. Some of the changes were required by the genre. For example, Shakespeare omits Rosader's internal debate on whether to save his brother, condensing the gist of this passage of over five hundred words into two and a half lines. Separate events are combined and compressed. Shakespeare omits the two reconciliations between Rosader and Saladyne and in place of the sequence where Rosader is chained as a lunatic by Saladyne and then set free by Adam with whose help he kills some of his brother's guests, Shakespeare has the brief third scene of the second act. Some material is rearranged so that major plot lines are not long lost to sight. Whereas in Lodge the Rosader-Saladyne plot is dropped for about fifteen pages when Alinda and Rosalynde appear in the forest, in Shakespeare Orlando flees to the forest at about the same time as the two girls. Lodge develops his three love affairs consecutively; one is virtually completed before the next is begun, and each is developed at almost equal length. Shakespeare quickly disposes of the Celia-Oliver romance and has Phebe fall in love with Ganymede much earlier than does Lodge. He is thus able to develop the love affairs concurrently, including the added one of Audrey and Touchstone, and to play them off one against the other. (Lodge has little of Shakespeare's ironic contrasts.)

Shakespeare retains little of the brutality of the novel. Orlando is far gentler than Rosader, the wrestler and his young opponents are injured rather than killed, and Saladyne's rescue of the ladies from a band of robbers is omitted. For the final battle in which Torismond, the usurper, dies, Shakespeare substitutes the miraculous conversion of Duke Frederick. The diminution of action and violence is in harmony with the spirit of the play and allows Shakespeare to develop contrasting emotions, values, and attitudes. Even when Shakespeare adheres to the general outline of a conversation in Lodge, he so alters the details that what is stilted in the novel becomes vivid, natural, engaging.

A few of Shakespeare's smaller changes can be mentioned here. In Lodge, the girls are not reluctant, as they are in Shakespeare, to watch the wrestling. Shakespeare gives far greater emphasis to Adam's age and long, faithful service. He links the two groups of court characters by making the two Dukes brothers and the dead Sir Rowland de Boys an enemy of Duke Frederick. In Lodge, Rosalynde and Alinda see Rosader-Orlando in the forest at the same time; in Shakespeare, Celia sees him first, and her report to Rosalind allows us to see Rosalind's impulsive reaction and to hear some witty byplay.

Perhaps the most significant change is the addition of Jaques and Touchstone (Audrey, William, Martext, and Le Beau are far less important additions). Jaques and Touchstone have little effect on the development of the plot, but the Forest of Arden would be a duller and less realistic place without their presence. They help transform a piece of prose fiction, which is charming and often skill-fully narrated but intellectually thin and sometimes tedious, into a play as rich in wisdom and knowledge as it is in laughter.

The following abridgment of Lodge's *Rosalynde* constitutes a little over a third of the whole. Summaries of the narrative portions omitted are given in brackets. The material reprinted is divided into fifteen sections, each preceded by a bracketed reference to the scene or passage from the play with which it can be compared.

THOMAS LODGE

Selections from "Rosalynde"

[Sir John of Bordeaux has gathered his three sons around his death-bed. After dividing his wealth among them, he bequeaths a moral legacy in which he cautions his sons to follow wisdom and to practice virtue.]

1. [I.i.1–166]

John of Bordeaux being thus dead was greatly lamented of his sons, and bewailed of his friends, especially of his fellow Knights of Malta, who attended on his funerals, which were performed with great solemnity. His obsequies done, Saladyne caused, next his epitaph, the contents of the scroll to be portrayed out, which were to this effect. . . .
Saladyne having thus set up the schedule [of moral axioms addressed by John of Bordeaux to his three sons], and hanged about his father's hearse many passionate poems, that France might suppose him to be passing sorrowful, he clad himself and his brothers all in black, and in such sable suits discoursed his grief; but as the hyena when she mourns is then most guileful, so Saladyne under this show of grief

shadowed a heart full of contented thoughts. The tiger, though he hide his claws, will at last discover his rapine; the lion's looks are not the maps of his meaning, nor a man's physnomy is not the display of his secrets. Fire cannot be hid in the straw, nor the nature of man so concealed, but at last it will have his course. . . . So fared it with Saladyne, for after a month's mourning was passed, he fell to consideration of his father's testament; how he had bequeathed more to his younger brothers than himself, that Rosader was his father's darling, but now under his tuition, that as yet they were not come to years, and he being their guardian, might, if not defraud them of their due, yet make such havoc of their legacies and lands, as they should be a great deal the lighter; whereupon he began thus to meditate with himself:

"Saladyne, how art thou disquieted in thy thoughts, and perplexed with a world of restless passions, having thy mind troubled with the tenor of thy father's testament, and thy heart fired with the hope of present preferment! By the one thou art counseled to content thee with thy fortunes, by the other persuaded to aspire to higher wealth. Riches, Saladyne, is a great royalty, and there is no sweeter physic than store. . . . Thy brother is young, keep him now in awe; make him not checkmate with thyself, for

Nimia familiaritas contemptum parit.[1]

Let him know little, so shall he not be able to execute much; suppress his wits with a base estate, and though he be a gentleman by nature, yet form him anew, and make him a peasant by nurture; so shalt thou keep him as a slave, and reign thyself sole lord over all thy father's possessions. As for Fernandyne, thy middle brother, he is a scholar and hath no mind but on Aristotle; let him read on Galen while thou riflest with gold, and pore on his book till thou dost purchase lands. Wit is great wealth; if he have learning it is enough: and so let all rest."

In this humor was Saladyne, making his brother Rosader his footboy, for the space of two or three years, keeping him in such servile subjection, as if he had been the son of any country vassal. The young gentleman bore all with

[1] Too much familiarity breeds contempt.

patience, till on a day, walking in the garden by himself, he began to consider how he was the son of John of Bordeaux, a knight renowned for many victories, and a gentleman famoused for his virtues; how, contrary to the testament of his father, he was not only kept from his land and entreated as a servant, but smothered in such secret slavery, as he might not attain to any honorable actions.

"Ah," quoth he to himself, nature working these effectual passions, "why should I, that am a gentleman born, pass my time in such unnatural drudgery? Were it not better either in Paris to become a scholar, or in the court a courtier, or in the field a soldier, than to live a footboy to my own brother? Nature hath lent me wit to conceive, but my brother denied me art to contemplate; I have strength to perform any honorable exploit, but no liberty to accomplish my virtuous endeavors; those good parts that God hath bestowed upon me, the envy of my brother doth smother in obscurity; the harder is my fortune, and the more his forwardness."

With that, casting up his hand, he felt hair on his face, and perceiving his beard to bud, for choler he began to blush, and swore to himself he would be no more subject to such slavery. As thus he was ruminating of his melancholy passions in came Saladyne with his men, and seeing his brother in a brown study, and to forget his wonted reverence, thought to shake him out of his dumps thus:

"Sirrah," quoth he, "what is your heart on your half-penny, or are you saying a dirge for your father's soul? What, is my dinner ready?"

At this question Rosader, turning his head askance, and bending his brows as if anger there had ploughed the furrows of her wrath, with his eyes full of fire, he made this reply:

"Dost thou ask me, Saladyne, for thy cates? Ask some of thy churls who are fit for such an office. I am thine equal by nature, though not 'by birth, and though thou hast more cards in the bunch, I have as many trumps in my hands as thyself. Let me question with thee, why thou hast felled my woods, spoiled my manor houses, and made havoc of such utensils as my father bequeathed unto me? I tell thee,

Saladyne, either answer me as a brother, or I will trouble thee as an enemy."

At this reply of Rosader's Saladyne smiled as laughing at his presumption, and frowned as checking his folly; he therefore took him up thus shortly:

"What, sirrah! Well, I see early pricks the tree that will prove a thorn; hath my familiar conversing with you made you coy, or my good looks drawn you to be thus contemptuous? I can quickly remedy such a fault, and I will bend the tree while it is a wand. In faith, sir boy, I have a snaffle for such a headstrong colt. You, sirs, lay hold on him and bind him, and then I will give him a cooling card for his choler."

This made Rosader half mad, that stepping to a great rake that stood in the garden, he laid such load upon his brother's men that he hurt some of them, and made the rest of them run away. Saladyne, seeing Rosader so resolute and with his resolution so valiant, thought his heels his best safety, and took him to a loft adjoining to the garden, whither Rosader pursued him hotly. Saladyne, afraid of his brother's fury, cried out to him thus:

"Rosader, be not so rash. I am thy brother and thine elder, and if I have done thee wrong I'll make thee amends. Revenge not anger in blood, for so shalt thou stain the virtue of old Sir John of Bordeaux. Say wherein thou art discontent and thou shalt be satisfied. Brothers' frowns ought not to be periods of wrath; what, man, look not so sourly; I know we shall be friends and better friends than we have been, for, *Amantium ira amoris redintegratio est.*"[2]

These words appeased the choler of Rosader, for he was of a mild and courteous nature. . . . Upon these sugared reconciliations they went into the house arm in arm together, to the great content of all the old servants of Sir John of Bordeaux.

Thus continued the pad hidden in the straw, till it chanced that Torismond, king of France, had appointed for his pleasure a day of wrestling and of tournament to busy his commons' heads, lest, being idle, their thoughts should run

[2] The quarrels of friends lead to the renewing of love.

upon more serious matters, and call to remembrance their old banished king. A champion there was to stand against all comers, a Norman, a man of tall stature and of great strength—so valiant, that in many such conflicts he always bare away the victory, not only overthrowing them which he encountered, but often with the weight of his body killing them outright. Saladyne hearing of this, thinking now not to let the ball fall to the ground, but to take opportunity by the forehead, first by secret means convented with the Norman, and procured him with rich rewards to swear that if Rosader came within his claws he should never more return to quarrel with Saladyne for his possessions. The Norman desirous of pelf—as *Quis nisi mentis inops oblatum respuit aurum?*[3]—taking great gifts for little gods, took the crowns of Saladyne to perform the stratagem.

Having thus the champion tied to his villainous determination by oath, he prosecuted the intent of his purpose thus. He went to young Rosader, who in all his thoughts reached at honor, and gazed no lower than virtue commanded him, and began to tell him of this tournament and wrestling, how the king should be there, and all the chief peers of France, with all the beautiful damosels of the country.

"Now, brother," quoth he, "for the honor of Sir John of Bordeaux, our renowned father, to famous that house that never hath been found without men approved in chivalry, show thy resolution to be peremptory. For myself thou knowest, though I am eldest by birth, yet never having attempted any deeds of arms, I am youngest to perform any martial exploits, knowing better how to survey my lands than to charge my lance. My brother Fernandyne he is at Paris poring on a few papers, having more insight into sophistry and principles of philosophy, than any warlike endeavors. But thou, Rosader, the youngest in years but the eldest in valor, art a man of strength, and darest do what honor allows thee. Take thou my father's lance, his sword, and his horse, and hie thee to the tournament, and either there valiantly crack a spear, or try with the Norman for the palm of activity."

[3] Who in his right mind will refuse a gift of gold?

The words of Saladyne were but spurs to a free horse, for he had scarce uttered them, ere Rosader took him in his arms, taking his proffer so kindly, that he promised in what he might to requite his courtesy. . . .

[Torismond holds his tournament.]

2. [I.ii.93–250]

At last, when the tournament ceased, the wrestling began, and the Norman presented himself as a challenger against all comers, but he looked like Hercules when he advanced himself against Achelous, so that the fury of his countenance amazed all that durst attempt to encounter with him in any deed of activity. Till at last a lusty franklin of the country came with two tall men that were his sons, of good lineaments and comely personage. The eldest of these doing his obeisance to the king entered the list, and presented himself to the Norman, who straight coped with him, and as a man that would triumph in the glory of his strength, roused himself with such fury, that not only he gave him the fall, but killed him with the weight of his corpulent personage; which the younger brother seeing, leaped presently into the place, and thirsty after the revenge, assailed the Norman with such valor, that at the first encounter he brought him to his knees; which repulsed so the Norman, that, recovering himself, fear of disgrace doubling his strength, he stepped so sternly to the young franklin, that taking him up in his arms he threw him against the ground so violently, that he broke his neck, and so ended his days with his brother. At this unlooked-for massacre the people murmured, and were all in a deep passion of pity; but the franklin, father unto these, never changed his countenance, but as a man of a courageous resolution took up the bodies of his sons without show of outward discontent.

All this while stood Rosader and saw this tragedy; who, noting the undoubted virtue of the franklin's mind, alighted off from his horse, and presently sat down on the grass, and commanded his boy to pull off his boots, making him ready to try the strength of this champion. Being furnished as he would, he clapped the franklin on the shoulder and said thus:

"Bold yeoman, whose sons have ended the term of their years with honor, for that I see thou scornest fortune with patience, and thwartest the injury of fate with content in brooking the death of thy sons, stand awhile, and either see me make a third in their tragedy, or else revenge their fall with an honorable triumph."

The franklin, seeing so goodly a gentleman to give him such courteous comfort, gave him hearty thanks, with promise to pray for his happy success. With that Rosader vailed bonnet to the king, and lightly leaped within the lists, where noting more the company than the combatant, he cast his eye upon the troop of ladies that glistered there like the stars of heaven; but at last, Love, willing to make him as amorous as he was valiant, presented him with the sight of Rosalynde, whose admirable beauty so inveigled the eye of Rosader, that forgetting himself, he stood and fed his looks on the favor of Rosalynde's face; which she perceiving blushed, which was such a doubling of her beauteous excellence, that the bashful red of Aurora at the sight of unacquainted Phaeton, was not half so glorious.

The Norman, seeing this young gentleman fettered in the looks of the ladies, drave him out of his *memento* with a shake by the shoulder. Rosader looking back with an angry frown, as if he had been wakened from some pleasant dream, discovered to all by the fury of his countenance that he was a man of some high thoughts; but when they all noted his youth and the sweetness of his visage, with a general applause of favors, they grieved that so goodly a young man should venture in so base an action; but seeing it were to his dishonor to hinder him from his enterprise, they wished him to be graced with the palm of victory.

After Rosader was thus called out of his *memento* by the Norman, he roughly clapped to him with so fierce an encounter, that they both fell to the ground, and with the violence of the fall were forced to breathe; in which space the Norman called to mind by all tokens, that this was he whom Saladyne had appointed him to kill; which conjecture made him stretch every limb, and try every sinew, that working his death he might recover the gold which so bountifully was promised him. On the contrary part, Rosader while he breathed was not idle, but still cast his eye upon Rosalynde, who to encourage him with a favor, lent him such an amorous look, as might have made the most coward desperate; which glance of Rosalynde so fired the passionate desires of Rosader, that turning to the Norman he ran upon him and braved him with a strong encounter. The Norman received him as valiantly, that there was a sore combat, hard to judge on whose side fortune would be prodigal. At last Rosader, calling to mind the beauty of his new mistress, the fame of his father's honors, and the disgrace that should fall to his house by his misfortune, roused himself and threw the Norman against the ground, falling upon his chest with so willing a weight, that the Norman yielded nature her due, and Rosader the victory.

The death of this champion, as it highly contented the franklin, as a man satisfied with revenge, so it drew the king and all the peers into a great admiration, that so young years and so beautiful a personage should contain such martial excellence; but when they knew him to be the youngest son of Sir John of Bordeaux, the king rose from his seat and embraced him and the peers entreated him with all favorable courtesy. . . .

As the king and lords graced him with embracing, so the ladies favored him with their looks, especially Rosalynde, whom the beauty and valor of Rosader had already touched; but she accounted love a toy, and fancy a momentary passion, that as it was taken in with a gaze, might be shaken off with a wink, and therefore feared not to dally in the flame; and to make Rosader know she affected him, took from her neck a jewel, and sent it by a page to the young gentleman. The prize that Venus gave to Paris was not half so pleasing to the Troyan as this gem was to Rosader; for if fortune had sworn to make him sole monarch of the world, he would rather have refused such dignity, than have lost the jewel sent him by Rosalynde. To return her with the like he was unfurnished, and yet that he might more than in his looks discover his affection, he stepped into a tent, and taking pen and paper wrote this fancy [love poem]. . . .

This sonnet he sent to Rosalynde, which when she read she blushed, but with a sweet content in that she perceived love had allotted her so amorous a servant.

[Rosader and Saladyne again quarrel. Adam Spencer reconciles them. Rosalynde, debating her passion with herself, overcomes her doubts when she recalls the appearance and virtue of Rosader.]

3. [I.iii.35 s.d.–136]

Scarce had Rosalynde ended her madrigal, before Torismond came in with his daughter Alinda and many of the peers of France, who were enamored of her beauty; which Torismond perceiving, fearing lest her perfection might be the beginning of his prejudice, and the hope of his fruit end in the beginning of her blossoms, he thought to banish her from the court: "for," quoth he to himself, "her face is so full of favor, that it pleads pity in the eye of every man; her beauty is so heavenly and divine, that she will prove to me as Helen did to Priam; some one of the peers will aim at her love, end the marriage, and then in his wife's right attempt the kingdom. To prevent therefore *had I wist* in all these actions, she tarries not about the court, but shall, as an exile, either wander to her father, or else seek other fortunes." In this humor, with a stern countenance full of wrath, he breathed out this censure unto her before the peers, that charged her that that night she were not seen about the court: "for," quoth he, "I have heard of thy aspiring speeches, and intended treasons." This doom was strange unto Rosalynde, and presently, covered with the shield of her innocence, she boldly brake out in reverent terms to have cleared herself; but Torismond would admit of no reason, nor durst his lords plead for Rosalynde, although her beauty had made some of them passionate, seeing the figure of wrath portrayed in his brow. Standing thus all mute, and Rosalynde amazed, Alinda, who loved her more than herself, with grief in her heart and tears in her eyes, falling down on her knees, began to entreat her father thus:

"If, mighty Torismond, I offend in pleading for my

friend, let the law of amity crave pardon for my boldness; for where there is depth of affection, there friendship alloweth a privilege. Rosalynde and I have been fostered up from our infancies, and nursed under the harbor of our conversing together with such private familiarities, that custom had wrought a union of our nature, and the sympathy of our affections such a secret love, that we have two bodies and one soul. Then marvel not, great Torismond, if, seeing my friend distressed, I find myself perplexed with a thousand sorrows; for her virtuous and honorable thoughts, which are the glories that maketh women excellent, they be such as may challenge love, and raze out suspicion. Her obedience to your majesty I refer to the censure of your own eye, that since her father's exile had smothered all griefs with patience, and in the absence of nature, hath honored you with all duty, as her own father by nurture, not in word uttering any discontent, nor in thought, as far as conjecture may reach, hammering on revenge; only in all her actions seeking to please you, and to win my favor. Her wisdom, silence, chastity, and other such rich qualities, I need not decipher; only it rests for me to conclude in one word, that she is innocent. If then, fortune, who triumphs in a variety of miseries, hath presented some envious person, as minister of her intended stratagem, to taint Rosalynde with any surmise of treason, let him be brought to her face, and confirm his accusation by witnesses; which proved, let her die, and Alinda will execute the massacre. If none can avouch any confirmed relation of her intent, use justice, my lord, it is the glory of a king, and let her live in your wonted favor; for if you banish her, myself, as copartner of her hard fortunes, will participate in exile some part of her extremities."

Torismond, at this speech of Alinda, covered his face with such a frown, as tyranny seemed to sit triumphant in his forehead, and checked her up with such taunts, as made the lords, that only were hearers, to tremble.

"Proud girl," quoth he, "hath my looks made thee so light of tongue, or my favors encouraged thee to be so forward, that thou darest presume to preach after thy father? Hath not my years more experience than thy youth, and the winter of mine age deeper insight into civil policy, than the prime of thy flourishing days? The old lion avoids the toils, where the young one leaps into the net; the care of age is provident and foresees much; suspicion is a virtue, where a man holds his enemy in his bosom. Thou, fond girl, measurest all by present affection, and as thy heart loves, thy thoughts censure; but if thou knowest that in liking Rosalynde thou hatchest up a bird to peck out thine own eyes, thou wouldst entreat as much for her absence as now thou delightest in her presence. But why do I allege policy to thee? Sit you down, housewife, and fall to your needle; if idleness make you so wanton, or liberty so malapert, I can quickly tie you to a sharper task. And you, maid, this night be packing, either into Arden to your father, or whither best it shall content your humor, but in the court you shall not abide."

This rigorous reply of Torismond nothing amazed Alinda, for still she prosecuted her plea in the defense of Rosalynde, wishing her father, if his censure might not be reversed, that he would appoint her partner of her exile; which if he refused to do, either she would by some secret means steal out and follow her, or else end her days with some desperate kind of death. When Torismond heard his daughter so resolute, his heart was so hardened against her, that he set down a definite and peremptory sentence, that they should both be banished, which presently was done, the tyrant rather choosing to hazard the loss of his only child than anyways to put in question the state of his kingdom; so suspicious and fearful is the conscience of an usurper. Well, although his lords persuaded him to retain his own daughter, yet his resolution might not be reversed, but both of them must away from the court without either more company or delay. In he went with great melancholy, and left these two ladies alone. Rosalynde waxed very sad, and sat down and wept. Alinda she smiled, and sitting by her friend began thus to comfort her:

"Why, how now, Rosalynde, dismayed with a frown of contrary fortune? Have I not oft heard thee say, that high minds were discovered in fortune's contempt, and heroical scene in the depth of extremities? Thou wert wont to tell ·

others that complained of distress, that the sweetest salve for misery was patience, and the only medicine for want that precious implaister of content. Being such a good physician to others, wilt thou not minister receipts to thyself? ... If fortune aimeth at the fairest, be patient Rosalynde, for first by thine exile thou goest to thy father; nature is higher prized than wealth, and the love of one's parents ought to be more precious than all dignities. Why then doth my Rosalynde grieve at the frown of Torismond, who by offering her a prejudice proffers her a greater pleasure? And more, mad lass, to be melancholy, when thou hast with thee Alinda, a friend who will be a faithful copartner of all thy misfortunes, who hath left her father to follow thee, and chooseth rather to brook all extremities than to forsake thy presence. ... Cheerly, woman; as we have been bedfellows in royalty, we will be fellow mates in poverty. I will ever be thy Alinda, and thou shalt ever rest to me Rosalynde; so shall the world canonize our friendship, and speak of Rosalynde and Alinda, as they did of Pylades and Orestes. ...

At this Rosalynde began to comfort her, and after she had wept a few kind tears in the bosom of her Alinda, she gave her hearty thanks, and then they sat them down to consult how they should travel. Alinda grieved at nothing but that they might have no man in their company, saying it would be their greatest prejudice in that two women went wandering without either guide or attendant.

"Tush," quoth Rosalynde, "art thou a woman, and hast not a sudden shift to prevent a misfortune? I, thou seest, am of a tall stature, and would very well become the person and apparel of a page; thou shalt be my mistress, and I will play the man so properly, that, trust me, in what company soever I come I will not be discovered. I will buy me a suit, and have my rapier very handsomely at my side, and if any knave offer wrong, your page will show him the point of his weapon."

At this Alinda smiled, and upon this they agreed, and presently gathered up all their jewels, which they trussed up in a casket, and Rosalynde in all haste provided her of robes, and Alinda, from her royal weeds, put herself in more homelike attire. Thus fitted to the purpose, away go these two friends, having now changed their names, Alinda being called Aliena, and Rosalynde Ganymede. They traveled along the vineyards, and by many byways at last got to the forest side. . . .

[In the forest Aliena and Ganymede find the verses of Montanus engraved on a tree.]

4. [IV.i.141–68, 192–95]

"No doubt," quoth Aliena, "this poesy is the passion of some perplexed shepherd, that being enamored of some fair and beautiful shepherdess, suffered some sharp repulse, and therefore complained of the cruelty of his mistress."

"You may see," quoth Ganymede, "what mad cattle you women be, whose hearts sometimes are made of adamant that will touch with no impression, and sometime of wax that is fit for every form. They delight to be courted, and then they glory to seem coy, and when they are most desired then they freeze with disdain; and this fault is so common to the sex, that you see it painted out in the shepherd's passions, who found his mistress as froward as he was enamored."

"And I pray you," quoth Aliena, "if your robes were off, what mettle are you made of that you are so satirical against women? Is it not a foul bird defiles the own nest? Beware, Ganymede, that Rosader hear you not; if he do, perchance you will make him leap so far from love, that he will anger every vein in your heart."

"Thus," quoth Ganymede, "I keep decorum. I speak now as I am Aliena's page, not as I am Gerismond's daughter; for put me into a petticoat, and I will stand in defiance to the uttermost, that women are courteous, constant, virtuous, and what not."

"Stay there," quoth Aliena, "and no more words. . . ."

[Aliena and Ganymede overhear the eclogue in which Montanus, the young shepherd, describes his love for Phoebe and Corydon, the older shepherd, warns against the pains and follies of love.]

5. [II.iv.18–100; III.ii.23–31, 73–77]

The shepherds having thus ended their eclogue, Aliena stepped with Ganymede from behind the thicket; at whose sudden sight the shepherds arose, and Aliena saluted them thus:

"Shepherds, all hail, for such we deem you by your flocks, and lovers, good luck, for such you seem by your passions, our eyes being witness of the one, and our ears of the other. Although not by love, yet by fortune, I am a distressed gentlewoman, as sorrowful as you are passionate, and as full of woes as you of perplexed thoughts. Wandering this way in a forest unknown, only I and my page, wearied with travel, would fain have some place of rest. May you appoint us any place of quiet harbor, be it never so mean, I shall be thankful to you, contented in myself, and grateful to whosoever shall be mine host."

Corydon, hearing the gentlewoman speak so courteously, returned her mildly and reverently this answer:

"Fair mistress, we return you as hearty a welcome as you gave us a courteous salute. A shepherd I am, and this a lover, as watchful to please his wench as to feed his sheep; full of fancies, and therefore, say I, full of follies. Exhort him I may, but persuade him I cannot; for love admits neither of counsel nor reason. But leaving him to his passions, if you be distressed, I am sorrowful such a fair creature is crossed with calamity; pray for you I may, but relieve you I cannot. Marry, if you want lodging, if you vouch to shroud yourselves in a shepherd's cottage, my house for this night shall be your harbor."

Aliena thanked Corydon greatly, and presently sat her down and Ganymede by her. Corydon looking earnestly upon her, and with a curious survey viewing all her perfections applauded in his thought her excellence, and pitying her distress was desirous to hear the cause of her misfortunes, began to question her thus:

"If I should not, fair damosel, occasion offense, or renew your griefs by rubbing the scar, I would fain crave so much favor as to know the cause of your misfortunes, and why, and whither you wander with your page in so dangerous a forest?"

Aliena, that was as courteous as she was fair, made this reply:

"Shepherd, a friendly demand ought never to be offensive, and questions of courtesy carry privileged pardons in their foreheads. Know, therefore, to discover my fortunes were to renew my sorrows, and I should, by discoursing my mishaps, but rake fire out of the cinders. Therefore let this suffice, gentle shepherd. My distress is as great as my travel is dangerous, and I wander in this forest to light on some cottage where I and my page may dwell: for I mean to buy some farm, and a flock of sheep, and so become a shepherdess, meaning to live low, and content me with a country life; for I have heard the swains say, that they drunk without suspicion, and slept without care."

"Marry, mistress," quoth Corydon, "if you mean so you came in good time, for my landlord intends to sell both the farm I till, and the flock I keep, and cheap you may have them for ready money; and for a shepherd's life, O mistress, did you but live awhile in their content, you would say the court were rather a place of sorrow than of solace. Here, mistress, shall not fortune thwart you, but in mean misfortunes, as the loss of a few sheep, which, as it breeds no beggary, so it can be no extreme prejudice; the next year may mend all with a fresh increase. Envy stirs not us, we covet not to climb, our desires mount not above our degrees, nor our thoughts above our fortunes. Care cannot harbor in our cottages, nor do our homely couches know broken slumbers. As we exceed not in diet, so we have enough to satisfy; and, mistress, I have so much Latin, *Satis est quod sufficit*."[4]

"By my troth, shepherd," quoth Aliena, "thou makest me in love with your country life, and therefore send for thy landlord, and I will buy thy farm and thy flocks, and thou shalt still under me be overseer of them both. Only for pleasure sake I and my page will serve you, lead the flocks to the field, and fold them. Thus will I live quiet, unknown, and contented."

[4] Sufficient is enough.

This news so gladded the heart of Corydon, that he should not be put out of his farm, that putting off his shepherd's bonnet, he did her all the reverence that he might. But all this while sat Montanus in a muse, thinking of the cruelty of his Phoebe, whom he wooed long, but was in no hope to win. Ganymede, who still had the remembrance of Rosader in his thoughts, took delight to see the poor shepherd passionate, laughing at Love, that in all his actions was so imperious.

[Aliena and Ganymede question Montanus about his love. They happily tend their flocks every day. Back at court Rosader has been chained by Saladyne. Freed by Adam, Rosader fights with Saladyne and the sheriff, after which he takes flight with Adam. They wander in the forest, where they almost perish for hunger.]

6. [II.vi.; II.vii.87s.d.–200]

As he [Adam] was ready to go forward in his passion, he looked earnestly on Rosader, and seeing him change color, he rose up and went to him, and holding his temples, said:

"What cheer, master? Though all fail, let not the heart faint; the courage of a man is showed in the resolution of his death."

At these words Rosader lifted up his eye, and looking on Adam Spencer, began to weep.

"Ah, Adam," quoth he, "I sorrow not to die, but I grieve at the manner of my death. Might I with my lance encounter the enemy, and so die in the field, it were honor and content; might I, Adam, combat with some wild beast and perish as his prey, I were satisfied; but to die with hunger, Oh Adam, it is the extremest of all extremes!"

"Master," quoth he, "you see we are both in one predicament, and long I cannot live without meat; seeing therefore we can find no food, let the death of the one preserve the life of the other. I am old, and overworn with age, you are young, and are the hope of many honors. Let me then die; I will presently cut my veins, and, master, with the warm blood relieve your fainting spirits; suck on that till I end, and you be comforted."

With that Adam Spencer was ready to pull out his knife, when Rosader full of courage, though very faint, rose up, and wished Adam Spencer to sit there till his return; "for my mind gives me," quoth he, "I shall bring thee meat." With that, like a madman, he rose up, and ranged up and down the woods, seeking to encounter some wild beast with his rapier, that either he might carry his friend Adam food, or else pledge his life in pawn for his loyalty.

It chanced that day, that Gerismond, the lawful king of France banished by Torismond, who with a lusty crew of outlaws lived in that forest, that day in honor of his birth made a feast to all his bold yeomen, and frolicked it with store of wine and venison, sitting all at a long table under the shadow of lemon trees. To that place by chance fortune conducted Rosader, who seeing such a crew of brave men, having store of that for want of which he and Adam perished, he stepped boldly to the board's end, and saluted the company thus:

"Whatsoever thou be that art master of these lusty squires, I salute thee as graciously as a man in extreme distress may; know that I and a fellow friend of mine are here famished in the forest for want of food; perish we must, unless relieved by thy favors. Therefore, if thou be a gentleman, give meat to men, and to such men as are every way worthy of life. Let the proudest squire that sits at thy table rise and encounter with me in any honorable point of activity whatsoever, and if he and thou prove me not a man, send me away comfortless. If thou refuse this, as a niggard of thy cates, I will have amongst you with my sword; for rather will I die valiantly, than perish with so cowardly an extreme."

Gerismond, looking him earnestly in the face, and seeing so proper a gentleman in so bitter a passion, was moved with so great pity, that rising from the table, he took him by the hand and bad him welcome, willing him to sit down in his place, and in his room not only to eat his fill, but be lord of the feast.

"Grammercy, sir," quoth Rosader, "but I have a feeble friend that lies hereby famished almost for food, aged and therefore less able to abide the extremity of hunger than myself, and dishonor it were for me to taste one crumb, before I made him partner of my fortunes; therefore I will run and fetch him, and then I will gratefully accept of your proffer."

Away hies Rosader to Adam Spencer, and tells him the news, who was glad of so happy fortune, but so feeble he was that he could not go; whereupon Rosader got him up on his back, and brought him to the place. Which when Gerismond and his men saw, they greatly applauded their league of friendship; and Rosader, having Gerismond's place assigned him, would not sit there himself, but set down Adam Spencer. Well, to be short, those hungry squires fell to their victuals, and feasted themselves with good delicates, and great store of wine. As soon as they had taken their repast, Gerismond, desirous to hear what hard fortune drave them into those bitter extremes, requested Rosader to discourse, if it were not any way prejudicial unto him, the cause of his travel. Rosader, desirous any way to satisfy the courtesy of his favorable host, first beginning his exordium with a volley of sighs, and a few lukewarm tears, prosecuted his discourse, and told him from point to point all his fortunes: how he was the youngest son of Sir John of Bordeaux, his name Rosader, how his brother sundry times had wronged him, and lastly how, for beating the sheriff and hurting his men, he fled.

"And this old man," quoth he, "whom I so much love and honor, is surnamed Adam Spencer, an old servant of my father's, and one, that for his love, never failed me in all my misfortunes."

When Gerismond heard this, he fell on the neck of Rosader, and next discoursing unto him how he was Gerismond their lawful king exiled by Torismond, what familiarity had ever been betwixt his father, Sir John of Bordeaux, and him, how faithful a subject he lived, and how honorable he died, promising, for his sake, to give both him and his friend such courteous entertainment as his present estate could minister, and upon this made him one of his foresters. Rosader seeing it was the king, craved pardon for his boldness, in that he did not do him due reverence, and humbly gave him thanks for his favorable courtesy. Gerismond, not satisfied yet with news, began to inquire if he had been lately in the court of Torismond, and whether he had seen his daughter Rosalynde or no? At this Rosader fetched a deep sigh, and shedding many tears, could not answer. Yet at last, gathering his spirits together, he revealed unto the king, how Rosalynde was banished. . . . This news drave the king into a great melancholy, that presently he arose from all the company, and went into his privy chamber, so secret as the harbor of the woods would allow him. The company was all dashed at these tidings, and Rosader and Adam Spencer, having such opportunity, went to take their rest. Where we leave them, and return again to Torismond.

[To get Saladyne's land, Torismond uses the pretext of Saladyne's cruelty to Rosader. Thrown into prison, Saladyne repents of his wickedness. In the forest Rosader carves verses on trees celebrating Rosalynde.]

7. [III.ii.1–10, 86–249]

One day among the rest, finding a fit opportunity and place convenient, desirous to discover his woes to the woods, he engraved with his knife on the bark of a myrtle tree, this pretty estimate of his mistress' perfection . . . In these and such like passions Rosader did every day eternize the name of his Rosalynde; and this day especially when Aliena and Ganymede, enforced by the heat of the sun to seek for shelter, by good fortune arrived in that place, where this amorous forester registered his melancholy passions. They saw the sudden change of his looks, his folded arms, his passionate sighs; they heard him often abruptly call on Rosalynde, who, poor soul, was as hotly burned as himself, but that she shrouded her pains in the cinders of honorable modesty. Whereupon, guessing him to be in love, and according to the nature of their sex being pitiful in that behalf, they suddenly brake off his melancholy by their approach, and Ganymede shook him out of his dumps thus:

"What news, forester? Hast thou wounded some deer, and lost him in the fall? Care not man for so small a loss; thy fees was but the skin, the shoulder, and the horns; 'tis hunter's luck to aim fair and miss; and a woodman's fortune to strike and yet go without the game."

"Thou art beyond the mark, Ganymede," quoth Aliena: "his passions are greater, and his sighs discovers more loss; perhaps in traversing these thickets, he hath seen some beautiful nymph, and is grown amorous."

"It may be so," quoth Ganymede, "for here he hath newly engraven some sonnet; come, and see the discourse of the forester's poems."

Reading the sonnet over, and hearing him name Rosalynde, Aliena looked on Ganymede and laughed, and Ganymede looking back on the forester, and seeing it was Rosader, blushed; yet thinking to shroud all under her page's apparel, she boldly returned to Rosader, and began thus:

"I pray thee tell me, forester, what is this Rosalynde for whom thou pinest away in such passions? Is she some nymph that waits upon Diana's train, whose chastity thou hast deciphered in such epithets? Or is she some shepherdess that haunts these plains whose beauty hath so bewitched thy fancy, whose name thou shadowest in covert under the figure of Rosalynde, as Ovid did Julia under the name of Corinna? Or say me forsooth, is it that Rosalynde, of whom we shepherds have heard talk, she, forester, that is the daughter of Gerismond, that once was king, and now an outlaw in the forest of Arden?"

At this Rosader fetched a deep sigh, and said:

"It is she, O gentle swain, it is she; that saint it is whom I serve, that goddess at whose shrine I do bend all my devotions; the most fairest of all fairs, the phoenix of all that sex, and the purity of all earthly perfection."

"And why, gentle forester, if she be so beautiful, and thou so amorous, is there such a disagreement in thy thoughts? Happily she resembleth the rose, that is sweet but full of prickles? Or the serpent Regius that hath scales as glorious as the sun and a breath as infectious as the Aconitum is deadly? So thy Rosalynde may be most amiable and yet unkind; full of favor and yet froward, coy without wit, and disdainful without reason."

[Rosader denies this and reads a poem describing Rosalynde's beauty.]

"Believe me," quoth Ganymede, "either the forester is

an exquisite painter, or Rosalynde far above wonder; so it makes me blush to hear how women should be so excellent, and pages so unperfect."

Rosader beholding her earnestly, answered thus:

"Truly, gentle page, thou hast cause to complain thee wert thou the substance, but resembling the shadow content thyself; for it is excellence enough to be like the excellence of nature."

"He hath answered you, Ganymede," quoth Aliena. "It is enough for pages to wait on beautiful ladies, and not to be beautiful themselves."

"O mistress," quoth Ganymede, "hold you your peace, for you are partial. Who knows not, but that all women have desire to tie sovereignty to their petticoats, and ascribe beauty to themselves, where, if boys might put on their garments, perhaps they would prove as comely; if not as comely, it may be more courteous. . . ."

[Rosader agrees to meet Ganymede and Aliena the next day to read them some more sonnets addressed to Rosalynde.]

"So Ganymede," said Aliena, the forester being gone, "you are mightily beloved; men make ditties in your praise, spend sighs for your sake, make an idol of your beauty. Believe me, it grieves me not a little to see the poor man so pensive, and you so pitiless."

"Ah, Aliena," quoth she, "be not peremptory in your judgments. I hear Rosalynde praised as I am Ganymede, but were I Rosalynde, I could answer the forester. If he mourn for love, there are medicines for love; Rosalynde cannot be fair and unkind. And so, madam, you see it is time to fold our flocks, or else Corydon will frown and say you will never prove good housewife."

[Rosalynde meditates on whether to serve Diana or Venus. She decides not to arouse the ire of Venus.]

The sun was no sooner stepped from the bed of Aurora, but Aliena was wakened by Ganymede, who, restless all night, had tossed in her passions, saying it was then time to go to the field to unfold their sheep. Aliena, that spied where the hare was by the hounds, and could see day at a little hole, thought to be pleasant with her Ganymede, and therefore replied thus:

"What, wanton! The sun is but new up, and as yet Iris' riches lie folded in the bosom of Flora; Phoebus hath not dried up the pearled dew, and so long Corydon hath taught me, it is not fit to lead the sheep abroad, lest, the dew being unwholesome, they get the rot. But now see I the old proverb true: he is in haste whom the devil drives, and where love pricks forward, there is no worse death than delay. Ah, my good page, is there fancy in thine eye, and passions in thy heart? What, hast thou wrapt love in thy looks, and set all thy thoughts on fire by affection? I tell thee, it is a flame as hard to be quenched as that of Aetna. . . .

"Come on," quoth Ganymede, "this sermon of yours is but a subtlety to lie still a-bed, because either you think the morning cold, or else I being gone, you would steal a nap. This shift carries no palm, and therefore up and away. And for Love, let me alone; I'll whip him away with nettles, and set disdain as a charm to withstand his forces: and therefore look you to yourself; be not too bold, for Venus can make you bend, nor too coy, for Cupid hath a piercing dart, that will make you cry *Peccavi.*"

"And that is it," quoth Aliena, "that hath raised you so early this morning." And with that she slipped on her petticoat, and start up; and as soon as she had made her ready, and taken her breakfast, away go these two with their bag and bottles to the field, in more pleasant content of mind than ever they were in the court of Torismond.

They came no sooner nigh the folds, but they might see where their discontented forester was walking in his melancholy. As soon as Aliena saw him, she smiled and said to Ganymede:

"Wipe your eyes, sweeting, for yonder is your sweetheart this morning in deep prayers, no doubt, to Venus, that she may make you as pitiful as he is passionate. Come on, Ganymede, I pray thee, let's have a little sport with him."

[Orlando again speaks of his love and reads some of his love poems to Aliena and Ganymede.]

8. [III.ii.338–90]

"Now, surely, forester," quoth Aliena, "when thou madest this sonnet, thou wert in some amorous quandary, neither too fearful as despairing of thy mistress' favors, nor too gleesome as hoping in thy fortunes."

"I can smile," quoth Ganymede, "at the sonettos, canzones, madrigals, rounds, and roundelays, that these pensive patients pour out when their eyes are more full of wantonness, than their hearts of passions. Then, as the fishers put the sweetest bait to the fairest fish, so these Ovidians, holding *amo* in their tongues, when their thoughts come at haphazard, write that they be rapt in an endless labyrinth of sorrow, when walking in the large lease of liberty, they only have their humors in their inkpot. If they find women so fond, that they will with such painted lures come to their lust, then they triumph till they be full-gorged with pleasures; and then fly they away, like ramage kites, to their own content, leaving the tame fool, their mistress, full of fancy, yet without even a feather. If they miss, as dealing with some wary wanton, that wants not such a one as themselves, but spies their subtlety, they end their amours with a few feigned sighs; and so their excuse is, their mistress is cruel, and they smother passions with patience. Such, gentle forester, we may deem you to be, that rather pass away the time here in these woods with writing amorets, than to be deeply enamored, as you say, of your Rosalynde. If you be such a one, then I pray God, when you think your fortunes at the highest, and your desires to be most excellent, then that you may with Ixion embrace Juno in a cloud, and have nothing but a marble mistress to release your martyrdom; but if you be true and trusty, eye-pained and heart-sick, then accursed be Rosalynde if she prove cruel; for, forester, I flatter not, thou art worthy of as fair as she." Aliena, spying the storm by the wind, smiled to see how Ganymede flew to the fist without any call; but Rosader, who took him flat for a shepherd's swain, made him this answer:

"Trust me, swain," quoth Rosader, "but my canzon was written in no such humor; for mine eye and my heart are relatives, the one drawing fancy by sight, the other entertaining her by sorrow. If thou sawest my Rosalynde, with what beauties nature hath favored her, with what perfection the heavens hath graced her, with what qualities the gods have endued her, then wouldst thou say, there is none so fickle that could be fleeting unto her. If she had been Aeneas' Dido, had Venus and Juno both scolded him from Carthage, yet her excellence, despite of them, would have detained him at Tyre. . . .

[After further conversation Rosader reads the last of his poems.]

9. [III.ii.391–425; IV.i.64–151]

Ganymede, pitying her Rosader, thinking to drive him out of this amorous melancholy, said that now the sun was in his meridional heat and that it was high noon, "therefore we shepherds say, 'tis time to go to dinner; for the sun and our stomachs are shepherds' dials. Therefore, forester, if thou wilt take such fare as comes out of our homely scrips, welcome shall answer whatsoever thou wantest in delicates."

Aliena took the entertainment by the end, and told Rosader he should be her guest. He thanked them heartily, and sat with them down to dinner, where they had such cates as country state did allow them, sauced with such content, and such sweet prattle, as it seemed far more sweet than all their courtly junkets.

As soon as they had taken their repast, Rosader, giving them thanks for his good cheer, would have been gone; but Ganymede, that was loath to let him pass out of her presence, began thus:

"Nay, forester," quoth he, "if thy business be not the greater, seeing thou sayest thou art so deeply in love, let me see how thou canst woo; I will represent Rosalynde, and thou shalt be as thou art, Rosader. See in some amorous eclogue, how if Rosalynde were present, how thou couldst court her; and while we sing of love, Aliena shall tune her pipe and play us melody."

"Content," quoth Rosader, and Aliena, she, to show her willingness, drew forth a recorder, and began to wind it. Then the loving forester began thus:

Rosader

I pray thee, nymph, by all the working words,
By all the tears and sighs that lovers know,
Or what or thoughts or faltering tongue affords,
I crave for mine in ripping up my woe.
Sweet Rosalynde, my love—would God, my love—
My life—would God, my life—aye, pity me!
Thy lips are kind, and humble like the dove,
And but with beauty pity will not be.
Look on mine eyes, made red with rueful tears,
From whence the rain of true remorse descendeth,
All pale in looks am I though young in years,
And nought but love or death my days befriendeth.
Oh let no stormy rigor knit thy brows,
Which love appointed for his mercy seat:
The tallest tree by Boreas' breath it bows;
The iron yields with hammer, and to heat.
  O Rosalynde, then be thou pitiful,
  For Rosalynde is only beautiful.

Rosalynde

Love's wantons arm their trait'rous suits with tears,
With vows, with oaths, with looks, with showers of gold;
But when the fruit of their affects appears,
The simple heart by subtle sleights is sold. . . .

When thus they had finished their courting eclogue in such a familiar clause, Ganymede, as augur of some good fortunes to light upon their affections, began to be thus pleasant:

"How now, forester, have I not fitted your turn? Have I not played the woman handsomely, and showed myself as coy in grants as courteous in desires, and been as full of suspicion as men of flattery? And yet to salve all, jumped I not all up with the sweet union of love? Did not Rosalynde content her Rosader?"

The forester at this smiling, shook his head, and folding his arms made this merry reply:

"Truth, gentle swain, Rosader hath his Rosalynde; but as Ixion had Juno, who, thinking to possess a goddess, only embraced a cloud. In these imaginary fruitions of fancy I resemble the birds that fed themselves with Zeuxis' painted grapes; but they grew so lean with pecking at shadows, that they were glad, with Aesop's cock, to scrape for a barley kernel. So fareth it with me, who to feed myself with the hope of my mistress's favors, sooth myself in thy suits, and only in conceit reap a wished-for content; but if my food be no better than such amorous dreams, Venus at the year's end shall find me but a lean lover. Yet do I take these follies for high fortunes, and hope these feigned affections do divine some unfeigned end of ensuing fancies."

"And thereupon," quoth Aliena, "I'll play the priest. From this day forth Ganymede shall call thee husband, and thou shalt call Ganymede wife, and so we'll have a marriage."

"Content," quoth Rosader, and laughed.

"Content," quoth Ganymede, and changed as red as a rose; and so with a smile and a blush, they made up this jesting match, that after proved to a marriage in earnest, Rosader full little thinking he had wooed and won his Rosalynde.

[Rosader rescues Saladyne from a lion and the two brothers are reconciled. They spend three days together, in which time Rosader is sorely missed by Ganymede. Shortly after he appears and accounts for his absence, a band of robbers sets upon them, hoping to steal Aliena. Rosader is wounded, but Saladyne, who is passing by, hears their cries and saves them. He and Aliena fall in love. Meditating on the pains and perils of love, Aliena consents in her mind to accept Saladyne. Ganymede praises Saladyne. While the two are tending their flocks and thinking of their loves, Corydon approaches and tells them where they can observe Montanus pleading with Phoebe.]

10. [V.ii.82–98; III.v.1–83]

Montanus, hearing the cruel resolution of Phoebe, was so overgrown with passions, that from amorous ditties he fell flat into these terms:

"Ah, Phoebe," quoth he, "whereof art thou made, that thou regardest not my malady? Am I so hateful an object that thine eyes condemn me for an abject? Or so base, that thy desires cannot stoop so low as to lend me a gracious look? My passions are many, my loves more, my thoughts loyalty, and my fancy faith: all devoted in humble devoir to the service of Phoebe; and shall I reap no reward for such fealties. . . . If, Phoebe, time may plead the proof of my truth, twice seven winters have I loved fair Phoebe; if constancy be a cause to farther my suit, Montanus' thoughts have been sealed in the sweet of Phoebe's excellence, as far from change as she from love. If outward passions may discover inward affections, the furrows in my face may decipher the sorrows of my heart, and the map of my looks the griefs of my mind. . . . If Phoebe cannot love, let a storm of frowns end the discontent of my thoughts, and so let me perish in my desires, because they are above my deserts; only at my death this favor cannot be denied me, that all shall say Montanus died for love of hardhearted Phoebe."

At these words she filled her face full of frowns, and made him this short and sharp reply:

"Importunate shepherd, whose loves are lawless, because restless, are thy passions so extreme that thou canst not conceal them with patience? Or art thou so folly-sick, that thou must needs be fancy-sick, and in thy affection tied to such an exigent, as none serves but Phoebe? Well, sir, if your market may be made nowhere else, home again, for your mart is at the fairest. Phoebe is no lettuce for your lips, and her grapes hangs so high, that gaze at them you may, but touch them you cannot. Yet, Montanus, I speak not this in pride, but in disdain; not that I scorn thee, but that I hate love; for I count it as great honor to triumph over fancy as over fortune. Rest thee content therefore, Montanus. Cease from thy loves, and bridle thy looks, quench the sparkles before they grow to a further flame; for in loving me thou shalt live by loss, and what thou utterest in words are all written in the wind. Wert thou, Montanus, as fair as Paris, as hardy as Hector, as constant as Troilus, as loving as Leander, Phoebe could not love, because she cannot love at all. . . .

Ganymede, overhearing all these passions of Montanus, could not brook the cruelty of Phoebe, but starting from behind the bush said:

"And if, damsel, you fled from me, I would transform you as Daphne to a bay, and then in contempt trample your branches under my feet."

Phoebe at this sudden reply was amazed, especially when she saw so fair a swain as Ganymede; blushing therefore, she would have been gone, but that he held her by the hand, and prosecuted his reply thus:

"What, shepherdess, so fair and so cruel? Disdain beseems not cottages, nor coyness maids; for either they be condemned to be too proud, or too froward. Take heed, fair nymph, that in despising love, you be not overreached with love, and in shaking off all, shape yourself to your own shadow, and so with Narcissus prove passionate and yet unpitied. Oft have I heard, and sometimes have I seen, high disdain turned to hot desires. Because thou art beautiful be not so coy; as there is nothing more fair, so there is nothing more fading—as momentary as the shadows which grows from a cloudy sun. Such, my fair shepherdess, as disdain in youth desire in age, and then are they hated in the winter, that might have been loved in the prime. A wrinkled maid is like to a parched rose, that is cast up in coffers to please the smell, not worn in the hand to content the eye. There is no folly in love to *had I wist*, and therefore be ruled by me. Love while thou art young, lest thou be disdained when thou art old. Beauty nor time cannot be recalled, and if thou love, like of Montanus; for if his desires are many, so his deserts are great."

Phoebe all this while gazed on the perfection of Ganymede, as deeply enamored on his perfection as Montanus inveigled with hers; for her eye made survey of his excellent feature, which she found so rare, that she thought the ghost of Adonis had been leaped from Elysium in the shape of a swain. When she blushed at her own folly to look so long on a stranger, she mildly made answer to Ganymede thus:

"I cannot deny, sir, but I have heard of Love, though I never felt love; and have read of such a goddess as Venus, though I never saw any but her picture; and perhaps"—and with that she waxed red and bashful, and withal silent; which Ganymede perceiving, commended in herself the bashfulness of the maid, and desired her to go forward.

"And perhaps, sir," quoth she, "mine eye hath been more prodigal today than ever before"—and with that she stayed again, as one greatly passionate and perplexed.

Aliena seeing the hare through the maze, bade her forward with her prattle, but in vain; for at this abrupt period she broke off, and with her eyes full of tears, and her face covered with a vermilion dye, she sat down and sighed. Whereupon Aliena and Ganymede, seeing the shepherdess in such a strange plight, left Phoebe with her Montanus, wishing her friendly that she would be more pliant to Love, lest in penance Venus joined her to some sharp repentance. Phoebe made no reply, but fetched such a sigh, that Echo made relation of her plaint, giving Ganymede such an adieu with a piercing glance, that the amorous girl-boy perceived Phoebe was pinched by the heel.

[Saladyne woos and wins Aliena. Phoebe becomes ill for love of Ganymede.]

11. [III.v.84–139; IV.iii.7–75]

The news of her sickness was bruited abroad through all the forest, which no sooner came to Montanus' ear, but he, like a madman, came to visit Phoebe. Where sitting by her bedside he began his exordium with so many tears and sighs, that she, perceiving the extremity of his sorrows, began now as a lover to pity them, although Ganymede held her from redressing them. Montanus craved to know the cause of her sickness, tempered with secret plaints, but she answered him, as the rest, with silence, having still the form of Ganymede in her mind, and conjecturing how she might reveal her loves. To utter it in words she found herself too bashful; to discourse by any friend she would not trust any in her amours; to remain thus perplexed still and conceal all, it was a double death. Whereupon, for her last refuge, she resolved to write unto Ganymede, and therefore desired Montanus to absent himself a while, but not to depart, for she would see if she could steal a nap. He was no sooner gone out of the chamber, but reaching to her standish, she took pen and paper, and wrote a letter to this effect. . . .

This letter and the sonnet being ended, she could find no fit messenger to send it by, and therefore she called in Montanus, and entreated him to carry it to Ganymede. Although poor Montanus saw day at a little hole, and did perceive what passion pinched her, yet, that he might seem dutiful to his mistress in all service, he dissembled the matter, and became a willing messenger of his own martyrdom. And so, taking the letter, went the next morn very early to the plains where Aliena fed her flocks, and there he found Ganymede, sitting under a pomegranate tree, sorrowing for the hard fortunes of her Rosader. Montanus saluted him, and according to his charge delivered Ganymede the letters, which, he said, came from Phoebe. At this the wanton blushed, as being abashed to think what news should come from an unknown shepherdess; but taking the letters, unripped the seals, and read over the discourse of Phoebe's fancies. When she had read and overread them Ganymede began to smile, and looking on Montanus, fell into a great laughter, and with that called Aliena, to whom she showed the writings. Who, having perused them, conceited them very pleasantly, and smiled to see how love had yoked her, who before would not stoop to the lure; Aliena whispering Ganymede in the ear, and saying, "Knew Phoebe what want there were in thee to perform her will, and how unfit thy kind is to be kind to her, she would be more wise, and less enamored. But leaving that, I pray thee let us sport with this swain." At that word Ganymede, turning to Montanus, began to glance at him thus:

"I pray thee, tell me, shepherd, by those sweet thoughts and pleasing sighs that grow from my mistress' favors, art thou in love with Phoebe?"

"Oh, my youth," quoth Montanus, "were Phoebe so far in love with me, my flocks would be more fat and their master more quiet; for through the sorrows of my discontent grows the leanness of my sheep."

"Alas, poor swain," quoth Ganymede, "are thy passions so extreme or thy fancy so resolute, that no reason will blemish the pride of thy affection, and raze out that which thou strivest for without hope?"

"Nothing can make me forget Phoebe, while Montanus forget himself; for those characters which true love hath stamped, neither the envy of time nor fortune can wipe away."

"Why but, Montanus," quoth Ganymede, "enter with a deep insight into the despair of thy fancies, and thou shalt see the depth of thine own follies. . . . I tell thee, Montanus, in courting Phoebe, thou barkest with the wolves of Syria against the moon, and rovest[5] at such a mark, with thy thoughts, as is beyond the pitch of thy bow, praying to Love, when Love is pitiless, and thy malady remediless. For proof, Montanus, read these letters, wherein thou shalt see thy great follies and little hope."

With that Montanus took them and perused them, but with such sorrow in his looks, as they betrayed a source of confused passions in his heart; at every line his color changed, and every sentence was ended with a period of sighs.

At last, noting Phoebe's extreme desire toward Ganymede and her disdain toward him, giving Ganymede the letter, the shepherd stood as though he had neither won nor lost. Which Ganymede perceiving wakened him out of his dream thus:

"Now, Montanus, dost thou see thou vowest great service and obtainest but little reward. . . . Then drink not willingly of that potion wherein thou knowest is poison; creep not to her that cares not for thee. . . ."

"I tell thee, Ganymede," quoth Montanus. . . . "Persuasions are bootless, reason lends no remedy, counsel no comfort, to such whom fancy hath made resolute; and therefore though Phoebe loves Ganymede, yet Montanus must honor none but Phoebe."

"Then," quoth Ganymede, "may I rightly term thee a

[5] shoot wildly

despairing lover, that livest without joy, and lovest without hope. But what shall I do, Montanus, to pleasure thee? Shall I despise Phoebe, as she disdains thee?"

"Oh," quoth Montanus, "that were to renew my griefs, and double my sorrows; for the sight of her discontent were the censure of my death. Alas, Ganymede, though I perish in my thoughts, let not her die in her desires. . . .

[Ganymede decides to visit Phoebe to cure her of her sickness and win her love for Montanus. Phoebe confesses her love to Ganymede.]

12. [V.ii.76–122]

At this she held down her head and wept, and Ganymede rose as one that would suffer no fish to hang on his fingers, made this reply.

"Water not thy plants, Phoebe, for I do pity thy plaints, nor seek not to discover thy loves in tears, for I conjecture thy truth by thy passions; sorrow is no salve for loves, nor sighs no remedy for affection. Therefore frolic, Phoebe; for if Ganymede can cure thee, doubt not of recovery. . . . Therefore, Phoebe, seek not to suppress affection, and with the love of Montanus quench the remembrance of Ganymede; strive thou to hate me as I seek to like of thee, and ever have the duties of Montanus in thy mind, for I promise thee thou mayest have one more wealthy, but not more loyal." These words were corrosives to the perplexed Phoebe, that sobbing out sighs, and straining out tears, she blubbered out these words:

"And shall I then have no salve of Ganymede but suspense, no hope but a doubtful hazard, nor comfort, but be posted off to the will of time? Justly have the gods balanced my fortunes, who, being cruel to Montanus, found Ganymede as unkind to myself; so in forcing him perish for love, I shall die myself with overmuch love."

"I am glad," quoth Ganymede, "you look into your own faults, and see where your shoe wrings you, measuring now the pains of Montanus by your own passions."

"Truth," quoth Phoebe, "and so deeply I repent me of

my frowardness toward the shepherd, that could I cease to love Ganymede, I would resolve to like Montanus."

"What, if I can with reason persuade Phoebe to mislike of Ganymede, will she then favor Montanus?"

"When reason," quoth she, "doth quench that love I owe to thee, then will I fancy him; conditionally, that if my love can be suppressed with no reason, as being without reason Ganymede will only wed himself to Phoebe."

"I grant it, fair shepherdess," quoth he; "and to feed thee with the sweetness of hope, this resolve on: I will never marry myself to woman but unto thyself."

And with that Ganymede gave Phoebe a fruitless kiss, and such words of comfort, that before Ganymede departed she arose out of her bed, and made him and Montanus such cheer, as could be found in such a country cottage; Ganymede in the midst of their banquet rehearsing the promises of either in Montanus' favor, which highly pleased the shepherd.

[Ganymede goes to join Aliena, who is with Rosader and Saladyne.]

13. [V.ii.13–74]

At last Corydon, who was with them, spied Ganymede, and with that the clown rose, and, running to meet him, cried:

"Oh sirrah, a match, a match! Our mistress shall be married on Sunday."

Thus the poor peasant frolicked it before Ganymede, who coming to the crew saluted them all, and especially Rosader, saying that he was glad to see him so well recovered of his wounds.

"I had not gone abroad so soon," quoth Rosader, "but that I am bidden to a marriage, which, on Sunday next, must be solemnized between my brother and Aliena. I see well where love leads delay is loathsome, and that small wooing serves where both the parties are willing."

"Truth," quoth Ganymede; "but a happy day should it be, if Rosader that day might be married to Rosalynde."

"Ah, good Ganymede," quoth he, "by naming Rosalynde, renew not my sorrows; for the thought of her perfections is the thrall of my miseries."

"Tush, be of good cheer, man," quoth Ganymede; "I have a friend that is deeply experienced in necromancy and magic; what art can do, shall be acted for thine advantage. I will cause him to bring in Rosalynde, if either France or any bordering nation harbor her; and upon that take the faith of a young shepherd."

Aliena smiled to see how Rosader frowned, thinking that Ganymede had jested with him. But, breaking off from those matters, the page, somewhat pleasant, began to discourse unto them what had passed between him and Phoebe; which, as they laughed, so they wondered at, all confessing that there is none so chaste but love will change. Thus they passed away the day in chat, and when the sun began to set they took their leaves and departed; Aliena providing for their marriage day such solemn cheer and handsome robes as fitted their country estate, and yet somewhat the better, in that Rosader had promised to bring Gerismond thither as a guest. Ganymede, who then meant to discover herself before her father, had made her a gown of green, and a kirtle of the finest sendal, in such sort that she seemed some heavenly nymph harbored in country attire.

[The characters assemble for the wedding of Aliena and Saladyne. Phoebe and Montanus speak of their unrequited loves to Gerismond.]

14. [V.iv.1–34; 107s.d.–148]

Gerismond, desirous to prosecute the end of these passions, called in Ganymede, who, knowing the case, came in graced with such a blush, as beautified the crystal of his face with a ruddy brightness. The king noting well the physnomy of Ganymede, began by his favors to call to mind the face of his Rosalynde, and with that fetched a deep sigh. Rosader, that was passing familiar with Gerismond, demanded of him why he sighed so sore.

"Because, Rosader," quoth he, "the favor of Ganymede puts me in mind of Rosalynde."

At this word Rosader sighed so deeply, as though his heart would have burst.

"And what's the matter," quoth Gerismond, "that you quite me with such a sigh?"

"Pardon me, sir," quoth Rosader, "because I love none but Rosalynde."

"And upon that condition," quoth Gerismond, "that Rosalynde were here, I would this day make up a marriage betwixt her and thee."

At this Aliena turned her head and smiled upon Ganymede, and she could scarce keep countenance. Yet she salved all with secrecy; and Gerismond, to drive away his dumps, questioned with Ganymede, what the reason was he regarded not Phoebe's love, seeing she was as fair as the wanton that brought Troy to ruin. Ganymede mildly answered:

"If I should affect the fair Phoebe, I should offer poor Montanus great wrong to win that from him in a moment, that he hath labored for so many months. Yet have I promised to the beautiful shepherdess to wed myself never to woman except unto her; but with this promise, that if I can by reason suppress Phoebe's love toward me, she shall like of none but of Montanus."

"To that," quoth Phoebe, "I stand; for my love is so far beyond reason, as will admit no persuasion of reason."

"For justice," quoth he, "I appeal to Gerismond."

"And to his censure will I stand," quoth Phoebe.

"And in your victory," quoth Montanus, "stands the hazard of my fortunes; for if Ganymede go away with conquest, Montanus is in conceit love's monarch; if Phoebe win, then am I in effect most miserable."

"We will see this controversy," quoth Gerismond, "and then we will to church. Therefore, Ganymede, let us hear your argument."

"Nay, pardon my absence a while," quoth she, "and you shall see one in store."

In went Ganymede and dressed herself in woman's attire . . . upon her head she wore a chaplet of roses, which gave her such a grace that she looked like Flora perked in the pride of all her flowers. Thus attired came Rosalynde in, and presented herself at her father's feet, with her eyes full of tears, craving his blessing, and discoursing unto him all her fortunes, how she was banished by Torismond, and how ever since she lived in that country disguised.

[Gerismond gives Rosalynde to Rosader and Phoebe accepts Montanus. After the three couples are married in church, Corydon sings a song, the first two lines of which are "A blithe and bonny country lass,/ Heigh ho, the bonny lass!"]

15. [V.iv.150s.d.–198]

As they were in the midst of their jollity, word was brought in to Saladyne and Rosader that a brother of theirs, one Fernandyne, was arrived, and desired to speak with them. Gerismond overhearing this news, demanded who it was.

"It is, sir," quoth Rosader, "our middle brother, that lives a scholar in Paris; but what fortune hath driven him to seek us out I know not."

... Fernandyne, as one that knew as many manners as he could points of sophistry, and was as well brought up as well lettered, saluted them all. But when he espied Gerismond, kneeling on his knee he did him what reverence belonged to his estate, and with that burst forth into these speeches:

"Although, right mighty prince, this day of my brother's marriage be a day of mirth, yet time craves another course; and therefore from dainty cates rise to sharp weapons. And you, the sons of Sir John of Bordeaux, leave off your amours and fall to arms. . . . For know, Gerismond, that hard by at the edge of this forest the twelve peers of France are up in arms to recover thy right; and Torismond, trooped with a crew of desperate runagates, is ready to bid them battle. The armies are ready to join; therefore show thyself in the field to encourage thy subjects. . . .

When the peers perceived that their lawful king was there, they grew more eager; and Saladyne and Rosader so behaved themselves, that none durst stand in their way, nor abide the fury of their weapons. To be short, the peers were conquerors, Torismond's army put to flight, and himself slain in battle. The peers then gathered themselves together, and saluted their king, conducted him royally into Paris, where he was received with great joy of all the citizens. As soon as all was quiet and he had received again the crown, he sent for Alinda and Rosalynde to the court, Alinda being very passionate for the death of her father, yet brooking it with the more patience, in that she was contented with the welfare of her Saladyne.

Well, as soon as they were come to Paris, Gerismond made a royal feast for the peers and lords of his land, which continued thirty days, in which time summoning a parliament, by the consent of his nobles he created Rosader heir apparent to the kingdom; he restored Saladyne to all his father's land and gave him the Dukedom of Nemours; he made Fernandyne principal secretary to himself; and that fortune might every way seem frolic, he made Montanus lord over all the forest of Arden, Adam Spencer captain of the King's Guard, and Corydon master of Alinda's flocks.

Commentaries

EDWARD DOWDEN

from *Shakspere: A Critical Study of His Mind and Art*

Shakspere, when he had completed his English historical plays, needed rest for his imagination; and in such a mood, craving refreshment and recreation, he wrote his play of *As You Like It*. To understand the spirit of this play, we must bear in mind that it was written immediately after Shakspere's great series of histories, ending with *Henry V* (1599), and before he began the great series of tragedies. Shakspere turned with a sense of relief, and a long easeful sigh, from the oppressive subjects of history, so grave, so real, so massive, and found rest and freedom and pleasure in escape from courts and camps to the Forest of Arden:

> Who doth ambition shun,
> And loves to live i' the sun,
>   Come hither, come hither, come hither.

From *Shakspere: A Critical Study of His Mind and Art* by Edward Dowden. 3rd ed. London, 1877. Reprinted by permission of Routledge & Kegan Paul, Ltd.

In somewhat the same spirit needing relief for an over-strained imagination he wrote his other pastoral drama, *The Winter's Tale*, immediately or almost immediately after *Timon of Athens*. In each case he chose a graceful story in great part made ready to his hand, from among the prose writings of his early contemporaries, Thomas Lodge and Robert Greene. Like the banished Duke, Shakspere himself found the forest life of Arden more sweet than that of painted pomp; a life "exempt from public haunt," in a quiet retreat, where for turbulent citizens, the deer, "poor dappled fools," are the only native burghers.

The play has been represented by one of its recent editors as an early attempt made by the poet to control the dark spirit of melancholy in himself "by thinking it away." The characters of the banished Duke, of Orlando, of Rosalind are described as three gradations of cheerfulness in adversity, with Jacques placed over against them in designed contrast.[1] But no real adversity has come to any one of them. Shakspere, when he put into the Duke's mouth the words, "Sweet are the uses of adversity," knew something of deeper affliction than a life in the golden leisure of Arden. Of real melancholy there is none in the play; for the melancholy of Jacques is not grave and earnest, but sentimental, a self-indulgent humor, a petted foible of character, melancholy prepense and cultivated; "it is a melancholy of mine own, compounded of many simples, extracted from many objects; and indeed the sundry contemplation of my travels, in which my often rumination wraps me in a most humorous sadness." The Duke declares that Jacques has been "a libertine, as sensual as the brutish sting itself"; but the Duke is unable to understand such a character as that of Jacques.[2] Jacques has been no more than a curious experimenter in libertinism, for the sake of adding an experience of madness and folly to the store of various superficial experiences which constitute his unpractical foolery of wisdom. The

---

[1] *As you Like it*, edited by the Rev. C. E. Moberly (1872), pp. 7–9.

[2] The Duke accordingly repels Jacques. *Jacques*—"I have been all this day to avoid him; he is too disputable for my company; I think of as many matters as he, but I give heaven thanks, and make no boast of them."

haunts of sin have been visited as a part of his travel. By and by he will go to the usurping Duke who has put on a religious life, because

> Out of these convertites
> There is much matter to be heard and learned.

Jacques died, we know not how, or when, or where; but he came to life again a century later, and appeared in the world as an English clergyman; we need stand in no doubt as to his character, for we all know him under his later name of Laurence Sterne. Mr. Yorick made a mistake about his family tree; he came not out of the play of Hamlet, but out of *As You Like It*. In Arden he wept and moralized over the wounded deer; and at Namport his tears and sentiment gushed forth for the dead donkey. Jacques knows no bonds that unite him to any living thing. He lives upon novel, curious, and delicate sensations. He seeks the delicious *imprévu* so loved and studiously sought for by that perfected French egoist, Henri Beyle. "A fool! a fool! I met a fool i' the forest!"—and in the delight of coming upon this exquisite surprise, Jacques laughs like chanticleer,

> Sans intermission
> An hour by his dial.

His whole life is unsubstantial and unreal; a curiosity of dainty mockery. To him "all the world's a stage, and all the men and women merely players"; to him sentiment stands in place of passion; an aesthetic, amateurish experience of various modes of life stands in place of practical wisdom; and words, in place of deeds. . . .

Jacques in his own way supposes that he can dispense with realities. The world, not as it is, but as it mirrors itself in his own mind, which gives to each object a humorous distortion, that is what alone interests Jacques. Shakspere would say to us, "This egoistic, contemplative, unreal manner of treating life is only a delicate kind of foolery. Real knowledge of life can never be acquired by the curious seeker for experiences." But this Shakspere says in his non-hortatory, undogmatic way.

Upon the whole, *As You Like It* is the sweetest and happiest of all Shakspere's comedies. No one suffers; no one lives an eager intense life; there is no tragic interest in it as there is in *The Merchant of Venice*, as there is in *Much Ado About Nothing*. It is mirthful, but the mirth is sprightly, graceful, exquisite; there is none of the rollicking fun of a Sir Toby here; the songs are not "coziers' catches" shouted in the nighttime, "without any mitigation or remorse of voice," but the solos and duets of pages in the wildwood, or the noisier chorus of foresters. The wit of Touchstone is not mere clownage, nor has it any indirect serious significances; it is a dainty kind of absurdity worthy to hold comparison with the melancholy of Jacques. And Orlando in the beauty and strength of early manhood, and Rosalind,

> A gallant curtle-axe upon her thigh,
> A boar-spear in her hand,

and the bright, tender, loyal womanhood within—are figures which quicken and restore our spirits, as music does, which is neither noisy nor superficial, and yet which knows little of the deep passion and sorrow of the world.

Shakspere, when he wrote this idyllic play, was himself in his Forest of Arden. He had ended one great ambition—the historical plays—and not yet commenced his tragedies. It was a resting place. He sends his imagination into the woods to find repose. Instead of the courts and camps of England, and the embattled plains of France, here was this woodland scene, where the palm tree, the lioness, and the serpent are to be found; possessed of a flora and fauna that flourish in spite of physical geographers. There is an open-air feeling throughout the play. The dialogue, as has been observed, catches freedom and freshness from the atmosphere. "Never is the scene within-doors, except when something discordant is introduced to heighten as it were the harmony."[3] After the trumpet tones of *Henry V* comes the sweet pastoral strain, so bright, so tender. Must it not be

[3] C. A. Brown, *Shakespeare's Autobiographical Poems*, p. 283.

all in keeping? Shakspere was not trying to control his melancholy. When he needed to do that, Shakspere confronted his melancholy very passionately, and looked it full in the face. Here he needed refreshment, a sunlight tempered by forest boughs, a breeze upon his forehead, a stream murmuring in his ears.

MAX BEERBOHM

At His Majesty's Theatre

October 12, 1907

"Jolly" is surely the right epithet for Mr. Oscar Asche's
production of *As You Like It;* and I think one might, without risk of hyperbole, strengthen that epithet by the adverb
"awfully." Yes, it is an awfully jolly affair, compact of good
will and hard work and "go" and "snap" and "ginger."
There is no shirking, no fumbling. Sharp's the word, and
there isn't a dull moment. The whole thing is on a level with
Mr. Asche's production of *The Taming of the Shrew*. But
that play is not, one must confess, on a level with *As You
Like It*. It is a capital farce, straightforward, full-blooded.
But it is not, does not set out to be, a masterpiece of poetry.
In *As You Like It* we have a delicate fantasy into which
Shakespeare breathed the very soul of spring. No other play
is so fragrant, through and through, with young lyrical
beauty. It is less like a play than like a lyric that has been
miraculously prolonged to the length of a play without
losing its airiness and its enchantment. If butterflies were
gregarious, one would liken *As You Like It* to a swarm of

From *Around Theatres* by Max Beerbohm. New York: Alfred A. Knopf,
Inc., 1930; London: Rupert Hart-Davis, Ltd., 1953; New York: Simon &
Schuster, Inc., 1954. Copyright 1930 by Max Beerbohm. Reprinted by per-
mission of Rupert Hart-Davis, Ltd.

butterflies all a-wing. I think it is rather a play for the reader's imagination than for the spectator's eyes and ears. What actual Rosalind, what actual Arden, could compete with the lady and the forest conjured up for us by the music of Shakespeare's words? Ah, let the butterflies hover in our imagination. Do not catch them for us. But, if catch them you will, be very tender with them. Rub off as little as you can of the bloom on their wings. As you are strong, be merciful.

Mr. Asche is strong, and I am sure he has meant to be merciful. Arden, as shown under his auspices, is a very beautiful place. But it is not, like Shakespeare's Arden, an enchanted place. It is a "lovely spot." One feels that it is mentioned by Baedeker, and reproduced in color on picture post cards. I see the knickerbockered tourist buying a pack of these bright missives at the village shop, and sending them off right and left to his best friends, with stylographic inscriptions: "This is where I am," "Glorious weather," "What's the matter with Arden?" and the like. I think it a pity that Mr. Ricketts, who designed the scenery for *Attila*, was not recalled to insinuate something of fantasy and mystery into the sterling naturalism of Mr. Harker's work. To explain why I think so, let me submit an hypothesis. You are a young man, desperately in love with a young woman. Circumstances force you to betake yourself to a forest. There you meet the young woman in a suit of masculine clothes. But you have not the faintest suspicion that it is she. You take her for a sympathetic gentleman, and confide to her the sorrow that is at your heart. You see her quite often, but never with an inkling of her identity. What think you of the hypothesis? You say it is a ludicrous one. Just so; and not less ludicrous seems the story of Rosalind and Orlando when it is enacted against a background that challenges, and successfully challenges, stark reality. Rosalind, we then feel, ought to be wearing a false beard and blue spectacles, and to be assuming a deep bass voice, in order to make the play verisimilar. Things have come to a pretty pass when we bother our heads about verisimilitude for such a dream as *As You Like It*. As I have suggested, not the greatest genius in design could give us an Arden so good as the Arden dimly conceived by us when we read the play. But it would not be difficult to get an Arden better than Mr. Harker's. I am not one of those who think that the only possible backgrounds to poetic plays are of the highly conventionalized type inaugurated by Mr. Craig and adapted by Mr. Ricketts. But assuredly Nature must not be slavishly reproduced, as by Mr. Harker it is.

Again, I am not one of those who would have dramatic expression, in poetic plays, utterly subordinated to the rhythm of the verse. I do not ask for monotonous chanting. But I think it essential that the rhythm of the verse should be recognizably preserved for us. And this can be done without any sacrifice of the verse's meaning. The greater part of *As You Like It* is in prose; and Shakespeare's prose has a rhythm as important, in its way, as the rhythm of his verse. To neither of these rhythms is enough importance attached by the players in *As You Like It*. Perhaps if they were not munching apples quite so assiduously, the verse and the prose would stand a better chance. According to the modern doctor, apples are a splendidly wholesome diet, and I should not like the players to risk their health by abstaining. But I suggest that two-thirds or so of the fruit consumed on the stage might with advantage be consumed in the dressing rooms. No doubt it is very natural that Jaques, for example, should be engaged on an apple while he describes the seven ages of man. No doubt the thoughts in that speech are not so profound that their thinker would have had to postpone his meal because of them. But I maintain that the speech is a beautifully written one, very vivid, quaint, and offering scope for great variety in enunciation. It ought to be given for all it is worth, and not in a series of grunts between mouthfuls. Was not Mr. Asche playing Frederick, some years ago, in the Benson company when Mr. Lyall Swete, as Jaques, enunciated the speech so tellingly? I have not forgotten Mr. Swete's performance, and I wonder that Mr. Asche can have managed to put it so completely out of his mind. Mr. Swete's personality was, of course, not incongruous with that of "Monsieur Melancholy"; and Mr. Asche's decidedly is. However sympathetically Mr. Asche might enter into the character, Nature would prevent him

from seeming very like Jaques. Still, he need not seem so
utterly dissimilar as he does. He has a natural dignity,
dignity unlike that of Jaques, but still dignity. Why should
he so carefully discard it throughout the play, to substitute
the manner of a "boer carousing"? Mr. Ainley, as Orlando,
is not undignified, but he seems thoroughly afraid of the
beauty of his part. He avoids lyric rapture as though it were
the plague. There is no nonsense about "the quotidian of
love upon" *him*. One would say that his occupation in the
forest was not to "hang odes on hawthornes and elegies on
brambles," but to find some fellow to challenge his catch-
as-catch-can championship. It is very natural that a handsome actor, who sailed into fame as Paolo, should be
anxious to escape the snares of sugariness and mawkishness
into which handsome actors are apt to slip. And it is quite
true that Orlando was a manly person. But Orlando was
very much in love, lyrically so. And so long as Mr. Ainley
eschews lyric rapture, he will not be Orlando. Miss Lily
Brayton, as Rosalind, pays more attention than anyone else
(except Mr. Brydone, as Adam) to the cadences of the verse
and prose; and gives a very clever, mettlesome performance,
somewhat lacking in softness. Mr. Courtice Pounds is
amusingly unctuous, yet light, as Touchstone. And I suppose
that if I were an Elizabethan in the cockpit, Miss Caldwell's
Audrey would keep me in fits of laughter. Being what I am,
I wish she would tone her performance down: it is very
much too wantonly ugly. Audrey was a slut, but a slut of
the woodland, not of the gin palace. Mr. Brydone plays
Adam with real imagination, pathos, and sense of beauty.

ARTHUR COLBY SPRAGUE

from *Shakespeare and the Actors*

Early in 1723, Charles Johnson's *Love in a Forest*, a
version of *As You Like It* with interpolated passages from
other Shakespearean plays, especially *A Midsummer Night's
Dream*, was put on at Drury Lane. Only some eighteen
years later was *As You Like It* itself revived. The play
prospered in the years to come, and of course accumulated
traditions. But the oldest of these traditions go back only
to a time long after any recollection of Elizabethan ways
had vanished.

Almost at once we have a physical encounter. "Wilt thou
lay hands on me?" Oliver cries. "Wert thou not my brother,"
says Orlando, "I would not take this hand from thy throat."
Oliver, one is sure, is the first to pass from words to deeds;
but what precisely he does, there is no way of telling. "Going to strike" is written, evidently by some early actor, in a
copy of the 1794 acting edition. Most frequently, Oliver has
"advanced and laid hold of him." In like manner, I have seen
an attempt by Adam to help Oliver to his feet made the
pretext for the latter's "Get you with him, you old dog!"

From *Shakespeare and the Actors* by Arthur Colby Sprague. Cambridge,
Mass.: Harvard University Press; London: Oxford University Press, 1944.
Copyright, 1944, by the President and Fellows of Harvard College. Re-
printed by permission of Harvard University Press.

In 1890, exception was taken to Ada Rehan's "rushing rapidly on the stage with a face all smiles, followed, after an interval sufficient to give the audience time to applaud, by Celia coming on in much the same manner, as if the two ladies were playing at a lively game of hide-and-seek." But leading ladies, like low comedians, have their privileges. Another note concerns Le Beau, who, at the St. James's five years before, carried "a live falcon on his wrist." This bit of antiquarianism worked out badly, for the bird flapped its wings "persistently through all his speeches."[1]

The Duke's guards form a ring. This was sometimes done with ropes and spears, sometimes by the guards kneeling and crossing their spears.[2] Then the wrestling begins. Godfrey Turner, writing in 1883, could remember only two occasions upon which it was done successfully: once at Drury Lane, in Macready's time; once at Sadler's Wells. There "Marston, a Lancashire lad, wrestled superbly, and was as agile as a cat." He

> allowed himself to be caught up by Charles, so as to lean over the wrestler's shoulder, while his own feet, being lifted clear above the ground, were coiled round the giant's firmly planted leg. For a few moments this statuesque position was retained; and then, just as Orlando appeared in utmost peril of being thrown, he suddenly regained his footing, reversed the situation, cross-buttocked Charles, and flung him heavily to earth.

Winter describes in detail Daly's arrangement of the bout. Hobart Bosworth, "who played *Charles*, was a large man of commanding presence, an athlete and a trained wrestler." He brought out "the savage animosity" Charles feels toward his adversary. After hurling Orlando from him twice, he rushed upon him "like a maddened bull." Whereupon, Orlando,

> stepping suddenly forward . . . whirled upon his heel, reaching over his own shoulder, grasped *Charles* about the neck, and, using as an aid the momentum of that swiftly rushing attack, heaved his body aloft and seemed to dash it upon

192 ARTHUR COLBY SPRAGUE

the ground, with killing force. The feat was, in reality, performed by Bosworth, using *Orlando's* shoulder to pivot upon.

Benson "in his earlier days . . . would lift Oscar Asche, even then no light weight, and throw him clear over his head."[3]
After the defeat of the wrestler come these speeches:

> *Duke.* How dost thou, Charles?
> *Le Beau.* He cannot speak, my lord.
> *Duke.* Bear him away.

But as early as 1774 (when Bell's edition appeared), Touchstone had appropriated Le Beau's line, and he continued in possession of it for more than a century. He even gagged it, in course of time, so that it became "*He says* he cannot speak, my lord."[4] Likewise, he took charge of the removal of Charles's body—and in one instance seems actually to have dragged it off himself.[5] Usually, however, following Kemble's direction (1810), the guards have carried away Charles, with Touchstone going, or rather, strutting before. In James Lewis's copy, the comedian wrote at "He cannot speak, my lord:"—"Puts End of Staff on Chas breast &c."

Rosalind rewards Orlando by hanging a chain about his neck. Helen Faucit stealthily kissed the chain in doing so. Mary Anderson, at Stratford in 1885, approached Orlando carrying a victor's wreath as well as her own chain, and, as she pressed the chain endearingly into his hand, Orlando let the wreath "drop unheeded to the ground."[6] One further variation comes from the so-called "William Warren Edition," based on Julia Marlowe's promptbook, where Orlando goes out at the end of the scene, "*kissing cross on chain.*"

A single note must suffice for the next three scenes. When Celia pleads with her father (I.iii.67), Julia Marlowe's Rosalind "*goes to bench and sits, weeping.*" Rosalind must do something here—or do nothing very well. But the actress was criticized for abandoning "herself to such a prone state of sobbing as she did, lying prostrate . . . after the tyrannical Duke's stumping exit up the terrace-steps." She might have "taken her banishment with no less apprehension but with less collapse."[7]

Act II, Scene 3, begins with Adam saying "Who's there?" and presently he warns Orlando not to come "within these doors." Francis Gentleman, in 1770, speaks of the scene's changing "to Oliver's house, Orlando appears knocking at the door, and is answered by Adam." Orlando not implausibly continued to knock on doors for over a century.[8] In two early promptbooks, Adam goes into the house for the gold. Later, he usually carried it about with him in a bag, going in, however, to fetch a staff and other small objects in preparation for his journey.[9]

Rosalind, Celia, and Touchstone find themselves in the Forest of Arden, at the beginning of Scene 4. Rosalind has a boar spear, of course, and should have a cutlass, instead of the little ax she was accustomed to wear at her belt in nineteenth-century performances. Celia often carried a shepherd's crook—and leaned heavily on Touchstone.[10] Touchstone has sometimes, indeed, quite forgotten his place. Thus, Lionel Brough, in 1880, laid Celia's "head on his shoulder, put his arm around her waist," and patted her cheek, as they went out together, at the end of the scene.[11] "Business and then Change Scene" is Buckstone's prompt-note at this point. The word "Business" standing alone can be most tantalizing—but not here! "Rosalind follows Corin off," reads the Howard Athenaeum (Boston) Promptbook, "Touchstone is following slowly when Celia calls. 'Touchstone.' he turns. recollects. goes back for her and they Exit together." The same pleasant bit of byplay turns up in at least three later acting versions.[12]

Daly's treatment of the songs in Scene 5 was justly praised:

> Sung as they were by Amiens half lying on the ground, with his brother exiles stretched on the sward around him ... they fitted naturally into the action. ... As usually given by a gentleman who advances to the footlights and sings not to his companions but across the orchestra to the audience, all the dramatic value of these lyrics is lost.[13]

Next we have Orlando and Adam; and Orlando should

carry Adam off. Not infrequently, however, he has shirked his assignment and merely led the old man away.[14] In the last scene in the act, it may be worth noting that in Lester Wallack's promptbook: "Duke—blesses—repast," just before Orlando rushes in; and "Jaq. Eats" after Orlando has forbidden it—which occasions his "but forbear, I say." At the end, it was usual for Amiens and Jaques to help Adam away, Orlando being now deeply engaged in talk with the Duke.[15]

As for the Seven Ages Speech, the old way was to accompany the "reading" of it with a full display of the actor's powers of mimicry. Darbyshire, in his *Art of the Victorian Stage*, describes a talk he had with Irving after a performance of *As You Like It* at the Prince's Theatre, Manchester, in 1902. " 'If these people are right,' " Irving is quoted as saying,

> "how terribly wrong we must have been; who ever heard of or saw Jacques on a rustic stool at a table, from which he gave the seven age speech, and never rose from it, not even on the delivery of the final line." . . . I reminded Sir Henry . . . that he gave the "To be or not to be" speech from an arm chair.

Oscar Asche was to carry informality a step further, and munch an apple during the delivery of the lines—a feat which took, he observes, much rehearsing.[16]

Upon his entrance in the second scene in Act III, Orlando certainly hangs his verses on a tree—or, in Elizabethan performances, on one of "the pillars of the heavens"—and the natural sequence is for Rosalind, when she appears, to find these verses rather than bring others with her. So, at any rate, she does in *Love in a Forest* and in most of the later acting editions.[17] Winter, in a characteristic effusion, describes Ada Rehan's entrance:

> When she dashed through the trees of Arden, snatching the verses of Orlando from their boughs, and cast herself at the foot of a great elm, to read those fond messages . . . her whole person, in its graceful abandonment of posture,

seemed to express an ecstasy of happy vitality and of victorious delight; her hands that held the written scrolls trembled with eager, tumultuous, and grateful joy.[18]

Mary Anderson had entered singing and sauntering, continued to sing negligently after she saw Orlando's poem, then stopped singing as she read it. It may be added that Ben Greet's Touchstone, in 1896, was pounced upon by Mr. Bernard Shaw for picking up and reading—as if they were still another of Orlando's compositions—"the impromptu burlesque" beginning "If a hart do lack a hind."[19]

Soon afterwards, Celia dismisses Corin and Touchstone. In Daly's version, Touchstone has been impertinently "*looking over her shoulder and reading in dumb show, winking at* Corin." At Celia's "Shepherd, go off a little," Touchstone "*orders* Corin *off with a gesture, when he turns—and is ordered off himself. He goes with comic abruptness, first picking up the paper, which he carries off, reading in dumb show.*" In the "William Warren Edition" when Celia says "Go with him, sirrah," Touchstone "*points to himself inquiringly;* Celia *points* L.; Corin *laughs.*"

Celia names Orlando as the writer of the verses, and Rosalind exclaims, "Alas the day! what shall I do with my doublet and hose?" At this point, the Victorian actress was likely to make a great to-do about her own legs. Mrs. Kendal put "her hands over her face" at "Alas the day," then after a pause crossed to where Celia was sitting and spoke, "half whispering in Celia's ear, 'What shall I do with my doublet and hose?' "[20] To a writer in *Blackwood's* for September 1890, Rosalind's words are merely an expression

of natural embarrassment, suddenly to find that here is the man to whom she has lost her heart, by whom "she would be woo'd, and not unsought be won," and that her man's attire stands in the way of her being so. . . . What can Miss Rehan mean by pulling down her doublet as she speaks the words, as though she would accomplish the impossible feat of hiding her legs under it,—an indelicacy of suggestion at which one can only shudder?

A. B. Walkley, playing "Devil's Advocate," complains that the American actress "made as much fuss as though she had been Susannah surprised by the Elders."[21] On the other hand, W. Graham Robertson writes of Mrs. Langtry that, as Rosalind, she gave "no new readings," spoke her lines

> simply, not chopping them up with "business" or strangling them with "suppressed emotion." . . . In short, she gave Shakespeare a chance. . . . One bit of original business I remember which I have never noticed in another Rosalind. She carefully avoided all vulgar clowning in passages referring to her male attire, but when she spoke the line—"Here, on the skirts of the forest, like fringe on a petticoat," she put out her hand with a perfectly natural gesture to pick up her own petticoat, and finding none, paused awkwardly for half a second.[22]

Meanwhile, Jaques and Orlando have entered, and Rosalind has overheard their talk (Ada Rehan could not forbear clapping her hands "vivaciously, though softly, on hearing Orlando's sentiments"). On the departure of "Monsieur Melancholy," the lover may well begin to "mar trees" once more[23]—and Rosalind will attract his attention with difficulty. Helen Faucit was praised for the manner in which she hugged Orlando's verses to her heart, as she talked with Orlando himself about them; and Mary Anderson used very similar business.[24]

On January 6, 1825, *The Edinburgh Dramatic Review*, in commenting upon a performance at the Theatre Royal the night before, praises the Audrey of Mrs. Nicol as

> most rich and felicitous. There was perhaps an anachronism in her munching a turnip; but, to be sure, since Shakspeare treated the forest of *Ardennes* with a lion, a little thing like this may be overlooked; *argale*, we were very much pleased with the effect of the turnip.

From the terms used, it is conceivable that the eating of turnips was new to Audrey, in Edinburgh, at any rate, but once she had begun it was long indeed before she tired of them. In the Boston, Howard Athenaeum Promptbook, of

1852, she is furnished at her entrance—arm in arm with Touchstone—with a "clasp knife turnip and large sunflower." At "Well, the gods give us joy," Cumberland's old direction, "*Capers clumsily up the Stage*," is kept, with the added note: "during this Sc Audrey produces a knife & turnip and after peeling it cuts and eats it occasionally offering Touchstone a piece." And at the end: "He takes her arm and they go up and off R3E she dancing and singing 'The gods give us joy &c.' "[25]

The natural affinity existing between Audrey and her turnip is made the subject of some highly curious reflections by Arthur Matthison in his essay, "Theatrical Properties," in *The Era Almanack* for 1882. "Woe to the day for *As You Like It*," he exclaims, "should Audrey venture on alone, or the turnip in a rash moment rush on its fate discoupled from its Audrey." That day was fast approaching. In 1885, when Mary Anderson played Rosalind at Stratford, Audrey, indeed, not only "gnawed" a turnip, but one which "had been plucked near Anne Hathaway's cottage." But Marion Lea, Mrs. Langtry's Audrey in 1890, spoke "Is it honest in deed and word? Is it a true thing?" simply and well, instead of drawling it "with a leer between two bites at a property turnip." And in Isabel Irving's performance with the Daly Company, "for the first time *Audrey* became a possible mate for *Touchstone*, and no mere turnip-munching, cherry-cheeked clod."[26] Daly's acting edition has her in the course of devouring "*a huge turnip*," early in the scene. "Touchstone, *annoyed, snatches it and throws it off*." Then she produces a succession of apples! In the "William Warren Edition" these apples again figure—but there is no turnip.

The scene of the mock marriage, early in Act IV, needs taste and tact if it is to be right. I fancy we should have liked the Orlando of Forbes-Robertson, which puzzled and somewhat offended *The Athenaeum* (October 27, 1888):

What can we make of an Orlando who accepts his mistress's challenge to woo her in her disguise as a Girton graduate might accept a proposal to analyze a case of modern witchcraft; who declines, until compelled, to kiss the small gloved hand?

But we read, too, of Adelaide Neilson that "her utterance of the simple words 'Woo me! woo me!' to Orlando, as her cheek was laid upon his shoulder, and her arm stole coyly about his neck, was sweet as a blackbird's call to his mate." And when all allowance has been made for the sentimentality of the description, the action described still seems wrong. In Fanny Davenport's pomptbook, when Rosalind, hearing that Orlando must be away from her until two o'clock, says " 'Tis but one cast away, and so, come death!" she "cries— Orlando taps her on shoulder—she turns laughing—he retreats"; and on his exit, "Ros. coughs—Orlando reenters— kisses her hand and then runs off." Both bits of business found their way into later acting texts.[27]

As for the episode of Rosalind's fainting near the end of the act, it is enough to note that Oliver had better not catch her, or do more than Celia asks him to do, take her by the arm; that he has sometimes slapped "Ganymede" cheerfully on the back, at "take a good heart and counterfeit to be a man"; and that Rosalind has occasionally indulged in a second (pretended) swoon, at "I pray you tell your brother how well I counterfeited. Heigh-ho!" Fanny Davenport, indeed, to get a strong curtain, closed with: "Ros. faints on bank C. Oliver on R. & Celia on L. of bank. . . . Picture."[28]

In the first scene in Act v, Touchstone has been accustomed to follow William about, threateningly, during the speech beginning "He, sir, that must marry this woman," the clown shrinking before him.[29]

In the concluding scene, Robson's Touchstone, at Cincinnati in 1885, is described with relish by Frederick Warde: "He strutted, he crowed, and to continue the simile, he flapped his wings with the triumphant satisfaction of a barnyard rooster."[30] "Salutation and greeting to you all," says Touchstone—and James Lewis wrote against the words, in his copy of *As You Like It*, "bows. Makes Audrey curtsy &c." What she does to occasion his reproving, "Bear your body more seeming, Audrey" is for the actress to decide. I have seen her hanging upon Touchstone here.[31] Or perhaps she merely stands in some ungainly posture gaping at the courtiers? The stage direction in Cumberland's edition,

"*Audrey,* L. *assumes a stiff and formal air,*" presupposes some such display of loutishness. On the other hand, the observant, if censorious author of "'*As You Like It*' à l'Américaine," in *Blackwood's* for September 1890, after remarking that the words are a hint to Audrey "not to slouch in country fashion before the great folks," is shocked to find that in Daly's production Touchstone here "turned round to Audrey, who is flirting with two courtiers (*proh pudor!*) and with these words swings her round to him with the roughness of an angry boor."[32]

Rosalind's final entrance, in early nineteenth-century editions, is slightly postponed. Hymen delivers his first stanza, then "*goes to the Top of the Stage, brings forward* Rosalind, *and presents her to the* Duke." Anna Seward, in a letter dated July 20, 1786, describes Mrs. Siddons at this moment in the play:

> One of those rays of exquisite and original discrimination, which her genius so perpetually elicits, shone out on her first rushing upon the stage in her own resumed person and dress; when she bent her knee to her father, the Duke, and said—
>
> "To you I give myself—for I am yours";
>
> and when, falling into Orlando's arms, she repeated the same words,—
>
> "To *you* I give myself—for I am *yours!*" . . .
>
> The tender joy of filial love was in the first [line]; the whole soul of enamoured transport in the second.

A century and more later, Julia Arthur was inspired to bring upon the stage "a lot of monks in an attempt to make the all-round marriage at the end realistic and spectacular." Norman Hapgood, who liked her production, calls this the "only impertinence" in it.[33]

Bibliographical Notes

PROMPTBOOKS

(a) ? Eighteenth Century Promptbook (N. Y. P.).
[Bell ed. annotated in old hand. What looks like "Carvers Gar:" (*sc.* "Garden") at beginning of I, 1—cf. Robert Carver, the scene painter, died 1791. Very few properties—e. g., a single "gilt chair" in I, 2.]

(b) Marked Copy of 1794 acting edition (Harvard).
[Old hand and faded ink. An actor's name (?) against "Oliver," p. 63, but this is in pencil and perhaps later, as is "write this myself," p. 51.]

(c) Aberdeen 1806 Promptbook (N. Y. P.).
[1775 ed. inscribed "Aberdeen Jany 1806."]

(d) "Prompt Book Theatres Sheffield & Doncaster. Novr 1834" (N. Y. P.).
[The "Sheffield &" are added, as if originally used at Doncaster. Later printed casts inserted, of Birmingham (1847) and Boston (1856) performances.]

(e) "Prompt Copy Marked & Corrected by Robert Jones Stage Manager Howard Athenaeum Boston 1852" (N. Y. P.).
[Jones became stage manager at the opening of the season of 1852–53 when *As You Like It* was played with Miss Kimberly as Rosalind, Oct. 4 and 15—Van Lennep.]

(f) Buckstone's Haymarket 1867 Inscribed Promptbook (A. C. S.).
[Stage directions in Lacy's Acting Edition almost invariably retained. Some penciled additions refer to Manchester performances.]

(g) Lester Wallack's Promptbook (N. Y. P.).
[Penciled cast that of the important revival Sept. 30, 1880—see Odell, XI, 220. Twice described as "Wallack's Copy."]

(h) James L. Carhart's Marked Copy (Harvard).
[Ed. "As Played by Mrs. Langtry," New York and London, c. 1883, with printed cast including Carhart as Duke. This part and that of Adam are marked.]

(i) Fanny Davenport's 1886 Promptbook (Harvard).

[Handwriting, cuts, business, etc. identify it with "j" and the Fanny Davenport—J. H. Barnes tour of 1886–87. See *Much Ado* "f."]

(j) Wilton Lackaye's Marked Copy (Harvard).
["Property of Miss Davenport," and "Oliver" (in pencil, "Lackaye") on cover. Lackaye appeared with Miss Davenport on 1886–87 tour. Two other marked copies are for "Phoebe" and "Banished Duke."]

(k) James Lewis's Marked Copy (Harvard).
["French's Standard Drama" ed. "James Lewis" on wrapper, and the part of Touchstone marked throughout. He played it, under Daly, in 1889.]

The "William Warren Edition," Boston [1907], is "based upon the Prompt Book of Miss Julia Marlowe."

Notes

[[Professor Sprague has the following introduction to his notes. "In order to cut down the number of notes as much as possible, references to authorities have frequently been grouped in sequences corresponding to those of the text, with semicolons used to distinguish one set of references from another. Thus, on page 66 of the text, I have written:

> Mamillius, early in the nineteenth century, was contented with such playthings as a horse and drum. But Ellen Terry, playing the part in Charles Kean's production, drew about a toy cart 'from an actual one, in terra-cotta, preserved in the British Museum.'[232]

Note 232 reads: 'Oxberry's edition; Kean's edition, William Archer, "The Winter's Tale," *The Nineteenth Century*, October 1887, Ellen Terry, *The Story of My Life*, photograph opposite page 12, etc.' Here 'Oxberry's edition' is my authority for the early toys; whereas 'Kean's edition' and the other two citations refer to Ellen Terry's go-cart."
Material in double brackets has been added by editor.]]

1. "*As You Like It* à l'Américaine," *Blackwood's*, September 1890; *Dramatic Review*, February 1, 1885.

2. Daly's acting edition (1890); Lester Wallack's promptbook, "William Warren Edition."

3. "Pittite Memories," *The Theatre*, November 1, 1883; [[William Winter]], *Shakespeare on the Stage*, Second Series [[New York, 1915]], pp. 278 ff.; [[Gordon]] Crosse, *Fifty Years of Shakespearean Playgoing* [[London, 1941]], 31. For an ingenious modern expedient for avoiding the danger of ridicule here, see Harcourt Williams, *Four Years at the Old Vic*, London [1935], pp. 189, 190.

4. He spoke the line as recently as 1886 (Lackaye's Marked Copy). For the gag, see [[Frederick]] Warde, *The Fools of Shakespeare* [[New York, 1913]], 48.

5. 1794 Marked Copy.

6. [Margaret Stokes,] "Helen Faucit," *Blackwood's*, December 1885, cf. Helen Faucit, *On Some of Shakespeare's Female Characters*, Edinburgh and London, 1891, p. 244; Winter, *Shakespeare on the Stage*, Second Series, p. 296.

7. "William Warren Edition"; C[harlotte] P[orter], in *Poet-Lore*, I (1889), p. 142.

8. *The Dramatic Censor*, I, 465. James Carhart's marked copy of Mrs. Langtry's acting edition (c. 1883) still has the knocking. It is absent in the Daly and "William Warren" editions.

9. Eighteenth Century (?) Promptbook in New York Public Library, Sheffield and Doncaster Promptbook; Howard Athenaeum and Wallack Promptbooks, Carhart's Marked Copy.

10. Cf. I, 3, 119, and R. G. White, *Studies in Shakespeare*, Boston and New York, 1886, p. 245; and, for the crook, Howard Athenaeum and other promptbooks, Daly's edition.

11. *The Theatre*, April 1, 1880, *Athenaeum*, March 6, 1880.

12. Wallack and Fanny Davenport Promptbooks, Daly's edition.

13. "*As You Like It* à l'Américaine," *Blackwood's*, September 1890.

14. As, e.g., in *Love in a Forest*, where, though Orlando still says, "Come I will bear thee to some Shelter," he goes out, and later returns, merely "*leading* Adam."

15. "Eighteenth Century," Howard Athenaeum, and Wallack Promptbooks.

16. E.g., *The Monthly Mirror*, N.S., viii (1810), p. 466, *Shakespeariana*, V (1888), p. 223, J. R. Towse, *Sixty Years of the Theater*, New York and London, 1916, p. 113; [[A.]] Darbyshire [[*The Art of the Victorian Stage*, London and Manchester, 1907]], 77, 78; Max Beerbohm, *Around Theatres*, New York, 1930, II, 616, Oscar Asche *His Life*, London [1929], p. 119. At "Even in the cannon's mouth . . . " Daly's edition has the listeners "nod to each other."

17. Exceptions are Bell's and the "William Warren" editions. Dover Wilson has Rosalind find the verses. Kittredge has her bring them.

18. *Shadows of the Stage*, Second Series, New York, 1893 (1898), p. 251, repeated in his *Wallet of Time*, II, 155. Ada Rehan carried one paper with her and took another from the tree (Daly's edition).

19. *Dramatic Review*, September 5, 1885, Winter, *Shakespeare on the Stage*, Second Series, p. 299; *Our Theatres in the Nineties*, II, 122.

20. *The Dramatic Review*, February 1, 1885.

21. *Playhouse Impressions*, London, 1892, p. 32, Clement Scott, *Thirty Years at the Play and Dramatic Table Talk*, London [1891], p. 216. See also, *The Athenaeum*, March 4, 1871 (on Mrs. Rousby), and the Daly and "William Warren" editions.

22. *Life Was Worth Living*, New York and London [1931], p. 71.

23. *Saturday Review*, July 26, 1890, "*As You Like It* à l'Américaine"; Wallack's promptbook, cf. Daly and "William Warren" editions.

24. [[Joseph]] Knight, *Theatrical Notes* [[London, 1893]], 17; Winter, *Shakespeare on the Stage*, Second Series, pp. 299, 300.

25. Cumberland's *British Theatre* (1826). Wallack's promptbook also gives her the sunflower, knife, and turnip. The sunflower is wanting in Fanny Davenport's promptbook.

26. Mary Anderson, *A Few Memories*, New York, 1896, p. 197; W. G. Robertson, *Life Was Worth Living*, 72; *The Theatre*, February 1, 1894. See also Dutton Cook, *Nights at the Play*, 2 vols., London, 1883, I, 247, and *The Theatre*, May 1, 1894. Much later, Elizabeth Fagan always ate "a big raw turnip," as Audrey with Benson's Company (*From the Wings*, London, etc. [1922,] p. 73).

27. L. Clarke Davis, "Gossip about Actors," *The Galaxy*, May 1873; "William Warren Edition," cf. *Poet-Lore*, I (1889), p. 144; Daly's edition. For the deer carried across the stage at many Stratford performances, in IV, 2, see C. E. Flower in [[*As You Like It*]], "Memorial Theatre Edition" [[London, 1885]], p. vi.

28. Mary Anderson's acting edition, New York, c. 1885, "William Warren Edition," cf. "*As You Like It* à l'Américaine"; Davenport Promptbook, Daly and "William Warren" editions; *Monthly Mirror*, XV (1803), p. 276, Daly's edition.

29. Lacy's Acting Edition (c. 1842), Howard Athenaeum Promptbook, etc.

30. *The Fools of Shakespeare*, 67, 68.

31. As reproduced in Daly's edition, the accompanying photograph [[in Sprague]] of Lewis and Isabel Irving has for text the words under discussion.

32. Cf. C. D., "Audrey—A Country Wench," in *The Theatre*, May 1, 1894. Later in the scene, Daly's edition has "Touchstone *seeing* Jaques de Bois, *seizes* Audrey, *puts her arm in his, and drags her up the stage.*"

33. Mrs. Inchbald's *British Theatre* (1808), Cumberland, etc.; Hesketh Pearson (ed.), *The Swan of Lichfield*, New York, 1937, pp. 91, 92; Hapgood, *The Stage in America* [[New York, 1901]], 169.

ROBERT H. GOLDSMITH

Touchstone in Arcadia

"Thou speak'st wiser than thou art ware of" (*A.Y.L.I.* II.iv.55), comments Rosalind of Touchstone, and the fool feeds the complacent superiority of the noble lady by agreeing with her. Jaques, in commending Touchstone to the Duke, gloats over his discovery, "He's as good at anything, and yet a fool" (V.iv.104). This is as far as Jaques may go in magnanimity. Earlier in the play, Rosalind hails the jester as "Nature's natural the cutter-off of Nature's wit" (I.ii.47). And Celia welcomes him with even less grace, for, says she, "always the dullness of the fool is the whetstone of the wits" (I.ii.52). Except for the Duke, whose penetrating comments on the witty fool are well known, the noble characters in the play seem to regard Touchstone as a natural or dull fool who sometimes serves to sharpen the wits of his betters. Certain otherwise astute critics seem to have been misled by these comments upon the fool. Tolman finds that Shakespeare's treatment of Touchstone's character is "somewhat wavering and uncertain."[1] Furness notes an inconsistency

From *Wise Fools in Shakespeare* by Robert H. Goldsmith. East Lansing, Michigan: Michigan State University Press, 1955. Copyright 1955 Michigan State University Press. Reprinted by permission of the author and the publisher.

between the "simpleton" of the First Act and the wise, satirical fool of Act Five. "Are there not here two separate characters?" he asks.[2]

As for any real or apparent inconsistencies in Touchstone's characterization, they may be explained by reference to certain facts of stage history. If Shakespeare had Will Kempe in mind for the part when he began to write *As You Like It*, he undoubtedly altered the role in some important respects to fit the temper of Robert Armin, the new clown who joined the Chamberlain's Men sometime in 1600.[3] Kempe had acted the roles of such louts as Dogberry and Peter, whereas Armin shows himself a connoisseur of court fools in his book *Foole upon Foole, or Six Sortes of Sottes* (1600). There is another explanation for any discrepancy between the "roynish clown" of Act I and the clever jester of the remainder of the play. It may be that Touchstone disguises his wits when at Frederick's court out of prudent regard for the usurper's authority. Recent bitter experience has taught us over again that tyrants always regard intelligence with suspicion. This theory would also explain Touchstone's freer and happier tongue when he has escaped to the forest.

The attitude of genial condescension which Rosalind and others express was implicit in the relationship of master to fool from the beginning. Fools served a double function: to entertain their masters and mistresses and at the same time to minister to their sense of self-importance. Frequently the fool criticized his lord but always from behind a cloak of assumed inferiority. Such were the hierarchical arrangements of medieval and renaissance society. But a mixture of amusement, contempt, and, sometimes, awe often characterized the popular feelings toward the allowed fool. This peculiar and paradoxical status was the price he had to pay for his relative freedom and license to criticize. The wise fool willingly paid the price and enjoyed the paradox. That he not only accepts his role but even revels in it marks Touchstone off from some less wise fools. Rowley's Will Summers, for example, is almost childishly vain of his shrewd wits. He is enormously pleased with himself when he sacrifices Patch to the King's displeasure and thereby saves himself from a

beating. Touchstone apparently acquiesces when Jaques
introduces him to the Duke as "the motley-minded gentleman" (V.iv.41), whereas Feste in jesting with Olivia insists:
"I wear not motley in my brain" (*Twel*. I.v.63). Touchstone
never pushes his' point or insists unduly on his own good
sense. After Rosalind has berated him as a dull fool and has
sharpened her metaphorical wit upon him, Touchstone
answers simply, "You have said; but whether wisely or no,
let the forest judge" (III.ii.121).

Touchstone exercises his wit through parody, and parody
is, of course, the sworn enemy of the didactic. The Duke
may read his pretty sermons in stones and running brooks,
Jaques may moralize upon the stricken deer, and Orlando
pin his lovesick poems to every tree, but the fool looks on
and laughingly mimics them. He even triumphs over the
robust wit of Rosalind by his burlesque wooing and
wedding of Audrey. Like the wise fool that he is, Touchstone alters his manner to fit the quality and the mood of
the persons on whom he jests. With his mistress and Rosalind, he is properly subservient except for the occasional
impertinence that breaks through. His gross parody of
Orlando's lyrics is amusing and apt for the most part. But
one can hardly blame a lady for resenting a poem which
likens her to a hind or a cat in heat or to a whore carted
through the streets of London (III.ii.101).[4] However, Touchstone's sallies are usually less crude and direct, and they
are further softened by a touch of self-mockery. Silvius'
recital of his unrequited love for Phebe arouses differing
responses in Rosalind and in Touchstone:

Ros. Jove, Jove! this shepherd's passion
  Is much upon my fashion.

Touch. And mine, but it grows something stale with me. [II.iv.58]

The gentleman in motley pretends to being on terms of
equality with Jaques. Whenever the two meet, Touchstone
observes the elaborate punctilios of courtesy between
Elizabethan gentlemen, with just a hint of patronizing

Jaques who has condescended to him: "Good even, good Master What-ye-call't. How do you, sir? You are very well met. Goddild you for your last company. I am very glad to see you. Even a toy in hand here, sir. Nay, pray be cover'd" (III.iii.70). Dr. Thümmel, in contrasting Touchstone with Feste, finds that the earlier fool is something of a parvenu courtier and that his courtesy is an affectation.[5] This seems to be a misreading of Touchstone's intentions, for he is obviously parodying courtly manners here just as he later makes fun of the etiquette of the duello.[6] To the Duke, who justly appreciates his intelligence, Touchstone is properly deferential and courteous. There is the accent of genuine humility in his reply to the Duke's praise:

Duke. S. By my faith, he is very swift and sententious.

Touch. According to the fool's bolt, sir, and such dulcet diseases.
[V.iv.63]

By recalling the old proverb, "a fool's bolt is soon shot," he shows that he takes himself no more seriously than he ought to.

But when he encounters the shepherds and rustics, Touchstone adopts a tone as patronizing as Jaques and the ladies take toward him. Corin must smart a little under the fool's assumed superiority:

Cor. You have too courtly a wit for me. I'll rest.

Touch. Wilt thou rest damn'd? God help thee, shallow man! God make incision in thee, thou art raw! [III.ii.69]

In saluting the clown William, he is a trifle more condescending than in his manner of greeting Jaques:

Touch. Good ev'n, gentle friend. Cover thy head, cover thy head. Nay, prithee be cover'd. How old are you, friend?

Will. Five-and-twenty, sir.

Touch. A ripe age. Is thy name William?

Will. William, sir.

Touch. A fair name. Wast born i' th' forest here?

Will. Ay, sir, I thank God.

Touch. "Thank God." A good answer.   [V.i.16]

Suddenly abandoning his friendly tone toward the lout, Touchstone bursts forth with a torrent of turgid and unprovoked abuse: "I will deal in poison with thee, or in bastinado, or in steel. I will bandy with thee in faction; I will o'errun thee with policy; I will kill thee a hundred and fifty ways. Therefore tremble and depart" (V.i.53). His bluster, of course, is not serious, and the storm dies as quickly as it arises. The furious fustian is not so much directed at poor William, who happens to lie in its path, as it is at poetasters like Marston who use this sort of bombast in all seriousness.[7]

While Touchstone's wit takes the form of parody, his temper is essentially realistic. He is the Vekke keeping watch in the Garden of the Rose, or Pandarus serving at the Court of Love. An even closer analogy to Touchstone in the Forest of Arden would be the garrulous nurse in *Romeo and Juliet*. Like the nurse and like Pandarus, Touchstone acts as a sort of comic catalyst in the golden world. Arden, however, is no less golden for Touchstone's presence there; on the contrary, it becomes infinitely more desirable and more comfortable than the gilt and tinsel world of conventional pastoral. With Touchstone one may sit down in Arden and scratch one's back or rub one's tired feet:

Ros. O Jupiter, how weary are my spirits!

Touch. I care not for my spirits, if my legs were not weary. [II.iv.1]

Touchstone is the critic inside the play. As C. S. Lewis has observed of the medieval dream-allegory: "Above all it protects itself against the laughter of the vulgar—that is, of all of us in certain moods—by allowing laughter and cynicism their place *inside* the poem. . . . In the same way, the comic figures in a medieval love poem are a cautionary

concession—a libation made to the god of lewd laughter. . ."[8] Touchstone's presence within the pastoral romance
is a concession to our sense of comic realism and protects
the play from corrosive criticism.

Realism surely borders on the grotesque in Touchstone's
wooing of Audrey. What romantic lover—what lover, for
that matter—would exclaim over his loved one, "Well,
praised be the gods for thy foulness! Sluttishness may come
hereafter" (III.iii.38)? Who would allude to his bride-to-be
as "A poor virgin, sir, an ill-favor'd thing, sir, but mine
own" (V.iv.58)? Who, but Touchstone? And the court fool
comes pressing in "amongst the rest of the country copulatives, to swear and to fórswear, according as marriage binds
and blood breaks" (V.iv.56). Do these speeches of the fool
show him to be a cynic, disillusioned with love and the
dream of fair ladies? Hardly! Touchstone is a genial
humorist, not a caustic critic.[9] True, he laughs good-
naturedly at the silly extravagances and conventions of
pastoral love, but at the same time he shows a wholesome
regard for the realities of marriage: "As the ox has his bow,
sir, the horse his curb and the falcon her bells, so man hath
his desires; and as pigeons bill, so wedlock would be nibbling" (III.iii.76). Nature must have her due. And who
knows this truth better than the court fool turned rustic
philosopher?

Whether we regard Touchstone as a grotesque philosopher
or as the realistic *punctum indifferens* of the play, we must
grant his wisdom. John Palmer has neatly summed up the
quality of the fool's wisdom in a sentence: "He will see
things as they are but without malice."[10] However, Mr.
Palmer's statement needs a slight emendation so that it
will read: "He will see things as they are *in nature* but without malice." For Touchstone is a natural philosopher and
realist. He is witty and penetrating enough to see physical
love behind the illusory mask of the pastoral lovers and to
note the peevishness and self-pity behind Jaques' affected
melancholy. Although he ironically joins the merry dance
to the altar at the end of the play, Touchstone is too hard-
headed to live happily in the forest of romance. This wise

fool is a critic, and the astringency of his wit is both his strongest asset and his chief liability. His mocking humor enables us to laugh at pretense and vulgar folly, but it cannot open our eyes to the true if transitory loveliness of the Arcadian dream. This unearthly charm is beyond the ken of the witty but worldly fool. While it is true that Shakespeare's conception of the wise fool grew and reached a finer flowering in the later plays, it is equally true that Touchstone is a wise and thoroughly witty fool.

Notes

1. *Falstaff and Other Shakespearean Topics* (New York, 1925), p. 75.

2. *As You Like It*, New Variorum ed. (Philadelphia, 1890), p. 309.

3. T. W. Baldwin, in "Shakespeare's Jester," *MLN*, XXXIX (1924), 447–55, presents convincing evidence for dating Armin's joining the Chamberlain's Men in 1600, after publication of his *Quips Upon Questions*. Chambers, in *Eliz. Stage*, II, 300, accepts the *Quips* as Armin's but somewhat inconsistently dates Armin's entry into Shakespeare's company 1599, because he describes himself on the title page of the first edition of *Quips* as "Clonnico de Curtanio Snuffe."

4. This diminishing or debasing of a thing or a person is known to rhetoricians as meiosis, or the disabler (Puttenham, Bk. III, Ch. xvii). Rosemond Tuve, in *Elizabethan and Metaphysical Imagery* (Chicago, 1947), p. 206, notes the "tempering or astringent effect" of such a figure and its ironical implications.

5. "Ueber Shakespeare's Narren," *Shakespeare Jahrbuch*, IX (Weimar, 1874), p. 104 f.

6. Whether Touchstone's parody on the courtly manner of quarreling specifically lampoons Vincentio Saviolo's *Honor and honorable Quarrels* (1595) or another work, *The Book of Honor and Arms* (1590) does not greatly matter. Through the fool, Shakespeare takes a dig at all such popular handbooks.

7. Cf. Feliche, in *Antonio and Mellida* (III, i, 226), on the fantastic, perfumed gull Castilio: "Honest musk-cod, twill not be so stitched together; take that, and that [striking him], and belie no Ladies love: sweare no more by Jesu: this Madam, that Ladie; hence goe, forsweare the presence, travaile three years to bury this bastinado: avoide, puffe paste, avoide."

8. *The Allegory of Love* (Oxford, 1948), pp. 172, 173.

9. For a contrary opinion, see F. S. Boas, *Shakspere and his Predecessors* (New York, 1896), pp. 339 f.: "Touchstone's wit takes always and with every one a caustic turn. . . . Thus while, like Feste, he has to do with each

of the characters in turn, he notes their special disposition, not to chime in with it, or to gently hint a cure for its defects, but to throw it up in all its worst lights." Such a description would fit Jaques more easily than Touchstone.

10. *Comic Characters of Shakespeare* (London, 1946), p. 36.

HELEN GARDNER

"As You Like It"

As its title declares, this is a play to please all tastes. It is the last play in the world to be solemn over, and there is more than a touch of absurdity in delivering a lecture, particularly on a lovely summer morning, on this radiant blend of fantasy, romance, wit and humor. The play itself provides its own ironic comment on anyone who attempts to speak about it: "You have said; but whether wisely or no, let the forest judge."

For the simple, it provides the stock ingredients of romance: a handsome, well-mannered young hero, the youngest of three brothers, two disguised princesses to be wooed and wed, and a banished, virtuous Duke to be restored to his rightful throne. For the more sophisticated, it propounds, in the manner of the old courtly literary form of the *débat*, a question which is left to us to answer: Is it better to live in the court or the country? "How like you this shepherd's life, Master Touchstone?", asks Corin, and receives a fool's answer: "Truly, shepherd, in respect of itself, it is a good life; but in respect that it is a shepherd's life, it is naught. In respect that it is solitary, I like it very well; but in respect that it is private, it is a very vile life." Whose society would you prefer, Le Beau's or Audrey's?

From *More Talking of Shakespeare*, ed. John Garrett. New York: Theatre Arts Books; London: Longmans, Green & Company, Ltd., 1959. © Longmans, Green and Co. Ltd. and Contributors 1959. Reprinted by permission of the publishers.

Would you rather be gossiped at in the court or gawped at in the country? The play has also the age-old appeal of the pastoral, and in different forms. The pastoral romance of princesses playing at being a shepherd boy and his sister is combined with the pastoral love-eclogue in the wooing of Phoebe, with the burlesque of this in the wooing of Audrey, and with the tradition of the moral eclogue, in which the shepherd is the wise man, in Corin. For the learned and literary this is one of Shakespeare's most allusive plays, uniting old traditions and playing with them lightly. Then there are the songs—the forest is full of music—and there is spectacle: a wrestling match to delight lovers of sport, the procession with the deer, which goes back to old country rituals and folk plays, and finally the masque of Hymen, to end the whole with courtly grace and dignity. This is an image of civility and true society, for Hymen is a god of cities, as Milton knew:

> There let *Hymen* oft appear
> In Saffron robe, with Taper clear,
> And pomp, and feast, and revelry,
> With mask, and antique Pageantry.

The only thing the play may be said to lack, when compared with Shakespeare's other comedies, is broad humor, the humor of gross clowns. William makes only a brief appearance. The absence of clowning may be due to an historic reason, the loss of Kempe, the company's funny man. But if this was the original reason for the absence of pure clowning, Shakespeare has turned necessity to glorious gain and made a play in which cruder humors would be out of place. *As You Like It* is the most refined and exquisite of the comedies, the one which is most consistently played over by a delighted intelligence. It is Shakespeare's most Mozartian comedy.

The basic story is a folk tale. The ultimate sources for the plots of Shakespeare's greatest tragedy and his most un-flawed comedy are stories of the same kind. The tale of the old king who had three daughters, of whom the elder two were wicked and the youngest was good, belongs to the same primitive world of the imagination as the tale of the knight who had three sons, the eldest of whom was wicked and robbed the youngest, who was gallant and good, of his inheritance. The youngest son triumphed, like Jack the Giant Killer, over a strong man, a wrestler, joined a band of outlaws in the forest, became their king, and with the aid of an old servant of his father, the wily Adam Spencer, in the end had his revenge on his brother and got his rights. Lodge retained some traces of the boisterous elements of this old story; but Shakespeare omitted them. His Orlando is no bully, threatening and blustering and breaking down the doors to feast with his boon companions in his brother's house. He is brave enough and quick-tempered; but he is above all gentle. On this simple story Lodge grafted a pastoral romance in his *Rosalynde*. He made the leader of the outlaws a banished Duke, and gave both exiled Duke and tyrant usurper only daughters, as fast friends as their fathers are sworn enemies. The wrestling match takes place at the tyrant's court and is followed by the banishment of Rosalynde and the flight of the two girls to the forest, disguised as shepherd and shepherdess. There the shepherd boy is wooed by the gallant hero, and arouses a passion of lovesickness in a shepherdess who scorns her faithful lover. The repentance of the wicked brother and his flight to the forest provide the necessary partner for the tyrant's good daughter, and all ends happily with marriages and the restoration of the good Duke. Shakespeare added virtually nothing to the plot of Lodge's novel. There is no comedy in which, in one sense, he invents so little. He made the two Dukes into brothers. Just as in *King Lear* he put together two stories of good and unkind children, so here he gives us two examples of a brother's unkindness. This adds to the fairy-tale flavor of the plot, because it turns the usurping Duke into a wicked uncle. But if he invents no incidents, he leaves out a good deal. Besides omitting the blusterings of Rosader (Orlando), he leaves out a final battle and the death in battle of the usurping Duke, preferring to have him converted offstage by a chance meeting with a convenient and persuasive hermit. In the same way he handles very cursorily the repentance of the wicked brother and his good fortune in love. In Lodge's story, the villain is cast into prison by the tyrant who covets his estates. In prison he repents, and it is as a penitent that he arrives in the forest. Shakespeare also omits the incident of the attack on Ganymede and Aliena by robbers, in which Rosader is overpowered and wounded and Saladyne (Oliver) comes to the rescue and drives off the assailants. As has often been pointed out, this is both a proof of the genuineness of his repentance and a reason, which many critics of the play have felt the want of, for Celia's falling in love. Maidens naturally fall in love with brave young men who rescue them. But Shakespeare needs to find no "reasons for loving" in this play in which a dead shepherd's saw is quoted as a word of truth: "Whoever lov'd that lov'd not at first sight." He has far too much other business in hand at the center and heart of his play to find time for mere exciting incidents. He stripped Lodge's plot down to the bare bones, using it as a kind of frame, and created no subplot of his own. But he added four characters. Jaques, the philosopher, bears the same name as the middle son of Sir Rowland de Boys— the one whom Oliver kept at his books—who does not appear in the play until he turns up casually at the end as a messenger. It seems possible that the melancholy Jaques began as this middle son and that his melancholy was in origin a scholar's melancholy. If so, the character changed as it developed, and by the time that Shakespeare had fully conceived his cynical spectator he must have realized that he could not be kin to Oliver and Orlando. The born solitary must have no family: Jaques seems the quintessential only child. To balance Jaques, as another kind of commentator, we are given Touchstone, critic and parodist of love and lovers and of court and courtiers. And, to make up the full consort of pairs to be mated, Shakespeare invented two rustic lovers, William and Audrey, dumb yokel and sluttish goat-girl. These additional characters add nothing at all to the story. If you were to tell it you would leave them out. They show us that story was not Shakespeare's concern in this play; its soul is not to be looked for there. If you were to go to *As You Like It* for the story you would, in Johnson's phrase, "hang yourself."

In an essay called "The Basis of Shakespearian Comedy"[1] Professor Nevill Coghill attempted to "establish certain things concerning the nature of comic form, as it was understood at Shakespeare's time." He pointed out that there were two conceptions of comedy current in the sixteenth century, both going back to grammarians of the fourth century, but radically opposed to each other. By the one definition a comedy was a story beginning in sadness and ending in happiness. By the other it was, in Sidney's words, "an imitation of the common errors of our life" represented "in the most ridiculous and scornefull sort that may be; so that it is impossible that any beholder can be content to be such a one." Shakespeare, he declared, accepted the first; Jonson, the second. But although *As You Like It*, like *A Midsummer Night's Dream*, certainly begins in sadness and ends with happiness, I do not feel, when we have said this, that we have gone very far toward defining the play's nature, and I do not think that the plot in either of these two lovely plays, or in the enchanting early comedy *Love's Labor's Lost*, which indeed has hardly any plot at all, can be regarded as the "soul" or animating force of Shakespeare's most original and characteristic comedies. Professor Coghill's formula fits plays which we feel rather uneasy about, *The Merchant of Venice* and *Measure for Measure*. It is precisely the stress on the plot which makes us think of these as being more properly described as tragicomedies than comedies. Neither of them is a play which we would choose as a norm of Shakespeare's genius in comedy. In *As You Like It* the plot is handled in the most perfunctory way. Shakespeare crams his first act with incident in order to get everyone to the forest as soon as he possibly can and, when he is ready, he ends it all as quickly as possible. A few lines dispose of Duke Frederick, and leave the road back to his throne empty for Duke Senior. As for the other victim of a wicked brother, it is far more important that Orlando should marry Rosalind than that he should be restored to his rights.

Mrs. Suzanne Langer, in her brilliant and suggestive book

[1] *Essays and Studies* (English Association: John Murray, 1950).

Feeling and Form,[2] has called comedy an image of life triumphing over chance. She declares that the essence of comedy is that it embodies in symbolic form our sense of happiness in feeling that we can meet and master the changes and chances of life as it confronts us. This seems to me to provide a good description of what we mean by "pure comedy," as distinct from the corrective or satirical comedy of Jonson. The great symbol of pure comedy is marriage by which the world is renewed, and its endings are always instinct with a sense of fresh beginnings. Its rhythm is the rhythm of the life of mankind, which goes on and renews itself as the life of nature does. The rhythm of tragedy, on the other hand, is the rhythm of the individual life which comes to a close, and its great symbol is death. The one inescapable fact about every human being is that he must die. No skill in living, no sense of life, no inborn grace or acquired wisdom can avert this individual doom. A tragedy, which is played out under the shadow of an inevitable end, is an image of the life pattern of every one of us. A comedy, which contrives an end which is not implicit in its beginning, and which is, in itself, a fresh beginning, is an image of the flow of human life. The young wed, so that they may become in turn the older generation, whose children will wed, and so on, as long as the world lasts. Comedy pictures what Rosalind calls "the full stream of the world." At the close of a tragedy we look back over a course which has been run: "the rest is silence." The end of a comedy declares that life goes on: "Here we are all over again." Tragic plots must have a logic which leads to an inescapable conclusion. Comic plots are made up of changes, chances and surprises. Coincidences can destroy tragic feeling: they heighten comic feeling. It is absurd to complain in poetic comedy of improbable encounters and characters arriving pat on their cue, of sudden changes of mind and mood by which an enemy becomes a friend. Puck, who creates and presides over the central comedy of *A Midsummer Night's Dream,* speaks for all comic writers and lovers of true comedy when he says:

[2] Routledge, 1953.

And those things do best please me
That befall preposterously.

This aspect of life, as continually changing and presenting fresh opportunities for happiness and laughter, poetic comedy idealizes and presents to us by means of fantasy. Fantasy is the natural instrument of comedy, in which plot, which is the "soul" of tragedy, is of secondary importance, an excuse for something else. After viewing a tragedy we have an "acquist of true experience" from a "great event." There are no "events" in comedy; there are only "happenings." Events are irreversible and comedy is not concerned with the irreversible, which is why it must always shun the presentation of death. In adapting Lodge's story Shakespeare did not allow Charles the wrestler to kill the Franklin's sons. Although they are expected to die, we may hope they will recover from their broken ribs. And he rejected also Lodge's ending in which the wicked Duke was killed in battle, preferring his improbable conversion by a hermit. But why should we complain of its improbability? It is only in tragedy that second chances are not given. Comedy is full of purposes mistook, not "falling on the inventor's head" but luckily misfiring altogether. In comedy, as often happens in life, people are mercifully saved from being as wicked as they meant to be.

Generalization about the essential distinctions between tragedy and comedy is called in question, when we turn to Shakespeare, by the inclusiveness of his vision of life. In the great majority of his plays the elements are mixed. But just as he wrote one masterpiece which is purely tragic, dominated by the conception of Fate, in *Macbeth*, so he wrote some plays which embody a purely comic vision. Within the general formula that "a comedy is a play with a happy ending," which can, of course, include tragicomedies, he wrote some plays in which the story is a mere frame and the essence of the play lies in the presentation of an image of human life, not as an arena for heroic endeavor but as a place of encounters:

Tragedy is presided over by time, which urges the hero onward to fulfill his destiny. In Shakespeare's comedies time goes by fits and starts. It is not so much a movement onward as a space in which to work things out: a midsummer night, a space too short for us to feel time's movement, or the unmeasured time of *As You Like It* or *Twelfth Night*. The comedies are dominated by a sense of place rather than of time. In Shakespeare's earliest comedy it is not a very romantic place: the city of Ephesus. Still, it is a place where two pairs of twins are accidentally reunited, and their old father, in danger of death at the beginning, is united to his long-lost wife at the close. The substance of the play is the comic plot of mistakings, played out in a single place on a single day. The tragicomic story of original loss and final restoration provides a frame. In what is probably his second comedy, *The Two Gentlemen of Verona*, Shakespeare tried a quite different method. The play is a dramatization of a *novella*, and it contains no comic place of encounters where time seems to stand still. The story begins in Verona, passes to Milan, and ends in a forest between the two cities. None of these places exerts any hold upon our imaginations. The story simply moves forward through them. In *Love's Labor's Lost*, by contrast, Shakespeare went as far as possible in the other direction. The whole play is a kind of ballet of lovers and fantastics, danced out in the King of Navarre's park. Nearby is a village where Holofernes is the schoolmaster, Nathaniel the curate, and Dull the constable. In this play we are given, as a foil to the lords and ladies, not comic servants, parasitic on their masters, but a little comic world, society in miniature, going about its daily business while the lovers are engaged in the discovery of theirs. Shakespeare dispensed with the tragicomic frame altogether here. There is no sorrow at the beginning, only youthful male fatuity; and the "putting right" at the close lies in the chastening of the lords by the ladies. The picture of the course of life as it appears to the comic vision, with young men falling in love and young women testing their suitors, and other men "laboring in their vocations" to keep the world turning and to impress their fellows, is the whole matter of the play. Much more magical than the sunlit park of the King of Navarre is the wood near Athens where Puck plays the part of chance. Shakespeare reverted here to the structural pattern of his earliest comedy, beginning with the cruel fury of Egeus against his daughter, the rivalry of Lysander and Demetrius and the unhappiness of the scorned Helena, and ending with Theseus's overriding of the father's will and the proper pairing of the four lovers. But here he not only set his comic plot of mistakings within a frame of sorrow turning to joy, he also set his comic place of encounters apart from the real world, the palace where the play begins and ends. All the center of the play takes place in the moonlit wood where lovers immortal and mortal quarrel, change partners, are blinded, and have their eyes purged.

Having created a masterpiece, Shakespeare, who never repeated a success, went back in his next play to tragicomedy, allowing the threat of terrible disaster to grow through the play up to a great dramatic fourth act. *The Merchant of Venice* has what *The Two Gentlemen of Verona* lacks, an enchanted place. Belmont, where Bassanio goes to find his bride, and where Lorenzo flees with Jessica, and from which Portia descends like a goddess to solve the troubles of Venice, is a place apart, "above the smoke and stir." But it is not, like the wood near Athens, a place where the changes and chances of our mortal life are seen mirrored. It stands too sharply over against Venice, a place of refuge rather than a place of discovery. *Much Ado About Nothing* reverts to the single place of *The Comedy of Errors* and *Love's Labor's Lost;* and its tragicomic plot, which also comes to a climax in a dramatic scene in the fourth act, is lightened not by a shift of scene but by its interweaving with a brilliant comic plot, and by all kinds of indications that all will soon be well again. The trouble comes in the middle of this play: at the beginning, as at the end, all is revelry and happiness. A sense of holiday, of time off from the world's business, reigns in Messina. The wars are over, peace has broken out, and Don Pedro and the gentlemen have returned to where the ladies are waiting for them to take up again the game of love and wit. In the atmosphere created by the first act Don John's malice is a cloud no bigger than a man's hand. And although it grows as the play proceeds, the crisis of the fourth act is like a heavy summer thundershower which darkens the sky for a time but will, we know, soon pass. The brilliant lively city of Messina is a true place of mistakings and discoveries, like the park of the King of Navarre; but, also like the park of the King of Navarre, it lacks enchantment. It is too near the ordinary world to seem more than a partial image of human life. In *As You Like It* Shakespeare returned to the pattern of *A Midsummer Night's Dream*, beginning his play in sorrow and ending it with joy, and making his place of comic encounters a place set apart from the ordinary world.

The Forest of Arden ranks with the wood near Athens and Prospero's island as a place set apart, even though, unlike them, it is not ruled by magic. It is set over against the envious court ruled by a tyrant, and a home which is no home because it harbors hatred, not love. Seen from the court it appears untouched by the discontents of life, a place where "they fleet the time carelessly, as they did in the golden age," the gay greenwood of Robin Hood. But, of course, it is no such Elysium. It contains some unamiable characters. Corin's master is churlish and Sir Oliver Martext is hardly sweet-natured; William is a dolt and Audrey graceless. Its weather, too, is by no means always sunny. It has a bitter winter. To Orlando, famished with hunger and supporting the fainting Adam, it is "an uncouth forest" and a desert where the air is bleak. He is astonished to find civility among men who

> in this desert inaccessible,
> Under the shade of melancholy boughs,
> Lose and neglect the creeping hours of time.

In fact Arden does not seem very attractive at first sight to the weary escapers from the tyranny of the world. Rosalind's "Well, this is the forest of Arden" does not suggest any very great enthusiasm; and to Touchstone's "Ay, now I am in Arden; the more fool I: when I was at home, I was in a better place: but travelers must be content," she can only reply "Ay, be so, good Touchstone." It is as if they all have to wake up after a good night's rest to find what a pleasant place they have come to. Arden is not a place for the young only. Silvius, forever young and forever loving, is balanced by Corin, the old shepherd, who reminds us of that other "penalty of Adam" beside "the seasons' difference": that man must labor to get himself food and clothing. Still, the labor is pleasant and a source of pride: "I am a true laborer: I earn that I eat, get that I wear, owe no man hate, envy no man's happiness, glad of other men's good, content with my harm; and the greatest of my pride is to see my ewes graze and my lambs suck." Arden is not a place where the laws of nature are abrogated and roses are without their thorns. If, in the world, Duke Frederick has usurped on Duke Senior, Duke Senior is aware that he has in his turn usurped upon the deer, the native burghers of the forest. If man does not slay and kill man, he kills the poor beasts. Life preys on life. Jaques, who can suck melancholy out of anything, points to the callousness that runs through nature itself as a mirror of the callousness of men. The herd abandons the wounded deer, as prosperous citizens pass with disdain the poor bankrupt, the failure. The race is to the swift. But this is Jaques's view. Orlando, demanding help for Adam, finds another image from nature:

> Then but forbear your food a little while,
> Whiles, like a doe, I go to find my fawn
> And give it food. There is a poor old man,
> Who after me hath many a weary step
> Limp'd in pure love: till he be first suffic'd,
> Oppress'd with two weak evils, age and hunger,
> I will not touch a bit.

The fact that they are both derived ultimately from folk tale is not the only thing that relates *As You Like It* to *King Lear*. Adam's somber line, "And unregarded age in corners thrown," which Quiller-Couch said might have come out of one of the greater sonnets, sums up the fate of Lear:

> Dear daughter, I confess that I am old;
> Age is unnecessary: on my knees I beg
> That you'll vouchsafe me raiment, bed, and food.

At times Arden seems a place where the same bitter lessons can be learned as Lear has to learn in his place of exile, the blasted heath. Corin's natural philosophy, which includes the knowledge that "the property of rain is to wet," is something which Lear has painfully to acquire:

> When the rain came to wet me once and the wind to make me chatter, when the thunder would not peace at my bidding, there I found 'em, there I smelt 'em out. Go to, they are not men o' their words: they told me I was everything; 'tis a lie, I am not ague-proof.

He is echoing Duke Senior, who smiles at the "icy fang and churlish chiding of the winter's wind," saying:

> This is no flattery: these are counselors
> That feelingly persuade me what I am.

Amiens's lovely melancholy song:

> Blow, blow, thou winter wind,
> Thou art not so unkind
>   As man's ingratitude....

> Freeze, freeze, thou bitter sky,
> That dost not bite so nigh
>   As benefits forgot...,

is terribly echoed in Lear's outburst:

> Blow, winds, and crack your cheeks! rage! blow!
> . . . .
> Rumble thy bellyful! Spit, fire! spout, rain!
> Nor rain, wind, thunder, fire, are my daughters:
> I tax not you, you elements, with unkindness;
> I never gave you kingdom, call'd you children....

And Jaques's reflection that "All the world's a stage" becomes in Lear's mouth a cry of anguish:

> When we are born, we cry that we are come
> To this great stage of fools.

It is in Arden that Jaques presents his joyless picture of
human life, passing from futility to futility and culminating
in the nothingness of senility—"sans everything"; and in
Arden also a bitter judgment on human relations is lightly
passed in the twice repeated "Most friendship is feigning,
most loving mere folly." But then one must add that hard
on the heels of Jaques's melancholy conclusion Orlando
enters with Adam in his arms, who, although he may be
"sans teeth" and at the end of his usefulness as a servant,
has, beside his store of virtue and his peace of conscience,
the love of his master. And the play is full of signal instances
of persons who do not forget benefits: Adam, Celia, Touchstone—not to mention the lords who chose to leave the
court and follow their banished master to the forest. In a
recent number of the *Shakespeare Survey* Professor Harold
Jenkins has pointed out how points of view put forward by
one character find contradiction or correction by another,
so that the whole play is a balance of sweet against sour, of
the cynical against the idealistic, and life is shown as a
mingling of hard fortune and good hap. The lords who have
"turned ass," "leaving their wealth and ease a stubborn
will to please," are happy in their gross folly, as Orlando is
in a lovesickness which he does not wish to be cured of.
What Jaques has left out of his picture of man's strange
eventful pilgrimage is love and companionship, sweet
society, the banquet under the boughs to which Duke
Senior welcomes Orlando and Adam. Although life in
Arden is not wholly idyllic, and this place set apart from
the world is yet touched by the world's sorrows and can be
mocked at by the worldly wise, the image of life which the
forest presents is irradiated by the conviction that the gay
and the gentle can endure the rubs of fortune and that this
earth is a place where men can find happiness in themselves
and in others.

The Forest of Arden is, as has often been pointed out, a
place which all the exiles from the court, except one, are
only too ready to leave at the close. As, when the short
midsummer night is over, the lovers emerge from the wood,
in their right minds and correctly paired, and return to the
palace of Theseus; and, when Prospero's magic has worked

the cure, the enchanted island is left to Caliban and Ariel, and its human visitors return to Naples and Milan; so the time of holiday comes to an end in Arden. The stately masque of Hymen marks the end of this interlude in the greenwood, and announces the return to a court purged of envy and baseness. Like other comic places, Arden is a place of discovery where the truth becomes clear and where each man finds himself and his true way. This discovery of truth in comedy is made through errors and mistakings. The trial and error by which we come to knowledge of ourselves and of our world is symbolized by the disguisings which are a recurrent element in all comedy, but are particularly common in Shakespeare's. Things have, as it were, to become worse before they become better, more confused and farther from the proper pattern. By misunderstandings men come to understand, and by lies and feignings they discover truth. If Rosalind, the princess, had attempted to "cure" her lover Orlando, she might have succeeded. As Ganymede, playing Rosalind, she can try him to the limit in perfect safety, and discover that she cannot mock or flout him out of his "mad humor of love to a living humor of madness," and drive him "to forswear the full stream of the world, and to live in a nook merely monastic." By playing with him in the disguise of a boy, she discovers when she can play no more. By love of a shadow, the mere image of a charming youth, Phoebe discovers that it is better to love than to be loved and scorn one's lover. This discovery of truth by feigning, and of what is wisdom and what folly by debate, is the center of *As You Like It*. It is a play of meetings and encounters, of conversations and sets of wit: Orlando versus Jaques, Touchstone versus Corin, Rosalind versus Jaques, Rosalind versus Phoebe, and above all Rosalind versus Orlando. The truth discovered is, at one level, a very "earthy truth": Benedick's discovery that "the world must be peopled." The honest toil of Corin, the wise man of the forest, is mocked at by Touchstone as "simple sin." He brings "the ewes and the rams together" and gets his living "by the copulation of cattle." The goddess Fortune seems similarly occupied in this play: "As the ox hath his bow, the horse his curb, and the falcon her bells, so man hath his

desires; and as pigeons bill, so wedlock would be nibbling."
Fortune acts the role of a kindly bawd. Touchstone's
marriage to Audrey is a mere coupling. Rosalind's advice
to Phoebe is brutally frank: "Sell when you can, you are
not for all markets." The words she uses to describe Oliver
and Celia "in the very wrath of love" are hardly delicate,
and after her first meeting with Orlando she confesses to
her cousin that her sighs are for her "child's father." Against
the natural background of the life of the forest there can be
no pretense that the love of men and women can "forget
the He and She." But Rosalind's behavior is at variance
with her bold words. Orlando has to prove that he truly is,
as he seems at first sight, the right husband for her, and show
himself gentle, courteous, generous and brave, and a match
for her in wit, though a poor poet. In this, the great coupling
of the play, there is a marriage of true minds. The other
couplings run the gamut downward from it, until we reach
Touchstone's image of "a she-lamb of a twelvemonth" and
"a crooked-pated, old, cuckoldy ram," right at the bottom
of the scale. As for the debate as to where happiness is to
be found, the conclusion come to is again, like all wisdom,
not very startling or original: that "minds innocent and
quiet" can find happiness in court or country:

> Happy is your Grace,
> That can translate the stubbornness of fortune
> Into so quiet and so sweet a style.

And, on the contrary, those who wish to can "suck melancholy" out of anything, "as a weasel sucks eggs."
   In the pairing one figure is left out. "I am for other than
for dancing measures," says Jaques. Leaving the hateful
sight of reveling and pastime, he betakes himself to the
Duke's abandoned cave, on his way to the house of penitents
where Duke Frederick has gone. The two commentators of
the play are nicely contrasted. Touchstone is the parodist,
Jaques the cynic. The parodist must love what he parodies.
We know this from literary parody. All the best parodies are
written by those who understand, because they love, the
thing they mock. Only poets who love and revere the epic

can write mock-heroic and the finest parody of classical tragedy comes from Housman, a great scholar. In everything that Touchstone says and does gusto, high spirits and a zest for life ring out. Essentially comic, he can adapt himself to any situation in which he may find himself. Never at a loss, he is life's master. The essence of clowning is adaptability and improvisation. The clown is never baffled and is marked by his ability to place himself at once *en rapport* with his audience, to be all things to all men, to perform the part which is required at the moment. Touchstone sustains many different roles. After hearing Silvius's lament and Rosalind's echo of it, he becomes the maudlin lover of Jane Smile; with the simple shepherd Corin he becomes the cynical and worldly-wise man of the court; with Jaques he is a melancholy moralist, musing on the power of time and the decay of all things; with the pages he acts the lordly amateur of the arts, patronizing his musicians. It is right that he should parody the rest of the cast, and join the procession into Noah's ark with his Audrey. Jaques is his opposite. He is the cynic, the person who prefers the pleasures of superiority, cold-eyed and cold-hearted. The tyrannical Duke Frederick and the cruel Oliver can be converted; but not Jaques. He likes himself as he is. He does not wish to plunge into the stream, but prefers to stand on the bank and "fish for fancies as they pass." Sir Thomas Elyot said that dancing was an image of matrimony: "In every daunse, of a most auncient custome, there daunseth together a man and a woman, holding eche other by the hande or the arme, which betokeneth concorde." There are some who will not dance, however much they are piped to, any more than they will weep when there is mourning. "In this theater of man's life," wrote Bacon, "it is reserved only for God and angels to be lookers on." Jaques arrogates to himself the divine role. He has opted out from the human condition.

It is characteristic of Shakespeare's comedies to include an element that is irreconcilable, which strikes a lightly discordant note, casts a slight shadow, and by its presence questions the completeness of the comic vision of life. In *Love's Labor's Lost* he dared to allow the news of a death to cloud the scene of revels at the close, and, through Rosa-

line's rebuke to Berowne, called up the image of a whole
world of pain and weary suffering where "Mirth cannot
move a soul in agony." The two comedies whose main
action is motivated by hatred end with malice thwarted but
not removed. In *The Merchant of Venice* and *Much Ado
About Nothing*, Shakespeare asks us to accept the fact that
the human race includes not only a good many fools and
rogues but also some persons who are positively wicked, a
fact which comedy usually ignores. They are prevented
from doing the harm they wish to do. They are not cured
of wishing to do harm. Shylock's baffled exit and Don John's
flight to Messina leave the stage clear for lovers and well-
wishers. The villains have to be left out of the party at the
close. At the end of *Twelfth Night* the person who is left out
is present. The impotent misery and fury of the humiliated
Malvolio's last words, "I'll be reveng'd on the whole pack
of you," call in question the whole comic scheme by which,
through misunderstandings and mistakes, people come to
terms with themselves and their fellows. There are some who
cannot be "taught a lesson." In Malvolio pride is not
purged; it is fatally wounded and embittered. It is characteristic of the delicacy of temper of *As You Like It* that its
solitary figure, its outsider, Jaques, does nothing whatever
to harm anyone, and is perfectly satisfied with himself and
happy in his melancholy. Even more, his melancholy is a
source of pleasure and amusement to others. The Duke
treats him as virtually a court entertainer, and he is a natural
butt for Orlando and Rosalind. Anyone in the play can put
him down and feel the better for doing so. All the same his
presence casts a faint shadow. His criticism of the world
has its sting drawn very early by the Duke's rebuke to him
as a former libertine, discharging his filth upon the world,
and he is to some extent discredited before he opens his
mouth by the unpleasant implication of his name. But he
cannot be wholly dismissed. A certain sour distaste for life
is voided through him, something most of us feel at some
time or other. If he were not there to give expression to it,
we might be tempted to find the picture of life in the forest
too sweet. His only action is to interfere in the marriage of
Touchstone and Audrey; and this he merely postpones. His

effect, whenever he appears, is to deflate: the effect does not last and cheerfulness soon breaks in again. Yet as there is a scale of love, so there is a scale of sadness in the play. It runs down from the Duke's compassionate words:

> Thou seest we are not all alone unhappy:
> This wide and universal theater
> Presents more woeful pageants than the scene
> Wherein we play in,

through Rosalind's complaint "O, how full of briers is this working-day world," to Jaques's studied refusal to find anything worthy of admiration or love.

One further element in the play I would not wish to stress, because though it is pervasive it is unobtrusive: the constant, natural and easy reference to the Christian ideal of loving-kindness, gentleness, pity and humility and to the sanctions which that ideal finds in the commands and promises of religion. In this fantasy world, in which the world of our experience is imaged, this element in experience finds a place with others, and the world is shown not only as a place where we may find happiness, but as a place where both happiness and sorrow may be hallowed. The number of religious references in *As You Like It* has often been commented on, and it is striking when we consider the play's main theme. Many are of little significance and it would be humorless to enlarge upon the significance of the "old religious man" who converted Duke Frederick, or of Ganymede's "old religious uncle." But some are explicit and have a serious, unforced beauty: Orlando's appeal to outlawed men,

> If ever you have look'd on better days,
> If ever been where bells have knoll'd to church . . . ;

Adam's prayer,

> He that doth the ravens feed,
> Yea, providently caters for the sparrow,
> Be comfort to my age!

and Corin's recognition, from St. Paul, that we have to
find the way to heaven by doing deeds of hospitality. These
are all in character. But the God of Marriage, Hymen,
speaks more solemnly than we expect and his opening words
with their New Testament echo are more than conventional:

> Then is there mirth in heaven,
> When earthly things made even
> Atone together.

The appearance of the god to present daughter to father
and to bless the brides and grooms turns the close into a
solemnity, an image of the concord which reigns in Heaven
and which Heaven blesses on earth. But this, like much else
in the play, may be taken as you like it. There is no need to
see any more in the god's appearance with the brides than
a piece of pageantry which concludes the action with a
graceful spectacle and sends the audience home contented
with a very pretty play.

Suggested References

The number of possible references is vast and grows alarmingly. (The *Shakespeare Quarterly* devotes a substantial part of one issue each year to a list of the previous year's work, and *Shakespeare Survey*—an annual publication—includes a substantial review of recent scholarship, as well as an occasional essay surveying a few decades of scholarship on a chosen topic.) Though no works are indispensable, those listed below have been found helpful.

1. Shakespeare's Times

Byrne, M. St. Clare. *Elizabethan Life in Town and Country.* Rev. ed. New York: Barnes & Noble, Inc., 1961. Chapters on manners, beliefs, education, etc., with illustrations.

Craig, Hardin. *The Enchanted Glass: the Elizabethan Mind in Literature.* New York and London: Oxford University Press, 1936. The Elizabethan intellectual climate.

Nicoll, Allardyce (ed.). *The Elizabethans.* London: Cambridge University Press, 1957. An anthology of Elizabethan writings, especially valuable for its illustrations from paintings, title pages, etc.

Shakespeare's England. 2 vols. Oxford: The Clarendon Press, 1916. A large collection of scholarly essays on a wide variety of topics (e.g., astrology, costume, gardening, horsemanship), with special attention to Shakespeare's references to these topics.

Tillyard, E. M. W. *The Elizabethan World Picture*. London: Chatto & Windus, 1943; New York: The Macmillan Company, 1944. A brief account of some Elizabethan ideas of the universe.

Wilson, John Dover (ed.). *Life in Shakespeare's England*. 2nd ed. New York: The Macmillan Company, 1913. An anthology of Elizabethan writings on the countryside, superstition, education, the court, etc.

2. Shakespeare

Bentley, Gerald E. *Shakespeare: A Biographical Handbook*. New Haven, Conn.: Yale University Press, 1961. The facts about Shakespeare, with virtually no conjecture intermingled.

Bradby, Anne (ed.). *Shakespeare Criticism, 1919–1935*. London: Oxford University Press, 1936. A small anthology of excellent essays on the plays.

Bush, Geoffrey Douglas. *Shakespeare and the Natural Condition*. Cambridge, Mass.: Harvard University Press; London: Oxford University Press, 1956. A short, sensitive account of Shakespeare's view of "Nature," touching most of the works.

Chute, Marchette. *Shakespeare of London*. New York: E. P. Dutton & Co., Inc., 1949. A readable biography fused with portraits of Stratford and London life.

Clemen, Wolfgang H. *The Development of Shakespeare's Imagery*. Cambridge, Mass.: Harvard University Press, 1951. (Originally published in German, 1936.) A temperate account of a subject often abused.

Chambers, E. K. *William Shakespeare: A Study of Facts and Problems*. 2 vols. London: Oxford University Press, 1930.

An invaluable, detailed reference work; not for the casual reader.

Craig, Hardin. *An Interpretation of Shakespeare.* New York: Citadel Press, 1948. A scholar's book designed for the layman. Comments on all the works.

Dean, Leonard F. (ed.). *Shakespeare: Modern Essays in Criticism.* New York: Oxford University Press, 1957. Mostly mid-twentieth-century critical studies, covering Shakespeare's artistry.

Granville-Barker, Harley. *Prefaces to Shakespeare.* 2 vols. Princeton, N.J.: Princeton University Press, 1946–47. Essays on ten plays by a scholarly man of the theater.

Harbage, Alfred. *As They Liked It.* New York: The Macmillan Company, 1947. A sensitive, long essay on Shakespeare, morality, and the audience's expectations.

Smith, D. Nichol (ed.). *Shakespeare Criticism.* New York: Oxford University Press, 1916. A selection of criticism from 1623 to 1840, ranging from Ben Jonson to Thomas Carlyle.

Spencer, Theodore. *Shakespeare and the Nature of Man.* New York: The Macmillan Company, 1942. Shakespeare's plays in relation to Elizabethan thought.

Stoll, Elmer Edgar. *Shakespeare and Other Masters.* Cambridge, Mass.: Harvard University Press; London: Oxford University Press, 1940. Essays on tragedy, comedy, and aspects of dramaturgy, with special reference to some of Shakespeare's plays.

Traversi, D. A. *An Approach to Shakespeare.* Rev. ed. New York: Doubleday & Co., Inc., 1956. An analysis of the plays, beginning with words, images, and themes, rather than with characters.

Van Doren, Mark. *Shakespeare.* New York: Henry Holt & Company, Inc., 1939. Brief, perceptive readings of all of the plays.

Whitaker, Virgil K. *Shakespeare's Use of Learning.* San Marino, Calif.: Huntington Library, 1953. A study of the relation of Shakespeare's reading to his development as a dramatist.

3. Shakespeare's Theater

Adams, John Cranford. *The Globe Playhouse*. Rev. ed. New York: Barnes & Noble, Inc., 1961. A detailed conjecture about the physical characteristics of the theater Shakespeare often wrote for.

Beckerman, Bernard. *Shakespeare at the Globe, 1599–1609.* New York: The Macmillan Company, 1962. On the playhouse and on Elizabethan dramaturgy, acting, and staging.

Chambers, E. K. *The Elizabethan Stage.* 4 vols. New York: Oxford University Press, 1923. Reprinted with corrections, 1945. An indispensable reference work on theaters, theatrical companies, and staging at court.

Harbage, Alfred. *Shakespeare's Audience.* New York: Columbia University Press; London: Oxford University Press, 1941. A study of the size and nature of the theatrical public.

Hodges, C. Walter. *The Globe Restored.* London: Ernest Benn, Ltd., 1953; New York: Coward-McCann, Inc., 1954. A well-illustrated and readable attempt to reconstruct the Globe Theatre.

Nagler, A. M. *Shakespeare's Stage.* Tr. by Ralph Manheim. New Haven, Conn.: Yale University Press, 1958. An excellent brief introduction to the physical aspect of the playhouse.

Smith, Irwin. *Shakespeare's Globe Playhouse.* New York: Charles Scribner's Sons, 1957. Chiefly indebted to J. C. Adams' controversial book, with additional material and scale drawings for model-builders.

Venezky, Alice S. *Pageantry on the Shakespearean Stage.*

New York: Twayne Publishers, Inc., 1951. An examination of spectacle in Elizabethan drama.

4. Miscellaneous Reference Works

Abbott, E. A. *A Shakespearean Grammar*. New edition. New York: The Macmillan Company, 1877. An examination of differences between Elizabethan and modern grammar.

Bartlett, John. *A New and Complete Concordance . . . to . . . Shakespeare*. New York: The Macmillan Company, 1894. An index to most of Shakespeare's words.

Bullough, Geoffrey. *Narrative and Dramatic Sources of Shakespeare*. 4 vols. Vols. 5 and 6 in preparation. New York: Columbia University Press; London: Routledge & Kegan Paul, Ltd., 1957–. A collection of many of the books Shakespeare drew upon.

Greg, W. W. *The Shakespeare First Folio*. New York and London: Oxford University Press, 1955. A detailed yet readable history of the first collection (1623) of Shakespeare's plays.

Kökeritz, Helge. *Shakespeare's Names*. New Haven, Conn.: Yale University Press, 1959; London: Oxford University Press, 1960. A guide to the pronunciation of some 1,800 names appearing in Shakespeare.

———. *Shakespeare's Pronunciation*. New Haven, Conn.: Yale University Press; London: Oxford University Press, 1953. Contains much information about puns and rhymes.

Linthicum, Marie C. *Costume in the Drama of Shakespeare and His Contemporaries*. New York and London: Oxford University Press, 1936. On the fabrics and dress of the age, and references to them in the plays.

Muir, Kenneth. *Shakespeare's Sources*. London: Methuen & Co., Ltd., 1957. Vol. 2 in preparation. The first volume, on the comedies and tragedies, attempts to ascertain what books were Shakespeare's sources, and what use he made of them.

Onions, C. T. *A Shakespeare Glossary*. London: Oxford University Press, 1911; 2nd ed., rev., with enlarged addenda, 1953. Definitions of words (or senses of words) now obsolete.

Partridge, Eric. *Shakespeare's Bawdy*. Rev. ed. New York: E. P. Dutton & Co., Inc.; London: Routledge & Kegan Paul, Ltd., 1955. A glossary of bawdy words and phrases.

Shakespeare Quarterly. See headnote to Suggested References.

Shakespeare Survey. See headnote to Suggested References.

5. *As You Like It*

Barber, C. L. *Shakespeare's Festive Comedy*. Princeton, N.J.: Princeton University Press; London: Oxford University Press, 1959.

Brown, John R. *Shakespeare and His Comedies*. London: Methuen & Co., Ltd., 1957.

Campbell, Oscar J. *Shakespeare's Satire*. New York and London: Oxford University Press, 1943.

Charlton, H. B. *Shakespearian Comedy*. 4th ed. London: Methuen & Co., Ltd., 1949.

Furness, H. H. (ed.). *As You Like It*. (New Variorum Ed.) Philadelphia, Pa.: J. P. Lippincott Company, 1890.

Halio, Jay L. " 'No Clock in the Forest': Time in *As You Like It*," *Studies in English Literature: 1500–1900*, II (1962), 197–207.

Hunter, G. K. *Shakespeare: The Late Comedies*. London: Longmans, Green & Co., Ltd., 1962.

Jenkins, H. "*As You Like It*," *Shakespeare Survey*, VIII (1955), 40–51.

Lascelles, Mary. "Shakespeare's Pastoral Comedy," *More Talking of Shakespeare*, ed. John W. P. Garrett. New York: Theatre Arts Books; London: Longmans, Green & Co., Ltd., 1959.

McIntosh, Angus. "*As You Like It*: A Grammatical Clue to Character," *A Review of English Literature*, IV (1963), 68–81.

Mincoff, Marco. "What Shakespeare Did to *Rosalynde*," *Shakespeare Jahrbuch*, XCVI (1960), 78–89.

Shaw, John. "Fortune and Nature in *As You Like It*," *Shakespeare Quarterly*, VI (1955), 45–50.

Smith, James. "*As You Like It*," *Scrutiny*, IX (1940), 9–32.

Stevenson, David L. *The Love-Game Comedy*. New York: Columbia University Press; London: Oxford University Press, 1946.

THE COMPLETE PLAYS OF

SHAKESPEARE

Superlatively edited paperbound volumes of Shakespeare's complete plays are now being offered in Signet Classic editions. Under the general editorship of Sylvan Barnet, Chairman of the English Department of Tufts University, each volume features a general Introduction by Dr. Barnet, special Introduction and Notes by an eminent Shakespearean scholar, critical commentary from past and contemporary authorities, and when possible, the actual source, in its entirety or in excerpt, from which Shakespeare derived his play. Among the volumes already available and priced at 50¢ each are:

KING LEAR. EDITED WITH INTRODUCTION AND NOTES BY RUSSELL FRASER, PRINCETON UNIVERSITY.　　　　(#CD160)

MACBETH. EDITED WITH INTRODUCTION AND NOTES BY SYLVAN BARNET, TUFTS UNIVERSITY.　　　　(#CD161)

OTHELLO. EDITED WITH INTRODUCTION AND NOTES BY ALVIN KERNAN, YALE UNIVERSITY.　　　　(#CD162)

RICHARD II. EDITED WITH INTRODUCTION AND NOTES BY KENNETH MUIR, UNIVERSITY OF LIVERPOOL.　　　　(#CD163)

THE WINTER'S TALE. EDITED WITH INTRODUCTION AND NOTES BY FRANK KERMODE, UNIVERSITY OF MANCHESTER.
　　　　(#CD164)

HAMLET. EDITED WITH INTRODUCTION AND NOTES BY EDWARD HUBLER, PRINCETON UNIVERSITY.　　　　(#CD169)

JULIUS CAESAR. EDITED WITH INTRODUCTION AND NOTES BY WILLIAM AND BARBARA ROSEN, UNIVERSITY OF CONNECTICUT.
　　　　(#CD170)

A MIDSUMMER NIGHT'S DREAM. EDITED WITH INTRODUCTION AND NOTES BY WOLFGANG CLEMEN, UNIVERSITY OF MUNICH.　　　　(#CD171)

TROILUS AND CRESSIDA. EDITED WITH INTRODUCTION AND NOTES BY DANIEL SELTZER, HARVARD UNIVERSITY. (#CD172)

GREAT PLAYS IN MENTOR EDITIONS

THE GENIUS OF THE EARLY ENGLISH THEATER
Barnet, Berman and Burto, editors
Complete texts including three anonymous plays—"Abraham and Isaac," "The Second Shepherd's Play," and "Everyman," and Marlowe's "Doctor Faustus," Shakespeare's "Macbeth," Jonson's "Volpone," and Milton's "Samson Agonistes." Also includes critical essays. (#MY730—$1.25)

THE GENIUS OF THE LATER ENGLISH THEATER
Barnet, Berman and Burto, editors
Complete plays, including Congreve's "The Way of the World," Goldsmith's "She Stoops to Conquer," Byron's "Manfred," Wilde's "Importance of Being Earnest," Shaw's "Major Barbara," and Golding's "The Brass Butterfly." With critical essays.
(#MQ448—95¢)

THE GENIUS OF THE IRISH THEATER
Barnet, Berman and Burto, editors
Complete texts of seven plays by Shaw, Synge, Lady Gregory, William Butler Yeats, Jack B. Yeats, Frank O'Connor, and Sean O'Casey. With critical essays. (#MT315—75¢)

EIGHT GREAT COMEDIES Barnet, Berman and Burto, editors
Complete English texts of "The Clouds," Machiavelli's "Mandragola," "Twelfth Night," "The Miser," "The Beggar's Opera," "Importance of Being Earnest," "Uncle Vanya," "Arms and the Man." With essays on the comic view. (#MQ343—95¢)

EIGHT GREAT TRAGEDIES Barnet, Berman and Burto, editors
Complete English texts of "Prometheus Bound," "Oedipus the King," "Hippolytus," "King Lear," "Ghosts," "Miss Julie," "On Baile's Strand," and "Desire Under the Elms." With essays on the tragic view. (#MQ461—95¢)

To Our Readers: If your dealer does not have the Signet and Mentor books you want, you may order them by mail enclosing the list price plus 10¢ a copy to cover mailing. (New York City residents add 5% Sales Tax. Other New York State residents add 2% plus any local sales or use taxes.) If you would like our free catalog, please request it by postcard. The New American Library, Inc., P. O. Box 2310, Grand Central Station, New York, N. Y. 10017.